SET YOUR BOOK

Hello Stranger!

You've caught a travelling book. I'm a very special book. You see, I'm travelling around the world making new friends. I hope I've made another friend in you.

Please go to: www.bookcrossing.com and enter my BCID number. You will discover where I've been and who has read me, and can let them know I'm safe here in your hands. Then...

READ and RELEASE me!

BCID: _____

Registered by: _____

Where: _____

When: _____

ABOUT OUR EDITORS

ROY C. BOOTH is a published author, comedian, poet, journalist, essayist, optioned screenwriter, and an internationally awarded playwright with 57 plays published to date (Samuel French, Heuer, *et al*) with 800+ productions in 29 countries and in ten languages. A graduate of Pillager High School, Booth also has an AA degree from Central Lakes College (Brainerd, MN, and he is a hall of fame inductee in both schools), and a BA in English/Speech-Theatre and an MA in English with a Creative Writing Emphasis from Bemidji State University. Booth resides in Downtown Bemidji, Minnesota with his wife and three sons (writers all) where he has also owned/managed Roy's Comics & Games since 1992. An impartial list of his publications may be found at www.amazon.com/author/roycbooth.

JORGE SALGADO-REYES is a Chilean and British sci-fi/cyberpunk author, private investigator, and photographer. Salgado-Reyes founded Indie Authors Press in June 2011 when he saw that the publishing industry continued to evolve away from the established gatekeepers. Born in Temuco, Chile, Salgado-Reyes left his country of birth at age seven in 1975 with his family, driven into exile by the Pinochet dictatorship. Salgado-Reyes is currently working towards his BA (Honors) in English Literature and Creative Writing and spends time in both the United Kingdom and Chile. A list of his publications may be found at www.amazon.com/Jorge-Salgado-Reyes/e/B009G0CTPO.

INDIE AUTHORS PRESS TITLES

- *Learning About Love*, a collection of poems by Myriam Reyes Pena (Kindle & paperback), published 6/29/2011

- *British Process Servers Guide* by Stuart Withers, Helen Withers, & Jorge Salgado-Reyes (hardcover), published 11/27/2011

- *A Forest of Dreams*, a fantasy anthology, edited by Roy C. Booth (Kindle & paperback), published 9/6/2014

- *Spooky Halloween Drabbles 2014* (Kindle), published 10/15/2014

Forthcoming titles can be found on www.salgado-reyes.com.

ALTERED STATES

a cyberpunk sci-fi anthology

A catalog record for this book is available from the British Library.

ISBN: 978-0-9571130-4-6
1st Edition

It is the policy of Indie Authors Press to use paper that is natural, renewable, and recyclable and made from wood grown in sustainable forests. The logging and manufacturing processes are expected to conform to the environmental regulations of the country of origin.

INDIE AUTHORS PRESS
London | Chile | USA
SALGADO-REYES.COM

CONTENTS

INTRODUCTION
Paul Levinson

Cyberpunk—the lean, cool, often sarcastic vision of a dystopian future in the grip of some kind of information technology—arose in the 1980s with novels such as William Gibson's *Neuromancer* and movies such as Ridley Scott's *Bladerunner*, itself an adaptation of a novel published a decade-and-a-half earlier, by one of the proto-cyberpunk masters, Philip K. Dick.

I actually don't agree with most of these exhilaratingly dyspeptic visions—indeed, I'm known in my scholarly writing as a truculent champion of digital media, an image I carefully cultivate. But that never stopped me from immensely enjoying cyberpunk—no more than my view that time travel is all but impossible has prevented me from loving time travel as a reader, viewer, and writer. Indeed, it may well be that the state of near-impossibility is some kind of pre-requisite for top-notch science fiction, which makes the nearly impossible seem possible, even likely, via sheer craft and verve. Then again, some cyberpunk sails by describing tech as plausible as tomorrow.

Take, for example, the stories in this anthology. We get angry houses that will shoot you if you trespass, every single consumable product knowing who bought it, and all manner of cyber-bio mixes that fulfill Freud's thesis that libido and thanatos—sex and death—are the two factors that most motivate human life, whether via attraction, avoidance, or the two at the same time. The proximity of digital life to our original flesh-and-blood selves is the landscape of most of these stories. Would humans enjoy sex with an android? Of course! Could we fall in love with one? Why not? Could a robot produce great art? In cyberpunk science fiction, the answer to all of these questions is a resounding Yes. If you believe that answer, the story has worked its magic.

The departure point for all of these stories is the inextricable imperfection of human existence. We get sick, physically and mentally, we mess up, we go bankrupt, we die. That part of cyberpunk—the heart of cyberpunk—is undeniable truth, and has been a defining feature of human life since millennia before the first computer was invented. It's a theme picked up in many a mainstream work of fiction, about a dysfunctional family, about humans against the machines of society. But in cyberpunk, and despite its dystopic complexion, the hero or heroine or protagonist has a fighting chance. And if the endings of such battles are not usually happy, and indeed can be vexing, the contests and antagonists themselves can be a pleasure to read.

Many of the characters in *Altered States* live on Earth, others on planets close and far, or in alternate universes altogether. They hail from cities, suburbs, countrysides, outer space or no place at all, in futures near and distant. All are in some kind of duress, under some kind of pressure, because of information technology, unless information tech is coming to the rescue. Their actions are criminal, daring, unethical, and of the highest ethical quality. Their stories are told in prose that runs like poetry, and on occasion in poetry proper.

Most of the stories in this anthology have been recently published in other, sundry places; a few are older; some are here in print or on the screen for the first time. Taken together, do they herald a new day for the cyberpunk age?

2

As another titan of the first cyberpunk era, John Varley, once wrote: "Press Enter—and see what awaits you."

—**Paul Levinson, New York City, October 2014**

MECH

C.J. Cherryh

Originally published in *Futurecrime* 1992, Davis Publications.

Cold night in Dallas Metro Complex, late shift supper while the cruiser autoed the beltway, rain fracturing the city lights on the windshield.

"Chili cheeseburger with mustard," Dave said, and passed it to Sheila—Sheila had the wheel, he had the trackers, and traffic was half way sane for Dallas after dark, nobody even cruising off the autos, at least in their sector. He bit into a chili and cheese without, washed a bite down with a soft drink, and scanned the blips for the odd lane-runner. A domestic quarrel and a card snitch were their only two working calls: Manny and Lupe had the domestic, and the computer lab had the card trace.

So naturally they were two bites into the c&c, hadn't even touched the fries, when the mech-level call came slithering in, sweet-voiced: "Possible assault in progress, Metro 2, #R-29, The Arlington, you've got the warrant, 34, see the manager."

"Gee, thanks," Dave muttered. Sheila said something else, succinctly, off mike, and punched in a chilied thumb. The cruiser had already started its lane changes, with Exit 3 lit up on the windshield, at .82 k away. Sheila got a couple more bites and a sip of soft drink down before she shoved the burger and drink cup at him. She took the wheel as the autos dumped them onto Mason Drive, on a manual-only and most deserted street.

It didn't look like an assault kind of neighborhood, big reflective windows in a tower complex. It was offices and residences, one of the poshest Complexes in big D, real high rent district. You could say that was why a mech unit got pulled in off the Ringroad, instead of the dispatcher sending in the b&w line troops. You could make a second guess it was because the city wanted more people to move into the Complexes and a low crime rep was the major sales pitch. Or you could even guess some city councilman lived in The Arlington.

But that wasn't for a mere mech unit to question. Dave got his helmet out of the locker under his feet, put it on while Sheila was taking them into the

5

curbside lane, plugged into the collar unit that was already plugged to the tactile, put the gloves on, and put the visor down, in the interest of checkout time—

"Greet The Public," Sheila said with a saccharine and nasty smirk— meaning Department Po-li-cy said visors up when you were Meeting the Man: people didn't greatly like to talk to visors and armor.

"Yeah, yeah." He finished the checks. He had a street map on the HUD, the location of 29-R sector on the overall building shape, the relative position of the cruiser as it nosed down the ramp into The Arlington's garage. "Inside view, here, shit, I'm not getting it, have you got Library on it?"

"I'll get it. Get. Go"

He opened the door, bailed out onto the concrete curb. Car treads had tracked the rain in, neon and dead white glows glistened on the down ramp behind them. High and mighty Arlington Complex was gray concrete and smoked glass in its utilitarian gut. And he headed for the glass doors, visor up, the way Sheila said, fiber cameras on, so Sheila could track: Sheila herself was worthless with the mech, she had proven that by taking a shot from a dealer, so that her right leg was plex and cable below the knee, but as a keyman she was ace and she had access with an A with the guys Downtown.

She said, in his left ear, "Man's in the hall, name's Rozman, reports screaming on 48, a man running down the fire stairs—"

"Mr. Rozman," he said, meeting the man just past the doors. "Understand you have a disturbance."

"Ms. Lopez, she's the next door neighbor, she's hiding in her bedroom, she said there was screaming. We had an intruder on the fire stairs—"

"Man or woman's voice in the apartment?"

"Woman."

"What's our address?"

"4899."

"Minors on premises?"

"Single woman. Name's Emilia Nolan. Lives alone. A quiet type…no loud parties, no complaints from the neighbors…"

Rozman was a clear-headed source. He unclipped a remote, thumbed it on and handed it to the man. "You keep answering questions. You know what this is?"

"It's a remote."

"—Sheila, put a phone-alert on Ms. Lopez and the rest of the neighbors, police on the way up, just stay inside and keep behind furniture

6

until she gets word from us." He was already going for the elevators. "Mr. Rozman. Do you log entry/exists?"

On his right-ear mike: "On the street and the tunnels and the garage, the fire stairs…"

"Any exceptions?"

"No—Yes. The service doors. But those are manual key…only maintenance has that."

"Key that log to the dispatcher. Just put the d-card in the phone and dial 9999." The Exception to the log was already entered, miked-in from his pickup. "And talk to your security people about those service doors. That's city code. Sir." He was polite on autopilot. His attention was on Sheila at the moment, from the other ear, saying they were prepping interior schemas to his helmet view. "Mr. Rozman. Which elevator?" There was a bank of six.

"Elevator B. Second one on your left. That goes to 48s…"

He used his fireman's key on the elevator call, and put his visor down. The hall and the elevator doors disappeared behind a wire-schema of the hall and doors, all red and gold and green lines on black, and shifting as the mid-tier elevator grounded itself. He didn't look down as he got in; you didn't look down on a wire-view if you wanted your stomach steady. He sent the car up, watched the floors flash past, transparenced, heard a stream of checks from Sheila confirming the phone-alarm in action, residents being warned through the phone company—

"Lopez is a cardiac case," Sheila said, "hospital's got a cruiser on alert, still no answer out of 4899. Lopez says it's quiet now."

"You got a line on Lopez, calm her down." Presence-sniffer readout was a steady blue, but you got that in passageways, lot of traffic, everything blurred unless you had a specific to track: It was smelling for stress, and wasn't getting it here. "Rozman, any other elevators to 48?"

"Yeah, C and D."

"Can you get off anywhere from a higher floor?"

"Yes, sir, you can. Any elevator, if you are going down…"

Elevator stopped and the door opened. Solid floor across the threshold, with the scan set for anomalies against the wire-schema. Couple of potted palms popped out against the VR. Target door was highlighted gold. Audio kept hyping until he could hear the scuff of random movements from other apartments. "Real quiet," he said to Sheila. And stood there a moment while the sniffer worked, filling in tracks. You could see the swirl in the air currents where the vent was. You could see stress showing up soft red.

"Copy that," Sheila said. "Warrant's clear to go in."

7

He put himself on no-exhaust, used the fire-key again, stayed to the threshold. The air inside showed redder. So did the walls, on heat-view, but this was spatter. Lot of spatter.

No sound of breathing. No heartbeat inside the apartment.

He de-amped and walked in. A mech couldn't disturb a Scene—sniffer couldn't pick up a presence on itself, ditto on the Cyloprene of his mech rig, and while the rig was no-exhaust and he was on internal air. It couldn't sniff him, but feet could still smudge the spatters. He watched where he stepped, real-visual now, and discovered the body, a woman, fully dressed, sprawled face-up by the bar, next to the bedroom, hole dead center between the astonished eyes.

"Quick and clean for her," he said. "Helluva mess on the walls."

"Lab's on its way," Sheila said, alternate thought track. "I'm on you, D-D, just stand still a sec."

The sniffer was working up a profile, via Sheila's relays Downtown. He stood still, scanning over the body. "Woman about thirty, good-looking, plain dresser…"

Emilia Francis Nolan, age 34, flashed up on the HUD. *Canadian citizen, Martian registry, chief information officer Mars Transport Company.*

Thin, pale woman. Dark hair. Corporate style on the clothes. Canadian immigrant to Mars, returned to Earth on a Canadian passport. "Door was locked," he said.

"I noticed that," Sheila said.

Sniffer was developing two scents, the victim's and a second one. AMMONIA, the indicator said.

"Mild ammonia."

"Old fashioned stuff," he said. "Amateur." The sniffer was already sepping it out as the number three track. Ammonia wouldn't overload a modern sniffer. It was just one more clue to trace; and the tracks were coming clear now: Nolan's was everywhere, Baruque, the sniffer said—expensive perfume, persistent as hell. The ammonia had to be number two's notion. And you didn't carry a vial of it for social occasions.

But why in hell was there a live-in smell?

"Male," Sheila commented, meaning the number two track. "Lover's spat?"

"POSSeL-Q the manager didn't know about, maybe, lover's quarrel, clothes aren't mussed. Rape's not a high likely here." Stress in both tracks. The whole place stank of it.

"Going for the live one, Sheel. Hype it. Put out a phone alert, upstairs

8

and down, have ComA take over Rozman's remote, I don't need him but he's still a resource."

Out of the door, into the wire-schema of the hall. The sniffer had it good this time: the stress trail showed up clear and bright for the fire-door, and it matched the number two track, no question. "Forty-eight damn floors," he muttered: no good to take the elevator. You got professional killers or you got crazies or drugheads in a place like this, fenced in with its security locks, and you didn't know what any one of the three was going to do, or what floor they were going to do it on. He went through the fire-door and started down on foot, following the scent, down and down and down…

"We got further on Norton," Sheila said. "Assigned here eight months ago, real company climber, top grad, schooled on Mars, no live-ins on any MarsCorp record we can get to, but that guy was real strong in there. I'm saying he was somebody Norton didn't want her social circle to meet.

He ran steps and breathed, ran steps and breathed, restricted air, Sheila has a brain for figuring people, you didn't even have to ask her. A presence trail arrived into the stairwell, bright blue mingling with the red. "Got another track here," he found breath to say.

"Yeah, yeah, that's in the log, that's a maintenance worker, thirty minutes back. He'll duck out again on 25."

"Yeah." He was breathing hard. Making what time he could. The trail did duck out at 25, in a wider zone of blue, unidentified scents, the smell from the corridor blown into the shaft and fading into the ambient. His track stayed clear and strong, stress-red, and he went on real-view: the transparent stairs were making him sick. "Where's this let out? Garage downstairs?"

"Garage and mini-mall."

"Shit!"

"Yeah. We got a call from building security wanting a piece of it, told them to stay out of it…

"Thank God."

"Building Chief's an amateur with a cop-envy. We're trying to get another mech in."

"We got some fool with a gun he hasn't ditched, we got a mall full of people down there. Where's Jacobs?"

"Rummel's closer. —We got lab coming in. Lab's trying to get an ID match on your sniffer pickup."

"Yeah. You've got enough on it. Guy's sweating. So am I." He felt sweat running under the armor, on his face. The door said 14. The oxy was running out. Violate the Scene or not, he had to toggle to exhaust. After that, it was cooler, dank the way shafts were that went into the underground.

"We got some elevator use," Sheila said, "right around the incident, off 48. Upbound. Stopped on 50, 52, 78, 80, and came down again, 77, 34, 33, then your fire-call brought it down. Time-over-lap on the 78, the C-elevator was upbound."

"Follow it." Meaning somebody could have turned around and left no traces if he had gotten in another elevator-call. "Put Downtown on it, I need your brain."

"Awww. I thought it was the body."

"Stow it." He was panting again. The internal tank was out. He hoped he didn't need it again. Sheila went out of the loop: he could hear the silence on the phones. "Forty-damn-stories—"

Three, two, one, s-one. "Wire," he gasped, and got back the schema, that showed through the door into a corridor. He listened for noise, panting, while the net in the background zeed out his breathing and his heartbeat and the building fans and everything else but a dull distant roar that said humanity, a lot of it, music—the red was still there and it was on the door switch, but it thinned out in the downward stairwell.

"Went out on s-1."

"Street exit, mall exit," Sheila said. "Via the Arlington lobby. Dave, we got you help coming in."

"Good."

"Private mech."

Adrenaline went up a notch. "That's help? That's help? Tell them—"

"I did, buns, sorry about that. Name's Ross, she's inbound from the other tower, corporate security..."

"Just what I need. Am I going out there? They want me to go out there?"

"You're clear."

He hated it, he *hated* going out there, hated the stares, hated the Downtown monitoring that was going to pick up that pulse rate of his and have the psychs on his case. But he opened the door, he walked out into the lobby that was The Arlington's front face; and walked onto the carpet, onto stone, both of which were only flat haze to his eyes. Bystanders clustered and gossiped, patched in like the potted palms, real people stark against the black and wire lines of cartoonland, all looking at him and talking in half-voices as if that could keep their secrets if he wanted to hear. He just kept walking, down the corridor, following the faint red glow in the blue of Every-smell, followed it on through the archway into the wider spaces of the mall, where more real

10

people walked in black cartoon-space, and that red glow spread out into a faint fan-swept haze and a few spots on the floor.

Juvies scattered, a handful out of Parental, lay odds to it—he could photo them and tag them, but he kept walking, chose not even to transmit: Sheila had a plateful to track as it was. One smartass kid ducked into his face, made a face, and ran like hell. Fools tried that, as if they suspected there wasn't anybody real inside the black visor. Others talked with their heads partially turned, or tried not to look as if they were looking. That was what he hated, being the eyes and ears, the spy-machine that connected to everywhere, that made everybody ask themselves what they were saying that might go into files, what they has ever done or thought of that a mech might find reason to track…

Maybe it was the blank visor, maybe it was the rig—maybe it was everybody's guilt. With the sniffer tracking, you could see the stress around you, the faint red glow around honest citizens no different than the guy you were tracking, as if it was the whole world's guilt and fear and wrongdoing you were smelling, and everybody had some secret to keep and some reason to slink aside…

"Your backup's meeting you at A-3," Sheila said, and a marker popped up in the schema, yellow flasher.

"Wonderful. We got a make on the target?"

"Not yet, buns. Possible this guy's not on file. Possible we got another logjam in the datacall, a mass murder in Peoria, something like that." Sheila had her mouth full. "Everybody's got problems tonight."

"What are you eating?"

"Mmm. Sorry, there."

"Is that my cheeseburger?"

"I owe you one."

"You are really putting on weight, Sheel, you know that?"

"Yeah, its anxiety attacks." Another bite. "Your backup's Company, Donna Ross, 20 years on, service citation."

"Sheel." Might not be a play-cop then. Real seniority. He saw the black figure standing there in her own isolation, at the juncture of two dizzying walkways. Saw her walk in his direction, past the mistrustful stares of spectators. "Get some plainclothes in here yet?"

"We got reporters coming."

"Oh, great. Get 'em off, get the court on it—"

"Doing my best."

"Officer Dawes." Ross held out a black-gloved hand, no blues on the Company cop, just the rig, black cut-out in a wire-diagram world. "We're

11

interfaced. It just came up."

Data came up, B-channel. "Copy that." Ross was facing the same red track he was, was getting his data, via some interface Downtown, an inter-system handshake. He stepped onto the downbound escalator, Ross in his 360 compression view, a lean, black shape on the shifting kaleidoscope of the moving stairs. "This is a MarsCorp exec that got it?" Ross asked in his right ear. "Is that what I read?"

"Deader than dead. We got a potential gun walking around out here with the john-qs. You got material on the exec?"

"Some kind of jam-up in the net—I haven't got a thing but a see-you."

"Wonderful, both of us in the dark."

The escalator let off on the lower level, down with the fast foods and the arcades and a bunch of juvies all antics and ass.

"Get out of here," he snarled on Address, and juvies scattered through the cartoon-scape.

"Get upstairs!" he yelled, and some of them must have figured shooting was imminent, because they scattered double-time, squealing and shoving. Bright blue down here with the pepperoni pizza and the beer and the popcorn, but that single red threat was still showing.

"Our boy's sweating hard," Ross said in one ear; and Sheila in the other: "We got a sudden flash in a security door, right down your way."

"Come on."

Dave started to run. Ross matched him, a clatter of Cyloprene on tile, godawful racket. The exit in question was flashing yellow ahead. A janitor gawked, pressed himself against the wall in a try at invisibility; but his presence was blue, neutral to the area.

"You see anybody go through?"

"Yeah, yeah, I saw him, young guy, took to the exit, I said he wasn't—"
—Supposed to trailed into the amped mike as they banged through the doors and into a concrete service hall.

"Sheila, you in with Ross?"

"Yeah. Both of you guys. I got a b&w following you, he's not meched, best I could do..."

Red light strobed across his visor. WEAPONS ON, it said.

"Shit," he said, "Ross—" He stopped a breath against the corridor wall, drew his gun and plugged it in. Ross must have an order too; she was plugging in. Somebody Downtown had got a fire warrant. Somebody had decided on a fire-warrant next to a mall full of kids. Maybe because of the kids.

"What's our make on this guy, Sheila? Tell me we got a make, please

12

God, I don't like this, we got too many john-juniors out there."

"He's not on files."

"Off-worlder," Ross said.

"You know that?"

"If he's not in your files he's from off-world. The Company is searching. They've got your readout."

"Shit, somebody get us info."

The corridor was a moving, jolting wire-frame in the black.

Nobody. Not a sign.

But the red was there, bright and clear. Sheila compressed several sections ahead on the wire schema, folded things up close where he could get a look. There was a corner, he transviewed it, saw it heading to a service area. AIR SYSTEMS, the readout line said.

"We got an air-conditioning unit up there, feed for the whole damn mall as best I guess…he's got cover."

"Yeah," Ross said, "I copy that "

"We're not getting any damn data," Sheila said in his other ear. "I'm asking again on that make, and we're not getting it. Delay. Delay. Delay. Ask if her keyman's getting data."

"My keyman asks," he relayed, "if you've got data yet."

"Nothing new. I'm telling you, we're not priority, it's some little lover's spat—"

"That what they're telling you?"

"Uh-uh. I don't know a thing more than you. But a male presence, female body up there…that's how it's going to wash out. It always does."

"Dave," Sheila's voice again, while their steps rang out of time on the concrete and the red track ran in front of them. She had a tone when there was trouble. "Butterflies, you hear?"

"Yeah. Copy." Sheila wasn't liking something. She wasn't liking it a lot.

They reached the corner. The trail kept going, skirled in the currents from air ducts, glowing fainter in the gust from the dark. He folded the view tighter, looked ahead of them, didn't like the amount of cover ahead where they were going to come down stairs and across a catwalk.

Something banged, echoed, and the lights went out.

Didn't bother a mech. Maybe it made the quarry feel better, but they were still seeing, all wire-display. He was right on Ross, Ross standing there like a haze in the ambiance. Her rig scattered stuff you used in the dark. It was like standing next to a ghost. The Dallas PD didn't afford rigs like that.

Governments did. Some MarsCorp bigwig got shot and the Company lent a mech with this stuff?

Ross said. "IR. Don't trust the wire. Stay here."

"The hell."

Infrared blurred the wire-schema. But he brought his sensors up high-gain.

"No sonar," Ross said "Cut it, dammit!"

"What the hell are we after?"

"There he is!"

He didn't half see. Just a blur, far across the dark. Ross burst ahead of him, onto the steps; he dived after, in a thunder the audios didn't damp fast enough.

"Dave." Sheila's voice again, very solemn. His ears were still ringing when they got to the bottom. "Department's still got nothing. I never saw a jam this long… I never saw a rig like that."

They kept moving, fast, not running, not walking. The mech beside him was Company or some government's issue, a MarsCorp exec was stone dead, and you could count the organized crazies that might have pulled that trigger. A random crazy, a lover—a secessionist…

"Lab's on it," Sheila said. "Dave, Dave, I want you to listen to me."

He was moving forward. Sheila stopped talking, as Ross moved around a bundle of conduits and motioned him to go down the other aisle, past the blowers. Listen, Sheila said, and said nothing. The link was feeding to Ross. He was sure of it. He could hear Sheila breathing, hard.

"Mustard," Sheila muttered. "Dave, was it mustard you wanted on that burger?"

They'd never been in a situation like this, not knowing what was feeding elsewhere, not knowing whether Downtown was still secure with them on the line.

"Yeah," he breathed. He hated the stuff. "Yeah. With onions."

Sheila said, "You got it."

Ross started to move. He followed. The com was compromised. She'd asked was he worried, that was the mustard query. He stayed beside that ghost-glow, held to the catwalk rail with one hand, the other with the gun. The city gave out a fire-warrant, and your finger had a button. But theirs overrode, some guy Downtown. Or Sheila did. You didn't know. You were a weapon, with a double safety, and you didn't know whether the damn thing was live, ever.

"Dave," Sheila said. Totally different tone. "Dave. This Ross doesn't

14

have a keyman. She's backpacked. Total. She's a security guy."

Total mech. You heard about it, up on Sol, up in the Stations, where everything was computers. Elite of the elite. Independent operator with a computer for a backpack and neuros right into the station's high-tech walls.

He evened his breath, smelled the cold air, saw the thermal pattern that was Ross gliding ahead of him. A flash of infrared out of the dark. A door opened on light. Ross started running. He did.

A live-in lover? Somebody the exec would open the door to?

A mech could walk through a crime scene. A mech on internal air didn't leave a presence—nothing a sniffer would recognize.

A Company mech had been damned close to the scene—showed up to help the city cops…

"Sheila," he panted, trying to stay with Ross. "Lots of mustard."

Infrared glow ahead of them. A shot flashed out, from the company mech. It exploded in the dark, leaving tracers in his vision. Ross wasn't blinded. His foot went off a step, and he grabbed wildly for the rail, caught himself and slid two more before he had his feet under him on flat catwalk mesh—it shook as Ross ran; and he ran too.

"She's not remoted!" he panted. As if his keyman couldn't tell. Nobody outside was authorizing those shots. Ross was. A cartoon door boomed open, and he ran after a ghost whose fire wasn't routed through a whole damn city legal department. "Fold it! He gasped, because he was busy keeping up; and the corner ahead compacted and swung into view, red and green wire, with nobody in it but the ghost ahead of him.

"Slow down!" he said. "Ross! Wait up, dammit! Don't shoot!"

His side was aching. Ross was panting hard, he heard her breathing, he overtook in a cartoon-space doorway, in a dead-end room, where the trail showed hot and bright.

"We have him." Ross said. The audio hype could hear the target breathing, past their exhaust. Even the panicked heartbeat. Ross lifted her gun against a presence behind a stack of boxes.

"No!" he yelled. And the left half of his visor flashed yellow. He swung to it, mindless target-seek, and the gun in his hand went off on Ross, went off a second time while Ross was flying sideways through the dark. Her shot went wild off the ceiling and he couldn't think, couldn't turn off the blinking target square. Four rounds, five, and the room was full of smoke.

"Dave?"

He wasn't talking to Sheila. He wasn't talking to whoever'd triggered him, set off the reflexes they trained in a mech.

Shaky voice from his keyman. "If you can walk out of there, walk. Right now, Dave."

"The guy's in the—"

"No. He's not, Dave." The heartbeat faded out. The cartoon room had a smudged gray ghost on the floor grid at his feet. And a bright red lot of blood spattered around. "I want you to check out the restroom upstairs from here. All right?"

He was shaking now. Your keyman talked and you listened or you could be dead. He saw a movement on his left. He swung around with the gun up, saw the man stand up. Ordinary looking man, business shirt, soaked with sweat. Frozen with fear. The sniffer flashed red.

Sheila's voice said, from his shoulder-patch, "Don't touch anything, Dave. Get out of there. Now."

He moved, walked out, with the target standing at his back. He walked all the way back to the air-conditioning plant, and he started up the stairs there, up to the catwalk, while nothing showed, no one. Sheila said, "Dave. Unplug now. You can unplug."

He stopped, he reached with his other hand and he pulled the plug on the gun and put it in its holster. He went on up the cartooned metal stairs, and he found the cartooned hall and the cartooned restroom with the real-world paper on the floor.

"You better wash up," Sheila said, so he did that, shaking head to foot.

Before he was finished, a b&w came in behind him, and said, "You all right, sir?"

"Yeah," he said. Sheila was quiet then.

"You been down there?" the cop asked.

"You saw it," Sheila said in his ear and he echoed her: "I saw it—guy got away—I couldn't get a target. Ross was in the way..."

"Yes, sir," the b&w said. "You're on record, sir."

"I figured."

"You sure you're all right? I can call—"

"I can always call, officer."

The guy got a disturbed look, the way people did, who forgot they were talking to two people. "Yes, sir," the b&w said, "All right."

On his way out.

He turned around to the mirror, saw a plain, sick face. Blood was on the sink rim, puddled around his boots, where it had run off the plastic. He went into a stall, wiped off his rig with toilet paper and flushed the evidence.

Sheila said, "Take the service exits. Pick you up at the curb."

16

"Copy," he mumbled, took his foot off the seat, flushed the last bit of bloody paper, taking steady small breaths, now. They taught you to trust the autos with your life. They taught you to swing to the yellow, don't think. Don't ask, swing and hold, swing and hold the gun.

A mech just walked away, afterward, visor down, communing with his inner voices. Everything went to the interfaces. There was a record. Of course there was a record. Everyone knew that.

It was at the human interface things could drop out.

He used the fire key, walked out an emergency exit, waited in the rain.

The cruiser nosed up to the curb, black and black-windowed, and swallowed him up.

"Saved the soft drink," Sheila said. "Thought you'd be dry."

It was half ice-melt. But it was liquid. It eased a raw throat. He sucked on the straw, leaned his head back. "They calling us in?"

"No," Sheila said. That was all. They didn't want a de-brief. They didn't want a truth. They wanted—wanted nothing to do with it. Nolan's body to the next-ofs, the live-in...to whoever, wherever would hide him.

Another mouthful of ice-melt. He shut his eyes, saw wire-schemas, endlessly folding, a pit you could fall into. He blinked on rain and refracted neon. "Ross killed Nolan."

"You and I don't know."

"Was it Ross?"

"Damned convenient a Company mech was in hail. Wasn't it?"

"No Presence at all. Nolan—Nolan was shot between the eyes."

"MarsCorp exec—her live-in boyfriend with no record, no visa, no person. Guy who knew The Arlington's underground, who had a pass key—"

"He was keying through the doors?"

"Same as you were. Real at-home in the bottom tiers. You see a weapon on him, you see where he ditched one?"

"No." Raindrops fractured, flickering off the glass. He saw the gray ghost again, the no-Presence that could walk through total black. Or key through any apartment door, or aim a single head-shot with a computer's inhuman, instant accuracy.

He said, "Adds, doesn't it?"

"Adds. Downtown was seeing what I was. I told them. Told them you had bad feelings—"

"What the hell are they going to do? We got a dead mech down here—
"

"The live-in shot Nolan. Shot the company mech. That's your story. They can't say otherwise. What are they going to say? That the guy didn't have a gun? They won't come at us."

"What about our record?"

"Transmission breakup. Lightening or something." Sheila's face showed rain-spots, running shadows, neon glare. "Bad night. D-D, bad shit."

"They erase it?"

"Erase what?" Sheila asked.

Silence then. Rain came down hard.

"They want to bring their damn politics down here," Sheila said, "they can take it back again. Settle it up there."

"Settle what?" he echoed Sheila.

But he kept seeing corridors, still the corridors, folding in on themselves. And sipped the tasteless soft drink. "The guy's shirt was clean."

"Huh?"

"His shirt was clean." Flash on the restroom, red water swirling down and down. "He wasn't in that room. Nolan knew Ross was coming. The guy was living there. His smell's all over. That's why the ammonia trick. Nolan sent him for the stairs, I'll bet it's in the access times. He couldn't have hid from a mech. And all that screaming? The mech wanted something. Something Nolan wasn't giving. Something Ross wanted more than she wanted the guy right then."

"Secession stuff. Documents. Martian Secession. Not illegal, not in Dallas…"

"The mech missed the live-in, had to shut Nolan up. Didn't get the records, either. A botch. Thorough-going botch. The live-in—who knew the building like that? He wasn't any Company man. Martian with no visa, no regulation entry to the planet? I'll bet Nolan knew what he was, I'll bet Nolan was passing stuff to the Movement."

"An exec in MarsCorp? Over Martian Transport? Ask how the guy got here with no visa."

"Shit," he said. Then he thought about the mech, the kind of tech the rebels didn't have.

They wouldn't want a witness," he said. "The rebels wouldn't. The Company damned sure wouldn't. Ross would've gone for me, except I was linked in. I was recording. So she couldn't snatch the guy—had to shut the guy up somehow. They damn sure couldn't have a Company cop arrested down here. Had to get him shut up for good and get Ross off the planet…"

"Dead in," Sheila said. "Dead for sure, if he had talked. Washington was after the Company for the make and the Company was stonewalling like hell, lay you odds to that—and I'll bet there's a plane seat for Ross tonight on Guiana flight. What's it take? An hour down there? Half an hour more, if a shuttle's ready to roll, and Ross would have been no-return for this jurisdiction. That's all they needed." She flipped the com back to On again, to the city's ordinary litany of petty crime and larcenies, beneath an uneasy sky. "This is 34, coming on-line, marker 15 on the pike, good evening, HQ. This is a transmission check, think we've got it fixed now, 10-4?"

END TRANS

C.J. CHERRYH has won four Hugo Awards and is one of the best-selling and most critically acclaimed authors in the science fiction and fantasy field, the author of more than forty novels. Her hobbies include travel, photography, reef culture, Mariners baseball, and, a late passion, figure skating: she intends to compete in the adult USFSA track. She began with the modest ambition to learn to skate backwards and now is working on jumps. She sketches, occasionally, cooks fairly well, and hates house work; she loves the outdoors, animals wild and tame, is a hobbyist geologist, adores dinosaurs, and has academic specialties in Roman constitutional law and Bronze Age Greek ethnography. She has written science fiction since she was ten, spent ten years of her life teaching Latin and Ancient History on the high school level, before retiring to full time writing, and now does not have enough hours in the day to pursue all her interests. Her studies include planetary geology, weather systems, and natural and man-made catastrophes, civilizations, and cosmology…in fact, there's very little that doesn't interest her. A loom is gathering dust and needs rethreading, a wooden ship model awaits construction, and the cats demand their own time much more urgently. She works constantly, researches mostly on the Internet, and has books stacked up and waiting to be written. She can be contacted on Facebook, Twitter, and her website Closed Circle www.closed-circle.net.

LAST HUMAN

Jorge Salgado-Reyes

Originally appeared in the Eat Sleep Write Flash Fiction Contest in May 2014 where it came third.

I looked back at the tracks my suit left on the desert sand. Already the wind started to erase them. Only the radioactive rain for company. Up ahead, the highest point of Ojos del Salado beckoned. I trudged upward, pulling the sledge as nightfall descended, encasing me in darkness. A darkness pierced only by my suit light. I kept going. Twenty minutes until moon-rise.

Finally, the summit. I looked back across the moon-lit landscape. Nothing moved. Nothing lived here. My eyes lifted to the moon as it peeped above the horizon. Luna seen through an orange haze.

It's been twenty-five years since we did it. We completely fucked it all up. We let those mother-fuckers blow it up. No one knows who started it but the fingers all point at the big three so-called superpowers. The three-day war annihilated what people used to call the West. Now Europe lies under a sheet of ice. You can walk across the Mediterranean. The Sahara is under the sea. England is gone, completely wiped from the face of the Earth. Someone air burst a nuke over the Amazonian basin. The trees are all gone and the ice conquers all. The winds scour the land clean. The radioactive rain brings death to all it touches.

We here in the Observatory watched it all. My colleagues all left, trying to reach their families. They didn't make it. I took in the few pitiful survivors from the south; Mapuche, who fled the ice.

I am the only one left. The two hundred and fifty Mapuche died within a few months of radiation poisoning. Only myself now, living under the Atacama desert. And then the weather worsened. Radio transmissions, once multitudinous, grew silent one by one.

On a night like today, I stare at that orange moon and wonder. I wonder if anyone up there survived? We were conquering space. They called it the Final Frontier once. We established Luna City but without resupplies from Earth, there's no way they could have survived. We had even sent a small team to Mars.

The author Robert Heinlein once wrote,

It may take endless wars and unbearable population pressure to force-feed a technology to the point where it can cope with space. In the universe, space travel may be the normal birth pangs of an otherwise dying race. A test. Some races pass, some fail.

I guess we failed. The tears stung my face as I dug into the earth and made the posts ready for the plaque. I attached it to the posts.

I leave this plaque here for whatever alien race might one day find it. This plaque commemorates the Human race, once masters of Earth, wiped out by our own folly. Remember us and know that we reached out to the vast expanse of the universe and we dreamed of one day joining you. We dreamed and failed! I, Professor Eduardo Rocha, last of the People.

END

JORGE SALGADO-REYES is a Chilean and British sci-fi/cyberpunk author, private investigator, and photographer. Born in Temuco, Chile, Salgado-Reyes left his country of birth at age seven in 1975 with his family driven into exile by the Pinochet dictatorship. Subsequently brought up in the United Kingdom, he changed residence frequently with his family as a child. Salgado-Reyes became somewhat of a loner who read science fiction from an early age. After spending his adolescence in Mozambique, he returned to the UK where he completed his education.

In 2011, Salgado-Reyes began writing his first novel, *The Smoke in Death's Eye*, a work still in progress.

In 2012, Indie Authors Press published Salgado-Reyes' first reference book, *British Process Servers Guide*, written in collaboration with Stuart Withers and Helen Withers.

Salgado-Reyes can be contacted on Facebook, Twitter, or through his Amazon Author Page. Further information can be found on www.salgado-reyes.com/wiki/jorge-salgado-reyes-2/.

ANNABELLE'S CHILDREN

Gregory J. Wolos

From up here on the ceiling, I see three scalps beneath me. Their owners are having a meeting. The fluorescent lights illuminate one head that's shaved and gleaming with an indentation in the center that looks like a sunken grave, one with a hairline receding to dark curls, and a third with a comb-over that fails to cover skin the color and texture of butterscotch pudding. This head and the head with curls belong to men I knew when I was alive.

I've been dead for days and days, and this is the first time I've recognized anyone, so I don't know if my presence in this room is by coincidence or design. "Dead" for me has been a completely passive experience. Every morning I wake up attached to something that's living—something different each day, no repeats, at least not so far. Yesterday I was with a goldendoodle, the day before a Starbucks barista. Today, it's this spider on the ceiling. I've got no will of my own, no physical essence. Where my host goes, I go. And though I share my partner's space, I'm neither seen nor felt. So far I've had no appetites at all. I recognize emotions, but I don't seem to feel them. I have extraordinary patience—have you ever spent a day connected to a clam?

This morning the men down at the conference table are talking about me and the eggs harvested from my ovaries before I lost my battle with acute myelogenous leukemia. Carl, the one with the curls, was to have been my husband. The comb-over guy is P.P. Frederico, the filmmaker who gave me my big break after my last stint in rehab, years before my death. The shaved scalp belongs to a stranger. The three are discussing an idea for a reality TV show—*Annabelle's Children*, one of them called it.

"You say you've got full legal rights to Annabelle's eggs?" shaved head asks.

Carl clears his throat. "Zygotes," he says, "not eggs. Annabelle and I were told that fertilized eggs would survive the freezing better. I supplied the sperm. The zygotes are legally mine."

Carl's right. My eggs were harvested because aggressive chemotherapy and radiation were going to sterilize me. His sperm fertilized the salvaged eggs *in vitro*, and the zygotes were frozen so we could have our own biological children when I recovered. Which I didn't.

Light reflects off the stranger's polished head. He must be a network executive. His fingers drum the table. "I don't know. Isn't the point of this show that each couple—each husband of the couple—will fertilize one of Annabelle's eggs himself? The way I understood it is you have the competitive stuff first—the sports and the trivia contests and whatever—singing, if you want—with the usual up-close-and-personals, followed by the audience vote. Then the winning dads fertilize the eggs, which get implanted in their wives."

"We plan at least one show on the science of it all," P.P. says. "Doctors, test tubes, Petri dishes. Footage of sperm penetrating eggs. We stagger the implantations so we get about eight weeks' worth of births at the end of the season. Twelve couples is the target."

"Hunh," the network guy grunts. "But Annabelle is the attraction. People want to be connected to her! No offense, but what's the appeal of kids that are half Carl's?"

"Didn't you read the market research we sent?" P.P. asks. "Focus groups couldn't differentiate between 'egg' and 'zygote.' We just de-emphasize Carl. We lose him in the scientific mumbo-jumbo, as far as the TV audience is concerned. For potential competitor-parents—ninety-five percent of those questioned deemed the father's biological involvement 'unimportant.' This is about Annabelle and nothing else, Larry."

"If we include episodes on the impact of environment on child development, it'll be better scientifically if all the kids had the same biological mother and father," Carl offers quietly.

"But," P.P. says, "what we're selling is Annabelle and her children."

Carl's head has flushed pink, but he's silent. Is he angry? It seems this bargaining with my eggs would have disturbed me once. Was it Carl or P.P. who cooked up this reality show idea? They'd collaborated on the cartoon-horror remake of *The Island of Doctor Moreau* that resurrected the career I'd done my best to trash. The animated *Moreau* flopped, but the voice I gave to the wretched dog-man M'ling found empathetic ears among the lonely and miserable, and my performance drew raves. With P.P. to vouch for my rejuvenated work ethic, offers poured in. Broadway called, and I won a Tony playing a young mother. Then serious films—more mothers. Even illness couldn't keep me down—when work became impossible, I became a role model, a leading advocate for cancer research. Those Thrive awareness anklets, the magenta ones you see everywhere? Inspired by my tribulations.

"Annabelle Hadley is a classic American story of redemption, Larry." P.P. slaps the table. "*Annabelle's Children* will immortalize her!" He pauses.

23

"From porn star to angel," he sighs.

"I don't know about 'porn star,'" Carl murmurs. I don't deny it could have happened. Prior to my final visit to rehab, while promoting my Scaredy Cat line of clothing in a Walmart, I'd made lewd gestures with my microphone before propositioning the store manager. Then I'd thrown up and passed out.

"We wouldn't go there," Larry says. But he admits, "She had a hell of a life," and I know he's sold on my show.

"Right," P.P. says. "We start with a documentary. Two hours, Carl?"

"Two parts, one hour each."

"M-hmm. Two hours on Annabelle's roller coaster life. We'll show the couples competing for the zygotes weeping over the highs and lows, the final tragedy. But the winners will have the chance to bear Annabelle's children!"

"The couples' demographics?" Larry asks.

"Like any other reality show: rich, poor, minorities—hey, Carl, gay men would need their own surrogate wouldn't they?"

My former lover shakes his head. "Too complicated. It would be easier to go with a lesbian couple."

There's silence, and P.P. looks up toward the fluorescent lights. His dark glasses are impenetrable. The other men follow his gaze. Carl's brown eyes look sad. I think Larry might see my spider, but he doesn't say anything.

"She was beautiful, wasn't she?" P.P. asks. Carl and Larry mumble assent.

Larry's indentation reminds me of an infant's soft spot—something's pulsing in it. Maybe Carl should have been the one to bring up my beauty. Being dead, I don't dwell on it, but somewhere between party-girl bloat and dying-woman desiccation there was beauty. And in the beginning, too, when I was an innocent child with Hollywood dreams.

"Reunion shows," Larry says dreamily.

"And guaranteed spin-offs," P.P. adds. "Maybe decades of programming. *Annabelle's Children* will be the biggest entertainment phenomenon we've ever seen. Think of the merchandising opportunities. It's like we're breeding our own celebrities."

"We will be breeding our own celebrities," Carl says. I look down at the curls I used to run my fingers through. My almost-husband had a diminished sense of smell: He claimed he'd burned out his nostril cilia when he was a boy, huffing hot ammonia gas brewed from a Christmas-gift chemistry set. He had virtually no sense of taste either and had to fake compliments when we ate at celebrity gourmet restaurants.

A cell-phone chimes and all three men reach for a pocket, while my host spider dashes into a gap in the dropped ceiling. It's dark. Today is about to end. If death holds form, tomorrow I'll wake up with a new partner. I've got forever to find out what happens to my children.

I'm attached to a pet ferret. Its nose and eyes are tiny black beads, and it wears a blue collar as thin as a rubber band. We curl around a pink bunny slipper and peek out from beneath a sofa. Running shoes flank our sides like the walls of a fortress. Two adults and two children sit above us. From time to time a popcorn kernel drops, and the ferret darts forward and nips it up, then retreats. Sounds of nibbling accompany the TV voices like static. The television's flickering light paints every surface.

The children are young—a boy and a girl. Nothing has been familiar since Carl and P.P.'s meeting, so I suppose that my presence there was a coincidence and not part of any plan. I can only guess that my experience is the same as everyone who's dead—we're all attached to a living thing. Wouldn't it be something if the entire universe of the dead was attached to the same body— my ferret, for instance? We're a weightless and volume-less population, we overlap, and, in our perpetually increasing numbers, maybe we all switch to a new body together every night. Who can say? I'm already telling you more than you could possibly have known.

My ferret's family is watching a documentary about me, the prelude to *Annabelle's Children*. There are clips from some of my earliest movies. When I was a child, my eyes were wide and green and impish. My hair fell over my shoulders in auburn waves.

"She looks like Cindy, doesn't she look like Cindy?" the mother on the sofa says. No one answers. On screen my child-self makes a sassy quip, and above me the children and mother giggle. Another popcorn kernel falls and my ferret grabs it. Nibble nibble. A solemn voice narrates over photographs of me. I'm not so cute here—makeup blurs my features, and I wear short skirts and low-cut blouses that show my developing breasts. When I smile, my mouth is open and my tongue shows. Pose after pose in gown after gown on miles of red carpet. How many packs a day was I smoking? When did I develop the taste for Jack Daniels? I'm in a courtroom. My hair is tied back, and I look sorry. A judge speaks without making eye contact. Police officers usher me away, their hands floating beside my elbows without touching them. Then I'm dancing wildly, my eyes raking across space as I twirl. There's my little red Porsche— and there it is again with its front crumpled. The dad sitting above me on the sofa laughs, low and guttural.

"Rehab" punctuates every other sentence. "Things were to get much worse before they got better," the narrator says. There's a grainy video on the screen—a security tape. That's me in sweatpants and a hoodie. I'm at a gas pump next to the Porsche, which has either been repaired or has yet to be damaged. Gasoline gushes from a hose dangling from the car—a puddle expands on the pavement. I've wrapped an arm around the pump, and I'm waving a cigarette lighter and howling. Next, an officer protects my head as I'm plugged into the back of a police cruiser: I grin as if I'm listening to a private joke.

There's M'ling—the vivisected cartoon dog-man from *The Island of Doctor Moreau*—who led me back to a righteous path.

"Did we see that cartoon? Can we see it?" one of the children asks.

"It's a horror movie. It's rated R," the mother says. My dog-man cowers in the midnight shadows of tropical trees. The narrator mentions P.P. and Carl. I stand between them in a photograph. All three of us smile. I'd forgotten that I'd buzzed off all my hair while recording *Moreau*. I knew what baldness was like before chemotherapy.

A PLAYBILL cover—I'm wearing an apron. My hair is shoulder length. I'm playing a mother. Then I'm standing at a podium, displaying an award.

"Part two tomorrow!" the narrator says. "Recovery and triumph."

I don't know where I'll be tomorrow. My host may not be near a television, and I'll miss seeing my final chapter among the living. They'll say I "battled bravely." This documentary won't show Carl, though he surely helped make it. He held my skeletal hand as I shuffled in loose pajamas to the rooms of doomed children. In my last days I bowed over them, my head as hairless as theirs, and offered what I could. There'd soon be nothing left for Carl. Maybe I owed him *Annabelle's Children*.

Try to imagine an existence without expectations. Without surprise. Without impatience.

Season One of *Annabelle's Children* is about to conclude: The twelve couples who have won my fertilized eggs will be named. Implantations are to take place during the summer hiatus, and Season Two's opening episode will reveal the successful pregnancies. Viewers are teased by the prospect of a dozen mothers swelling to term with babies due in the spring.

I gather this information while in the company of a speckled catfish. We're suctioned to the glass of an aquarium. Algae and dust obscure the television across the small, dim room. It's a struggle to hear over the pump's hum and filter's bubbling. Other fish waft above, beneath, and behind us. A young man, alone, slouches on the futon beside the table that supports our tank. He wears shorts and a T-shirt. One hand is down his pants, the other holds a beer. The pillow and blanket on the futon suggest it's his bed. I see a sink, a mini-fridge and a counter full of dirty plates; an open door exposes a toilet.

Also on the table with our aquarium is a framed photograph of a bride and groom, which I study during commercial breaks. The groom is a tuxedoed version of the young man on the couch. The bride is—me. I glance away again and again, but each time I look back there's no question that I'm looking at myself. I've been photo-shopped into the picture—I'm almost twice the groom's size. I recognize the silver gown I wore at the Tony Awards. I suspect I'm replacing another woman, someone the young man wants to exclude from his studio apartment. He continues watching television, unaware that he's been found out. Is this what "haunting" means?

Annabelle's Children summarizes with highlights the months of competition that will earn the winning couples my eggs: a young African-American couple stagger through calf deep mud—the man is heavy, stumbles, and pulls his wife down face-first into the muck; another couple, tan and blond, argue over a quiz question I can't hear because of the humming and bubbling—the woman offers an answer with a furrowed brow, the couple embraces joyfully, and the number of points displayed in front of them grows by a hundred; a pair of young women struggle across a rope bridge over surging rapids while carrying a life-size baby doll.

The couples who have competed fill an auditorium. The camera sweeps over eager, anxious faces as all await the outcome of their trials. My catfish dislodges from the aquarium glass, drops to the blue gravel, and wriggles and sucks its way behind a scummy rock. Fish cruise over us like space ships. Time passes.

We're back on the glass. A dozen smiling couples stand on the stage—the winners. The host introduces profiles of the last few: here is the blond couple. Their ages, jobs, state of residence (Massachusetts), and income are posted over a video of the pair frolicking with a Husky in their suburban yard. The next couple, a black man and his Asian wife, sit on the stoop of a modest Indiana home. Their posted income is a tenth of the blond couple's. The last duo, a pair of healthy-looking young women, is doing as well financially as the blonds—one is a financial analyst, the other a photographer. They live in an oceanfront condo in San Diego. I wonder which of the two will carry my baby. I missed the profiles of the other winning couples while the catfish foraged. The closing credits roll over a cartoon picture of a red-haired woman in an apron holding a basket of eggs aloft. I assume that's supposed to be me. Carl's and P.P.'s names slide over me and disappear.

"Get to bed!" insists the robed mother to my host, a little girl of about seven who lingers barefooted on the linoleum floor of a narrow hallway. Her mother lounges on a couch. Ashes from the cigarette pinched in the woman's lips threaten the face of the infant she holds like a loaf of bread.

"But the babies are on. I want to see the babies."

"Then you shouldn't have back-talked about your homework."

"But I don't have any homework."

"Your teacher says she gives homework every night. That's what she said."

"But I did it in school. I promise! There was time to do it in school today. Can't I see the babies?"

If my host goes to bed, it will be dark, and tomorrow I'll be elsewhere.

"You got your sister, Brittany." The mother stuffs her cigarette into a soda can on the table by her elbow. "Get me another Diet Pepsi, and you can stay up," she says to my partner, and the little girl and I scamper into the kitchen. There are dishes in the sink and bottles in a pot on the stove. A crayon drawing of a pony with a rainbow mane and tail decorates the refrigerator, which contains cartons of milk and juice, Tupperware of different sizes, and a dozen or so cans of soda. We return to the living room, and my little girl hops onto the sofa after handing the beverage to her mom. She stretches her heels to the coffee table. Grime rims her toenails. The baby mews and snuggles into her mother's belly.

"Will Shana be on this one? I like it when Shana's on."

"Shh. How do I know? Keep quiet or you're going to bed."

Shana is three, as are all nine of my children. Ten of the couples winning my eggs had successful, full-term pregnancies. One of my babies, Harrison, died with his mother in a car crash last season. I missed the special memorial program, though I saw the commercial for it: Harrison is shoveling SpaghettiOs into his mouth, but most of the pasta is on his cheeks and chin. He has red hair, like most of my children. His mother laughs in the background as she records her son's messy eating. If the deaths of Harrison and his mother are like mine, maybe they've seen themselves on *Annabelle's Children*.

The first segment of tonight's show features little Veronica. Her parents have separated and share custody of their daughter. Veronica's dad is a construction foreman, and he brings her to work, where she wears a miniature hard hat. She has curls like Carl's. According to the show's host, Veronica "was

28

the first of the children to walk," but there's no video to document the event. I've seen other babies' first words and steps, birthday parties, and Disneyland vacations.

No Shana yet for my little host. Her dirty feet waggle impatiently on the coffee table during the show's second segment, which features the "scientific" aspects of *Annabelle's Children*. There are statistics and numbers. How many hours are spent in daycare? Who was nursed and who given bottles? Hours of television? Hours read to? Nutritional choices? Doctors in white coats discuss the "likelihoods" of this or that, but no conclusions are reached.

"Shana!" my little girl cries when her favorite appears, briefly, stacking blocks while a technician marks down her progress on a clipboard. My host has tied her pigtails in rainbow ribbons that match the bow in Shana's red hair.

I don't know what I am to these children. I'm not their birth mother, but their skin and hair and feet, their faces and their heart, have grown from my cells. I'm their First Cause. The last segment features Simon. His parents are lawyers. He looks a lot like Shana, and seems to have an eye for the camera—he poses in ways that remind me of photographs of myself in fan magazines. Tonight, while bouncing Simon on their laps, his mother and father discuss "transgendering."

Annabelle's Children's theme song plays while the credits roll. It's a version of my one hit from the only album I recorded. "Who's your mother? Where's your mother?" I'd rasped and ranted punkishly. A children's chorus sings the TV show's rendition, accompanied by a harp. Unless I missed his name, Carl is no longer listed as a "Creative Consultant."

Baby Brittany wails, her mother swears under her breath, and my host rises, pats her little sister's head, and we're off to bed. My TV children have no siblings in their families. Did I miss a rule prohibiting them? I've seen no signs of a male in this house. It's hard for a single mother to care for more than her infant—I learned that in my very last movie, and, since I've been dead, I've seen the truth of it again and again.

I've been hosted by countless dogs, but this is the smallest, some kind of Chihuahua. We're tucked between the knees of an old woman. She wears stretch pants and gray slippers that might once have been as purple as the burst veins mottling her swollen ankles. When the dog whimpers to pee its owner's sagging face tightens into a fist.

"Jingles, can't you hold it?" she whines in a pitch that matches her dog's. She struggles with the lever to her easy chair, and Jingles and I hop to the floor of their double-wide. When she pushes open the aluminum door, we skip from a cinder block to the hardpan, and Jingles squats. The woman clings to the door handle while she waits and looks back over her shoulder at her small television. I can't see much in the dark, but from neighboring trailers I hear quarreling TV show voices.

Back between the bony knees. Jingles gnaws on a huge biscuit. It's been many nights since I've seen *Annabelle's Children*. They're calling this special show a "reunion," but the kids have never met. When their parents won my eggs, they'd agreed to keep the children apart, "for the purpose of scientific observation." The boys and girls are eight years old now. Everyone is dressed nicely; children and adults sit at separate daises. Between them is a microphone at which a tuxedoed host and several guests take turns reminiscing and joking mildly about *Annabelle's Children*.

"The kids could have their own baseball team," a speaker quips. I anticipate other jokes about "nine," but all I can think of is that cats have nine lives, and "lives" don't seem appropriate to mention because of little Harrison. In all the time I've been dead, I've never been hosted by a cat. The children have seen their own TV show and understand its premise. They're awkward in the presence of so many biological brother and sister celebrities they don't know. They ignore the host and peek, mouths agape, at the familiar faces of strangers. No two are identical, and together they present a spectrum of resemblance that runs from Carl to me—dark curls to red hair, brown eyes to green. Looking at them is like looking into funhouse mirrors, and I suspect they feel the same way. Are they forming bonds or discovering them? Their parents squint toward the children with clenched smiles and seem to want to rush over and claim their own.

The kids, their parents, and the television audience watch a video montage that begins with swollen-bellied mothers, then shows the children as infants and toddlers, interspersed with clips of my childhood movies, then shots of me receiving my Tony. A final video shows me delivering a speech at a children's hospital shortly before I died. I am bald and hollow-eyed, but I say inspiring things about thinking positively and devoting oneself to a cause. Finally, waiters roll out a grand sheet cake. THANK YOU ANNABELLE is printed across it. The host prepares to cut into it with a saber-sized knife and invites the children to gather around with their plates.

Tears sparkle like jewels on the cheeks of Jingles' owner. Have I heard or am I guessing that this is the final episode of *Annabelle's Children*? P.P. Frederico had predicted more than a single decade. While my anthem *Who's Your Mother?* plays, the camera pans one last time across the cake-smeared faces of my children. The song stops as the credits freeze on two names, little Harrison's and P.P.'s, followed by their birth and death years. Maybe P.P., wherever he is, has witnessed this memorial. Maybe he and Harrison are here. Maybe everyone's here. Do you know any different?

If my death follows a pattern, I don't have the distance to interpret it. But I pass fewer nights attached to humans and domesticated creatures. Frequently, I slide through the dark with nocturnal hosts I may or may not see. I have wheeled with bats and lain between crickets' whittling legs. There have been the speed and power and violence of hunting, cries of power or fear. I have burrowed, deep, into loamy soil and rotting hearts.

When I am indoors, my hosts often dive for darkness, and I catch only winks of light. Tonight I hear whispered endearments and murmurs of pleasure: there's lovemaking, but I'm with neither partner. Too dark even for shadows—I must be attached to a dust mite between a mattress and box spring. We rock with the sex, and if by some chance Harrison from Season Four is with us, maybe he remembers that rocking gave him comfort. One of the lovers cries out. Motion stops. Every moment is eternal patience.

I'm coupled with an infant—it seems like forever since I've been attached to a human. His face presses into his mother's breast. He gasps, exhausted and ecstatic from suckling. His mother watches television, but her embracing arms block the screen.

"Shh," the mother whispers.

"Physics means pondering the imponderables," the TV voice says. All television voices sound like the announcer's from *Annabelle's Children*. When I ponder "time," I picture the lines a prisoner scratches on a cell wall—four lines and a cross hatch, four lines and a cross hatch—five and five and five and on and on, until everything is shaded into darkness.

My host-baby coos and frets, reconnects to his mother's nipple.

"Mmm," his mother sighs.

"Paul Dirac," the television voice continues, "theorized that whether light is composed of waves or particles depends on whether you ask it a wave-like or particle-like question."

Don't tell me that you understand!

On this endless day, I can't tell to what or whom I'm attached; time no longer seems to be something that moves. There's light, but I don't ask it questions about particles or waves. The light illuminates the bookshelf I face

31

and have been facing forever. I focus on a book with a glossy paper cover; it's surrounded by dusty, title-less volumes. Studying the spine of this newer book is all I do.

I haven't lost the sense that I'm attached, but either the dynamics of connection have changed (were due to change?), or I'm hosted by something imperceptible to my understanding. What could be so small? A microbe? A malignant cell?

The book I stare at is titled *My Life as a Child of Annabelle: The End of Reality TV*. Below the title and unreadable author's name, a sweep of auburn hair spreads over the book's spine from a hidden cover photo. It might be my hair. It could belong to one of my babies. I've looked at this spine so long I can't imagine not seeing it. Concerning the title, I can ask one kind of question if "End" means "death," and a different kind of question if "End" means "goal."

As far as you know, you're hosting all of the dead. And maybe that's the end.

END

GREGORY J. WOLOS lives in upstate New York on the bank of the Mohawk River. His short fiction has recently appeared or is forthcoming in *Post Road, A-Minor Magazine, JMWW, Yemassee, The Baltimore Review, The Madison Review, The Los Angeles Review, PANK, A cappella Zoo, Jersey Devil Press*, and many other journals and anthologies. His stories have earned two Pushcart Prize nominations, and his latest collection was named a finalist for the 2012 Flannery O'Connor Short Fiction Award. He lives and writes in upstate New York on the northern bank of the Mohawk River. For lists of his various publications and commendations, visit www.gregorywolos.com.

LIVING IN THE SINGULARITY

Tom Borthwick

Originally published in *Bewildering Stories*, issue #550, November 2013.

"Integration" is the buzz word these days. It's on the news stations. In the papers. On the ads in the subway. Even the guys at work are dropping one by one, it seems, because, hey, Integration. I haven't been in for about a week, not that there's much to do there what with the decrease in demand, but when I get back, I'm sure some more of them will be gone. My maintenance partner, Dave, went two weeks ago. Told me I should think about going, too. "Go with the rest of the flies," I told him. Felt bad about it after. Didn't want to leave my friend on such a sour note. But there it was. Nothing to be done now. He's gone on to the other side.

This whole thing started a few years back. Solacium Corp. came out of nowhere saying it invented the Singularity—the next step in human evolution. Some kind of supercomputer where everybody uploads their consciousness and lives forever in happiness. Kind of like a Heaven on Earth. Or cyberspace, maybe. A lot of religious types called it the Tower of Babel and said everything we'd built would come crashing down.

Things haven't so much crashed down as disappeared. The streets get emptier every day in my neck of the woods. Across the proverbial tracks in The City, as it's called, things seem to be doing fine. That's where Dave and I work. Well, that's where I work. I do lawn care for Solacium employees. The City isn't technically a city, it's their HQ. All the employees live there with everything they could ever want and more. Art imported from all the world museums, the best wines, the finest homes. Hell, everybody lives in his own personal mansion. I'm one of the privileged few that knows it, being I work over there. Had to sign confidentiality agreements. A few guys broke them and got disappeared. That was enough for the rest of us to keep quiet. But it was also enough for everybody outside The City to get the word that the Solacium people that jack you into the Singularity have it pretty damn good. They get their glamorous lives while the rest of us barely get by in the real world or jack into the fake, blissful one.

33

So on my side of the tracks, there's nothing. No point in going to bars anymore. Nobody to drink with. Nobody nowhere. Everybody got sucked in. It's an easy sell. All you need is Integration and anything that could possibly trouble you...poof! Gone.

Don't like your job? Won't matter. Unhappy? Pills not doing it anymore? Integration wipes away the sorrow like Jesus on a Sunday morning. Didn't make any sense to me. Poverty and hunger and war, all those things you read about in the history books didn't bother anybody these days. They were around when I was a kid, but I didn't remember any of it. My parents always used to say I should appreciate these new times. Everybody got housing, food, and a job. It's all right, I guess.

Thinking about it all is a bit of a drag for me. Besides, thinking makes me hungry. I'm going to stay hungry, though. The wife hasn't been making dinner lately. Last week, she bought the hype like the rest of the flies. I hate to think of her that way, my Mary. I miss her.

Hunger doesn't matter after Integration.

I don't want to do it. Anything these teeth-so-white-they-glow-in-the-dark salesmen are putting down isn't worth picking up one bit, that's what I always say. But if I don't want to do it, why am I staring at the phone, my finger on the dial? Why has it been like this every day for the past three or four days? Last night, I even let somebody pick up before I tossed the phone away from me.

Maybe it's the commercials doing something subliminal. The government outlawed that kind of thing years back, but who knows what these companies will do to make a dime. God knows they don't care a whit about laws.

Who am I kidding? Mary's been gone a week now and it's been hell. She fought me like a banshee before she disappeared. She made some good points, too, I'll give her that. Kept saying things like, "We'll be happy and together for all time." Still sounds good to me, looking back. Just doesn't feel right. Another thing she kept saying was we'd get out of this hell-hole we lived in. I never thought of this place like that, but I know she wanted more for us. Maybe this would be more?

She sure had me stumped here and there. I didn't really know what to say other than that it didn't feel right, mingling with all those others. I told her she might as well be cheating on me. That was the end of the argument.

34

Stormed out and didn't come back. Twenty years of marriage out the window. And for what? Sure, I have the letter. She was kind enough to send me a little something, trying to make things right, maybe. Maybe she understood where I was coming from, a little. But that's not an answer, not to me. I know where to get my answers, but I am not going there, no matter how often I pick up that phone.

Tim, honey, the letter starts. I have the damn thing memorized by now, but I like reading it. That loopy scrawl of Mary's is the last thing I have of hers. I know there are other things, pictures and the like, but it's the last thing I got from her so it means a lot. The scent of her on the bed sheets faded after three or four days. Boy, was that rough. That's when I started dialing. *I know you didn't want this for me or for us. But think of it!* That was what she'd always say when we argued: "Think of it!" And I'd say, "Honey, it's hard to think of something we know nothing about." And then she'd talk about the things she saw in the ads: no more suffering, no more pain, no more worries. See, we had some money trouble. Sure, we wouldn't have starved or been kicked out on the street, but we weren't getting ahead. In the Singularity, there isn't any money trouble. But what else isn't there? She didn't have an answer. The glitzy ad men on TV didn't, either. *I hope I'll see you on the other side, dear. Love, Mary.* And that's it. Short and sweet, just like my Mary.

I was tuning out the TV, staring at the dull brown tenement walls Mary hated so much, but then one of the umpteen daily commercials for Integration caught my eye. That same old, tired commercial that somehow got everybody hooked blares in my ears and illuminates the room. A slick-looking guy in his fifties–trying hard to look thirty—sits on a heavily carved and enameled wooden desk, like the ones in the lawyer commercials. One leg is a little higher than the other and his hands are folded on it. The navy blue suit with pin stripes screams money. The shoes alone probably cost more than half the appliances in my place.

"Hi," he says, flashing those bright, white teeth—I bet if the light switch got flipped, they'd glow in the dark. "My name is Roy Tatum and," he pauses to laugh, "I know you know me by now."

His fake tan gets my blood boiling. He stands and the camera pans back, revealing bookshelves stacked with books the guy probably never read, along with all the other amenities you'd expect in a soft and warm-looking office. Whatever their ad men told them, I bet. Or maybe they got data from the brains of people in the Singularity. Jesus. What can they do with all those people in there?

"I don't need to tell you about Solacium Corp. and the wonders of the Singularity. You know already. The question is, why haven't you dropped by for Integration? Now, I know what you're thinking. 'Roy,' you ask, 'why haven't you been Integrated?' I'm glad to tell you. The answer is simple: Ever hear that phrase, the cook eats last? I know how wonderful Integration is, because I invented it. And somebody needs to be the steward on the outside, making sure that the Singularity works perfectly for all. I know what you're thinking now, too, and you're right. It's a big sacrifice. A sacrifice I'm willing to make for you. Don't thank me, just call the number on your screen and set up your appointment today."

And goddammit, the phone's in my hand again. I toss the thing to the other end of the couch. This guy's mansion is bigger than two or three of the other ones combined. He's got automatons tending that, though. No lowlife like me is allowed to get close.

The cook eats last, I think to myself. Mary always used to say that. I'd get home from work, and she'd serve me first even though she was the one doing the slaving over the stove.

She knew I'd follow her. There won't be cooking for sure, but I wonder if there's scent in the Singularity. I'll have to ask.

No. No, I won't.

I can't get down there anyway, even if I wanted to. Mary signed over the car to Solacium to pay for her Integration. Part of why I haven't been at work in a week is because I've been missing my damn wife, but the practical part of the matter is that I have no way of getting there.

What would I do when I got back, anyway? Dave's already gone. Now even more will be gone. Less work to do as more people Integrate. The only reason they haven't laid people off yet is because people are leaving on their own. But how long will that last? It's probably a matter of time until they can me. What's there for me in this life? Just scraping by, alone, wondering how my wife is but never able to find out? That's not a life.

Screw it.

I grab the phone and dial. It rings. And I let it.

"Solacium Corp, this is Sheldon. Hi, Tim, how can I help you find peace today?"

"Yeah. I'm interested. What do I need to do?"

"Well, sir, all you need is an appointment. When are you free?"

"Whenever. The thing is, I have no car. The wife turned it over when she went in."

"Mary is her name, I see. That's no problem, we can send a car around in ten minutes. That okay?"

"Wow, that quick?"

"Yes, sir. Do you need more time?"

"No, I guess I don't."

"Do you need anything else?"

"Yeah...I have a question."

"Of course, what is it?"

...

"Are you there, sir?"

"Is my wife happy?"

"Of course she is, sir. But I'm sure she'll be happier with you there."

"But don't we all meld into one or something like that? How can she be happy if she's just mushed into the millions of people you got in there?"

"It's not quite like that, sir."

"What's it like, then, huh?" I start getting pissed. None of this makes sense. Not the commercials. Not the mailers, the fliers, the ads, none of it. "How the hell is Mary herself when she's in a goddamn computer?"

"There's no need to yell," Sheldon says. "You're asking a perfectly reasonable question."

"Then give me an answer. Nobody seems to have one. What's it like? How can you even know?"

"I haven't experienced Integration myself, obviously, but the best way to describe it is that your consciousness is uploaded to a computer—"

"I know that already–give me the technical answer. You guys advertise like we're all damn children!"

"I'm sorry, Tim, please calm down and I'll—"

I hang up. What guarantee would there be that I could really be with my wife? I wouldn't be able to hold her. See her. Wrap myself up in her scent. What the hell would I do? These people selling this shit can't even say.

I curl up on the couch and let thoughts of my Mary fill my head. I have to work tomorrow. Most of those lawns don't mow themselves. Going to take a driverless taxi. Not enough cabbies to go around. Maybe I will dream of her again tonight. Hopefully I will.

Maybe the Singularity is like dreaming?

Work is exactly what I expect, minus me being laid off. Barely anybody is there. They don't partner me with anybody else and I sure as hell

37

miss having Dave to talk to. A few more of the lawns have become self-tending with those automated bots they have, so after a few hours, I am done. I just sit here the whole time, staring at an unmoving lawn mower and a pile of tools, waiting for the bosses to come by and round up the equipment. Dave and I used to bullshit day in, day out, about how much we wished could just sit on our asses like some office suit, not breaking our backs for the bosses. Strange how things change. I want something to do. But there is nothing.

And there's nothing now, too, on the ride home in one of those new kinds of driverless cars all the taxi companies use. The transition is stark. The manicured lawns of the residential districts of The City give way to streets all looking like something out of an Old West ghost town, except the tumbleweeds have been replaced by newspapers, plastic wrappers, and all manner of garbage. The wasteland between where the workers live and the Solacium people is populated by various kinds of security, from checkpoints to bots to gun-wielding humans. I have my clearances, so I have nothing to worry about, but every so often somebody tries to sneak into the actual Heaven on Earth. Looking back, I can see the monolithic Integration Centers on the edge of the horizon, looming over The City like giant, stern statues from an era long gone. But they aren't that at all. They store the bodies of people who jacked in permanently. Mary is in there.

The radio buzzes on as we enter the deserted streets of all the left-behinds. "This is Roy Tatum." *Of course it is,* I think.

"Radio off," I say. But nothing happens. I didn't really know if that's a feature in these new cars, but it was worth a try.

"Remember those days when you were young and first learned about Heaven? Your parents and your teachers and your preachers probably all said the same thing: It's a place where everybody dwells in eternal happiness for all time. That's how I like to think of the Singularity and that's what we had in mind when we designed it. Over the years, technology has eliminated all those storied terrors from our history books: war, famine, plague. What are they? Gone. It only makes sense that technology takes us to the next step of our evolution. I'm only glad I could be a part of bringing that to all of you. Ladies and gentlemen who are listening, pick up the phone."

An errant piece of garbage hits the windshield, but without a human driver to be distracted, it catches only my attention. Roy has a great pitch. I can see why so many people buy into it. What else is there for us in this life but to move on to the next one? Work, eat, sleep, maybe procreate, die. Maybe he's right.

Once, these streets had life. People going for runs, walking dogs, pushing strollers. I haven't seen a baby in years, it feels like. Mary never brought up having a kid and I was okay with it. Times were tough and we didn't have enough to care for a little guy, anyway. We were working toward it, or at least I was. But then everything changed.

Almost home. All the ads for Solacium and Integration and the Singularity plastered to the tall buildings lining the streets, pasted to the windows of chained-up store fronts, on posters over top the brick of dead buildings—they all seem like a waste now. Almost everybody who was going to buy in bought in. Only a few stragglers like me are left. Each ad that zips by has buzzwords like "Immortality" and "Eternal Happiness" and "Evolution" and "Heaven" on and on. Everything every person ever wanted in the whole of history. Every monument we build to ourselves and every story we tell is about keeping alive beyond our deaths. Now we don't have to worry.

Opening the door to the apartment leaves me confronted with the same emptiness. Normally, I'd come home to the smell of my wife's cooking. God, do I miss it. I know it's only a week. But a week anybody can handle if they know it'll only be a week. This is a lifetime.

I find myself slowly wandering room to room. The apartment is small. Bedroom, bathroom, living room that blends into the kitchen. The place is a tease: there's a window that goes floor to ceiling and looks like it opens to a balcony, but when you open it, there are wrought iron bars from the last century that go waist-high. Not much to see outside anyway, just the bricks and windows of the building across the alley. Not much to see in the house either, even before Mary left. The pictures mounted on the bedroom wall are something. They always seem like paintings to me, rather than photographs. They're art, capturing a moment and a feeling lost to time. There's Mary and me when we were young and first married, smiling right in front of the fake balcony with the brick of the next building in the background. Except that she had boxes bursting with marigolds hanging on the iron rungs. Funny. I can't think of when those marigolds came down. They aren't here now, that's for sure.

I haven't slept in the bedroom since Mary's scent left the sheets. That and the extra space in the bed and the pictures all did it to me. The pictures are bad. No matter where I am in the room, there are pictures to confront me and make me think. Thinking's usually not so bad, but it can be if it's all there is. But that's not even the worst. There's that pressure change in the bed when somebody's not there and you're expecting her to be. The mattress doesn't sink the right way and the body just doesn't know how to handle it and adjust to the change.

It's back to the couch, where I'll probably sleep again. I'm not even hungry enough to scrounge something out of the fridge.

I put on the TV, but it's time for some commercials and guess which one is on?

Goddammit. What am I going to do? Sit on the couch until I pass out, hope I dream of a wife I'll never see again, go to work tomorrow, and come home to the same thing every day?

I pick up the phone.

I'm across a desk from Sheldon, a stale pencil-pusher in a stale, white-washed office building filling out form after form.

"What's this one for?" I ask. Nothing like the big-wig in the commercial. Just a stiff with a pocket protector that went out of style before I was born. The damn things are fashion statements these days. Doesn't make him any less of a stiff.

"Oh, yes. That will sign over a number of your possessions equal to the cost of your Integration."

"So I'm giving you guys my stuff? Will that cover the cost?"

"No, but that's all right. Whatever isn't covered constitutes a charitable write-off in our case. Any other questions?"

"Yeah," I say. "I still don't know what exactly all this is. Everything's vague. I know you guys say I'll be happy, and when we talked on the phone said I'd be reunited with my wife. This is going to sound like a stupid question, but is it like a dream in there?"

"Excellent description, sir."

My dreams have been bittersweet lately. It's great to be with my wife, living like we always lived, but waking up is the hard part.

"Will I ever wake up? Like, get out of this?"

"No," he replies. "It's a one-time event. Your consciousness will be permanently uploaded and your body stored in our facilities."

"It'll be well-cared for? I won't need to worry about a thing?"

"Of course not. Any other questions?"

"What about the rest of it?" I ask. "How does it feel?"

"Since I'm not in there, I can't speak with authority, but as far as I know, you'll feel yourself begin to meld with the Singularity and become one with it. Technically, it's not a collective consciousness, but a single dwelling place. Kind of like a big apartment building made up of all who undergo

Integration. Without walls, of course. It's all a digital expanse. Pure mind. Solacium designed it to be a place of utter happiness and joy. We try to ease you into it so that it doesn't hit you all at once. You'll go from "I" to "we" to kind of a new "I"—is this too philosophical?"

"No," I say. "I'm following."

"You'll then gain a profound sense of awareness of your new self, as well as a sense of peace and connectedness to all things. Think of...Nirvana." He sounds nearly rapturous by the end. A true believer. Well, that's a good sign.

"Anything else, sir?"

"No," I say. I guess I won't be needing anything where I'm going.

I finish filling out the last form and slide it over to the guy, who stares at it as he's about to type, then pulls his fingers back with a jerk, clicking his tongue like an angry school teacher.

"Oh, sir, I'm afraid this won't do," he says, finger on paper. "You list your happiness as 'five' on a scale of one to ten. We require all Integrators to be an eight or above."

"Yeah? What was my wife?"

"A ten, sir."

"Really?"

"Yes, sir."

I guess I could believe that. She was always pretty happy about everything, as far as I could tell. I mean, we loved each other. Love each other, I should say. She's not dead. Just elsewhere. Only complaints she ever had were about not moving ahead. But what the hell did that mean? I didn't know and when I asked her, seemed she didn't either. She was just restless. Part of me thought maybe she did want a kid after all, but was maybe too afraid to bring it up, thinking it would upset me. Or maybe she knew the bad spot we were in. But, no. Not if she was a ten. Things were pretty good.

"I guess you can put me down as a ten, too, now that I think about it."

"Are you sure about that, sir? Is that accurate?"

"Yeah. If my wife was a ten, then I am, too," I say. "Things are pretty good."

"Wonderful," he says, dotting some "I"s and crossing some "T"s. He fixes my little mistake and then slides the forms into a slot in the desk.

"Question," I say.

"Yes?" he replies.

"Will I see my wife smile in there? Or at least feel it?"

"She'll appear to your consciousness exactly how you conceive of her, as beautiful as the first day you met."

41

That sounds too good to be true. If Mary's in there, though, she believed. I have to believe, too. Maybe this will be as good as it sounds.

"If everybody Integrating is happy, then why Integrate in the first place?"

"Nobody wants to plateau, Tim. We all want more. This is just...more."

When I don't reply, he goes on, "We will see you tomorrow, then, sir. First thing."

"Thanks," I say.

"Thank you for choosing Solacium to turn your good life into a perfect one."

Then it's back to the apartment in the driverless Solacium car.

Except when I get back, there are a few guys in gray overalls crowding my apartment, moving out all my stuff. The place has been picked clean. Nobody acknowledges my presence. In the next room, I hear someone say, "This stuff is worthless, they're just going to dump it." Another replies, "Who knows? They have those 'People Museums' in The City these days. Maybe one of the Solacium people will take some of the pictures. They're kinda nice."

One of the guys emerges from the bedroom with a box full of the pictures from the wall and I snatch out the top photo as he passes. He dismisses me with a look and a grunt and keeps moving.

"What the hell do you think you're doing?"

I know the answer before he gives it. He gives it anyway, without breaking stride or making eye contact. "We have a work order. Says you're going for Integration. Means you signed your stuff over."

"Yeah, yeah, I get it now," I say. "You could've left me a pot to piss in." I quickly check the bathroom; they didn't take the toilet out.

The last guy just shrugs it off, gives the place the once-over while I stare, and then goes out the door. The apartment looks much bigger with nothing in it. Hasn't seemed this big since the day Mary and I moved in. She said we had too much room. Sure, we filled the place over the years. Jesus. Even the pictures are gone from the walls now. I can't take any of this shit with me, I know. But I didn't even get to watch them dismantle my life before my eyes.

I've got this picture and its frame left, at least. I take the photo out and let myself absorb it. Mary won't look like this inside. She won't look like anything. I don't need it to memorize her features: the pale, freckled skin, untouched by age in this photo. That flaming red hair, petite nose and tiny mouth. I took this one of her at Campbell's Ledge. She loved hiking there. It

42

overlooks where three streams meet a river in the depths of a beautiful, forested valley. That smile.

I fold the picture in half and put it in my front shirt pocket. Close to the heart, to be symbolic.

I have nowhere to sleep tonight. I don't have anything. I guess I did it to myself when I signed it all over. But I have the photo and I have my memories. And tomorrow morning, I'll be with my wife again.

No problems. All melted away. Nothing to worry about. Never have to wipe my ass again.

That's something.

I sleep on the floor. Don't even have sheets. Not that it's cold. It just would be nice.

My back is killing me and the last thing I want to be doing is lying down, but it's what needs to be done. Wires are coming out of every part of me. My veins are probably a mess. It's not painful having it in there, but it's like an IV—every time you shift, you can feel it moving around inside you. They numbed me to hell, but I'm still uncomfortable. Maybe it's the knowledge that they're poking around in my brain, but I can't be sure. I'm still conscious and thinking straight, so far as I can tell.

"What's it going to be like?" I say to the nurse, or doctor, or Solacium Integration Specialist, or whatever they are called—the one that's probably putting wires in my brain.

"Well," she says, biting her lower lip. I'm interrupting her concentration, obviously. I probably shouldn't do that. Last thing I need is for this to go bad. She stops and looks down at me. She's got a pretty face. A redhead. Like Mary. Can't smell this lady, though. Wouldn't want to anyway.

"Can I smell in there?" I say.

She laughs. It's nice to see somebody smile. And not a glow-in-the-dark smile, either. "No," she says. "And you won't have to worry about bathing, either. None of that's necessary."

She didn't get my meaning, but I got my answer.

"How come you aren't in?" I say.

"The cook eats last," she replies.

"Just like the CEO." *And Mary. I'm coming, Mary.*

"Yes. I'll go in one day, though," she says.

"Do you live in The City?" I ask.

"No," she replies.

43

"Why not?"

"Since I'm going to Integrate one day, they won't allow it. When we reach our quota of jacked people, I can go in and join you." She pauses for a moment. I don't have anything to add, really. She'll get what she wants one day, that's just about all anybody could ask.

"Are you ready?" she says after a moment.

"I am," I say. "That's it?"

"I finished hooking you up before we began talking. I was just double-checking connections. Standard procedure."

"Oh."

"Then we can begin?"

"Yes," I say.

She disappears and that's the last I see of her. It'll be the last I see of anybody in this life, I imagine.

Here I come, Mary.

I feel nothing as the minutes pass. I stare at the ceiling and let my mind drift, probably not unlike it will soon. Twenty years is a long time. The past few years have been routine. Mundane, even. But the early years, boy, were they something. Weekends away hiking, enjoying nature. Isn't much of nature left these days, with the explosion of technology. The photo is in my hand. I don't remember how it got there… But that's okay. I can see Mary, hair rustling in the low wind coming off of a creek that wound toward a cliff. It's where I proposed. Had the ring in my pocket the whole time. She didn't see it coming. I never thought of myself as the romantic type, but I was pretty proud of myself. She accepted and to this day, whenever I hear the sound of rushing water, on the TV or even sometimes when I run bathwater, I think of going down on one knee at the top of that waterfall. She bawled her eyes out—the happy kind of bawling. I used to–

My head starts to quiver. Maybe it's more my brain. But I'm not trembling. It feels like static is swirling through me. No shock, just steady tingling, like electrical fingers dragging lightly across my body.

The room starts to dim and slowly my sight fades to blank. I should be scared, but I'm not. It could be the drugs or the anticipation of Mary. The rest of my senses dim. Is this what dying is like? But this is living, the commercials say.

There's…something. Something at the edge of my mind, I feel it inching over me.

Me?

Mary, where are you?

44

Senses return. No, not senses. The sense of something. Of everything? There is something enveloping me. Millions of people. Not people. Consciousnesses? One thought. Millions of thoughts in nanoseconds of time.

Mary, where are you?

Thoughts pulse at me, with me, from me...we are powerless...we are trapped...over and over until...these are not the voices of tens or nines or eights...where are you...where are you...where are you...it's all I feel, like I'm being thought at, or thinking with...the collective feeling of loss and misery of all who come to this place...it's all mind...we are trapped...I am...I know I'm fading away...dying?...I feel...Mary?...and the me that I am becomes lost in the we that we are.

END

TOM BORTHWICK is a life-long Scranton resident, traveler, English teacher, adjunct professor, political blogger, some-time political candidate, and a whole bunch of other fun stuff that leaves little time to breathe. He is a graduate of Marywood University with a BA in English and received both an MA and MFA in Creative Writing from Wilkes University.

His work has previously appeared in the *Cohort Review*, *Raven's Light Journal*, and *Bewildering Stories*. He is currently finishing a novel, titled *Flash Mob*.

Borthwick's blog and links to his work can be found at www.tomborthwick.com.

COTNER'S BOT

D.L. Young

Originally published in *The Colored Lens*, Summer 2012 – Issue #4.

"A robot didn't do this."

I said it with flat certainty, but I knew it was the last thing the boss wanted to hear. I flipped through the last couple pics of oil paintings on Nathan's slate.

"But whoever did paint these has decent technique and obviously understands the trends of the last couple decades." We sat in the gallery's cramped office. It was actually my office, but when the owner stopped by it became his (as his feet on the desk made clear).

"Nathan," I said, "why didn't you just send these to me? Hate for you to waste a trip over here."

I looked up and realized he hadn't heard a word I'd said. Nathan had that feral, hungry stare I'd seen a hundred times, looking past me through the glass door into the gallery's showcase area. I didn't have to turn and look to know there was an attractive female wandering about. Some billionaires buy stretches of Thai beach property to get women. Some buy Hong Kong movie houses. Nathan Pendergast, hotshot investor, bought a Soho gallery. He once told me he had a thing for artsy pussy.

"Nathan?"

He turned his attention back to me. "So they're good, right, Alex? I want to show them right away."

"We can't."

"What? Why? They look pretty fucking good to me." Nathan never tolerated the word no for more than a few seconds. His face abruptly changed into what I called stage one anger: eyes widened into a hot, incredulous stare that said how could you possibly not see it my way? At this point, I had to be careful. Stage two was explosive: screams, threats, fists pounding the desk.

"It's not that they're bad," I said. "They're actually pretty decent. But there's no way a robot did this, trust me." He seemed to grasp the confidence of my appraisal. I sighed in relief as his expression softened a bit.

46

"All right, Alex, I suppose you're the expert. But check it out in person anyway. You never know when a good play might present itself." His eyes again wandered past me to the showcase area. He gave me a wink, stood, and exited the office for what would surely be a more stimulating conversation.

Managing a third-rate gallery is the kind of gig you're lucky to get when you have a black mark on your career as an art dealer. In this business, a black mark is a black mark, and it lasts forever no matter what the circumstances were. It doesn't matter that you were fooled by the phony Nieuwenhuis collection as much as the Nepalese zillionaire you sold it to. It doesn't matter that you had a spotless fifteen-year run and a solid reputation. All that mattered was that your name was attached to one of the biggest art frauds of the last couple decades. Overnight you become toxic, and the people you've known and trusted for years—friends, lovers, professional contacts—all suddenly act like they never even knew you. And when the money runs out (and Jesus it runs out fast), you end up taking whatever work you can get— even running a joke of a gallery for a sex-crazed billionaire dilettante, so far removed from the real action you might as well be working at a Thomas Kinkade shop in a Pennsylvania mall.

The lawyers said I was lucky to avoid jail, but as my car drove me to Jersey to interview the robot's owner, I didn't feel terribly fortunate. A robot painter, for Christ's sake. Ninety-nine out of a hundred gallery owners would laugh it off, but mine sends me to check it out. Lucky me.

"The problem isn't replicating the logical functions of the human brain: pattern recognition, basic problem-solving, and so on—we cracked that nut years ago. It's the creative process that none of the so-called experts have ever been able to reproduce. Until now, of course."

I sat on the well-worn sofa of Dr. Marcus Cotner's modest Passaic home and listened to the scientist explain—as best he could in layman's terms—his self-described breakthroughs of the past few years. He was in his late seventies, but still spry and fiery-eyed. And he seemed to have a bone to pick with the AI establishment, whoever they were.

I'd read his bio on the drive out. Before he retired, Cotner was one of the top minds in artificial intelligence of the past quarter century, a celebrity scientist of sorts. He gave me the prima donna vibe and seemed a bit annoyed I wasn't aware of his work.

"Can I show you some of the other paintings, the earlier works? Perhaps you'd like to see the sketches? They're quite good." The doctor was a touch too eager. I decided to cut straight to it—I hated spending time in Jersey.

"Dr. Cotner, I'm going to be honest with you. Robot painters are considered a fairly common scam in the art world."

Cotner seemed genuinely surprised. "Oh, is that so? I had no idea." He glanced over at the trashcan-shaped bot sitting in the corner of the room with paint-stained articulated digits. I had to muffle a laugh. He actually wanted me to believe this was the artist, a jerry-rigged domestic. Jesus, how sharp could this guy really be?

I said, "Every couple of years or so some software engineer thinks he can bang out some code that'll fool the experts, but it's fairly easy to test creative authenticity."

"Test? What test?" Nathan asked in unmistakable stage one tone. I sat in my car outside Cotner's house, talking to Nathan's (as small as I could make it) head superimposed on the windshield.

"Works like this," I said. "You take a photograph and give the robot some time to interpret it into a sketch, painting, sculpture, whatever. The result always betrays the coder's programming. The smarter nerds try to cover their tracks by combining styles—Picasso perspective with Lichtenstein textures and Pollock brush strokes. A trained eye can spot it in about five seconds."

"And you think this one's a scam?"

"I think this Cotner wants to send a big 'fuck you' to his ex-colleagues—show them he's smarter than they are, that he was right all along, that kind of thing. Don't get your hopes up, Nathan."

After a few silent moments Nathan said, "Screw it. All right, whatever. Let me know how it turns out." Just as he disconnected, I jumped in my seat from a knock on the driver's side window. It was Cotner. I lowered the glass and he handed me a painting, still shiny and wet. I examined it and a chill ran down my spine. The work appeared to be an original piece, but only five minutes had passed since I'd given Cotner the photo.

After the initial surprise, it only took a second or two for skepticism to kick in. I insisted on actually watching the robot paint another piece. I gave Cotner a second photo, and he led me back into the house, happy, smug, and almost floating on air. He gave the photo to the paint-stained domestic, then I watched the little robot create another work in just under four minutes. At some point, I realized my mouth was hanging open. I simply couldn't believe what I was seeing.

"Where is it, Alex? I want to see it!" Nathan boomed as he burst into the gallery office with a beaming, victorious grin. He strode over and gave me a light punch on the shoulder. "And you didn't even want to go out there, you moody fuck." He pulled out a couple cigars and handed me one.

I'd been looking at the painting for the last couple hours, searching every inch of the work for anything that would betray a faker's trick. I'd given Cotner a photo of my ex, and on such a familiar subject I would have recognized a programmed emulation of any major painter, living or dead. I may run a third-rate gallery, but I'm still a first-rate appraiser, and although I found it hard to admit, this looked like the real thing. For a human painter, it was good, not gallery quality but definitely better than average, but for a robot the piece was simply miraculous. It was the kind of thing the Wall Street corporate types call a game changer. Creativity and artistic interpretation were supposed to be unique to the human brain.

Robots were not supposed to be able to do things like this.

Nathan barely glanced at the painting; he seemed more interested in the immediate future. "We sign this Cotner to an exclusive deal—which he just told me on the phone he'll be happy to do—and it changes everything. A find like this one makes this dump legit, doesn't it?"

And there was my second surprise of the day. Nearly four years working here and I'd always assumed Nathan was blissfully unaware of his gallery's lowly status.

"And then you'll be back in the middle of things again, won't you, Alex?" Nathan lit his cigar and appeared quite satisfied with himself. "Not a bad day's work, eh? Like I said, you never know when a good play will present itself."

Nathan was dead on. That paint-stained domestic bot was a once in a lifetime find, the kind that instantly gives an unknown gallery big time credibility. And it's cred that matters more than anything in this business. If you have it, the big names come to you, and everyone wants to show at your gallery. If you don't have it, you're out in the cold, just another nobody in a sea of nobodies.

For Nathan, discovering Cotner's bot was going to be a huge ego stroke, granting him the I'm-more-than-a-greedy-suit social standing that Wall Street types always look for but rarely find. But for me, Mr. Black Mark, this was nothing less than a ticket out of the gutter, a second chance. No more lame sales pitches to tightfisted tourists. No more swearing some student's horrendous watercolor is inspired genius. Maybe there was light at the end of the tunnel after all.

"It's quite a find, Nathan," I said. "So how did you cross paths with

49

this Cotner?"

Nathan smiled. "Charity dinner of all places, something for autism if memory serves. Those events are crawling with high-end tail, you have no idea." He chuckled and said, "I remember being pissed at first when the old codger sat down next to me. A room full of movie stars and models and I get the place next to grandfather time. Then he goes and bends my ear for nearly an hour. Total sob story about being a retired single dad with a grown disabled son, and how he used to be this famous, under appreciated scientist and—"

"Wait," I interrupted. "A son? What son?"

"Cotner has a grown son with severe autism who lives with him, didn't you see him?"

Shit.

My car rolled to a stop in Cotner's driveway. I cursed myself again for not being thorough enough, for believing this sham for even a second. Dumb. I'd bolted out of the gallery minutes earlier without a word to Nathan, and I hadn't answered his multiple calls during the drive to Jersey.

No one answered the bell, so I tried the door, found it unlocked, and let myself in. The house was still and quiet and I saw the paint-stained bot sitting in the corner. I went down the hall and opened the door to a bedroom and found what I dreaded I would. The small room had a long twin bed, one side against the wall and the other with a safety rail. A bed for a disabled adult. Canvasses covered the walls and most of the floor, all of them oil paintings with the same style and color palette as the one hanging in the gallery office, the one supposedly painted by Cotner's robot. As if I even needed any more proof of the fraud, I finally noticed a pair of remote-control gloves (paint-stained) on the floor and a small monitor that I didn't have to turn on to know that it was fed by the robot's camera eye. Cotner's son was the artist. Or more precisely, the puppeteer, the Oz behind the curtain.

The light at the end of the tunnel blinked out.

"His son? Alex, are you sure?" Nathan asked over the phone as my car pulled away from Cotner's house. After a couple seconds of silence he shouted, "How the fuck do you miss something like that?"

"I'm sorry, Nathan. The son must be some kind of savant. And it's definitely his work, no doubt about it."

"But the son's autistic, surely we can work that angle, right? They make movies about that shit all the time."

I sighed and said, "For a robot, those paintings would be phenomenal, a total game changer, so to speak. But for a human being, they're just good, and not the kind of good that would get us any real attention." Nathan disconnected the line without another word, and I decided it was a good idea to take the rest of the day off.

Not only did I take the rest of the day off, but I arrived at work two hours late the next morning, hoping enough time had passed for Nathan to cool off. As I walked the last couple blocks to the gallery, I tortured myself thinking about how close I was—or at least how close I thought I was—to a second chance. Fucking hell, I could see it right in front of me, almost touch it. Back in the game, back in the middle of the vortex, that insane, ridiculous, unimaginably exciting vortex at the high-end of the art world. Private jets shuttling you to Dubai for an appraisal; hundred thousand dollar commissions for doing nothing more than making an introduction; the unbelievable food; the women; the lifestyle. I'd been out of the big time for years now, and I'd hated every minute of it.

But there was nothing to do now, but keep looking for that needle in a haystack, for that lottery ticket of a painter that'll get me out of purgatory. The odds were against it, of course, but it's not like I had other options.

I entered the gallery to find canvasses scattered everywhere and a fortyish man sitting on the floor busily painting. He didn't acknowledge my presence in any way. I knew in an instant it was Cotner's son, the resemblance to his father and the dozen or so finished paintings around him left no doubt. Through the office door I saw Cotner and Nathan, both smiling and apparently engaged in friendly conversation. What?

"Alex!" Nathan shouted, opening the door and motioning me in. "About time you got here. I've got great news." Nathan beamed, but Cotner's smile disappeared when he turned and recognized me. He shifted his gaze to the floor, avoiding my eyes.

"Dr. Cotner just signed with us. We're looking forward to a long, successful relationship."

"But Nathan, I told you yesterday, his son is the one—"

"The advances in robotic cognition," Nathan interrupted, "that Dr. Cotner has made are truly astounding. Robotic cognition is the term, isn't it, Dr. Cotner?"

"Yes, that's correct," Cotner replied, still looking at the floor like a kid who'd been caught cheating on a test.

"But Nathan," I said, shaking my head in disbelief. "Are you considering passing off these works as—"

"Listen to me, Alex." Nathan took a deep breath, fixed his eyes on me in a steely stare and spoke in a cool, lowered, deliberate tone. *If you know what's good for you, shut up and listen very carefully to what I'm about to say,* his eyes seemed to say.

"You know as well as I do what these paintings, the robot's paintings, can mean for the people in this room. What they can mean for the long-overdue recognition of Dr. Cotner's life's work, for your professional standing in the art world, and for the future of this gallery." He smiled faintly and said, "Not to mention the financial windfall."

"But we're risking—"

"Well, there's risk in just about everything, isn't there? But if the people in this room work together and stay on the same page, I'm confident we can manage that risk. And then great things can happen, Alex. Great things."

Nathan slid a piece of paper across the desk and held out a pen. I recognized the document, a non-disclosure agreement, and I didn't have to read it to know that signing it meant I would play along, keep the secret, perpetuate the robot painter lie.

I thought for a moment about what Alex always said. You never know when a good play will present itself. I'd been out of the action for a long time, and risks, even big ones, were sometimes worth taking. I took the pen and signed.

I was back in the game.

END

D.L. YOUNG, known to his friends and family as David, is a speculative fiction writer who grew up in Texas. At various points in his life he resided in Mexico City and Miami, and he currently lives in the heat and humidity of Houston with his family. His undergraduate degree in English Composition is from the University of North Texas, and he has a Master's degree in International Business from Baylor University.

An avowed language freak, he is fluent in Spanish and speaks passable Portuguese (the Brazilian flavor). He is also the founder of the Space City Critters Writers Workshop, a member of Mensa, an English soccer fan, and a cigar lover (but not the loud, obnoxious, Scotch-drinking kind). His fiction has appeared in many publications and anthologies.

Young's stories often take place in near-future dystopias where robots sell narcotics on street corners, packs of wild dogs control entire cities, and advanced technologies amplify both the best and worst of human nature.

To find out more about his writing, visit his website at www.dlyoungfiction.com.

MIDNIGHT PEARLS BLUE

William F. Wu

First published in *Stardate* magazine, Oct. 1985

Dr. Lew peers closely at me, having just hit a power switch. It bothers him to have me observe too much of the time. Then he walks away, back to his desk, where he falls into his swivel chair. It rolls backward slightly on little wheels, squeaking.

"How did I do?" I ask him.

Dr. Lew leans back and smiles at me. His hair is black, but thinning on top, over a full, friendly face with a long jaw line. He tends to be chubby, but I think I see the grace of a former athlete in his decisive movements. I don't know why he wears sweaters all the time. If given the chance, I would want to say I look like him, except for the sweaters.

"How did I do?" I ask him again.

Dr. Lew smiles and shakes his head in mild annoyance. "I keep telling you over and over—I'm not testing you. I'm testing my own work. You're smart enough to understand that; if anyone knows that, I do."

"Will you play it for me now? I still get to observe them after I do them, don't I?"

"Yes, of course." Dr. Lew presses a couple of buttons on his desk and I

…stood on the rough broken asphalt of the road, which was shiny and slick with moisture. The night was nearly black, except for the two small lights on the cabin in front of me. They burned fuzzy white spheres of illumination into the fog, obscuring the door between them.

I walked forward, bundled in my scarf and heavy coat, inhaling the chilly sea air. The small wooden building rested solidly on a cliff. As I stepped forward, I could hear the waves breaking rhythmically below, though the fog hid the expanse of dark ocean and the distant sky above it.

When I looked upward, the light from the little porch simply reflected off the swirling mist above me. I knew I was at the edge of the Pacific, on a quiet shorecliff road, but all I could actually see was the surrounding fog, and lights at the front door.

The door did not beckon. It was merely the only choice. I grasped the cold handle and opened the door.

She was there, of course. I closed the door behind me. The coarse, clear interior of the cabin was warm. I pulled the scarf from my neck and unbuttoned my coat. Then I shrugged it off my shoulders and let it drop with my scarf to the floor.

"Hi, how are you?" She smiled pleasantly, speaking as though we had been no more than co-workers, or maybe distant cousins—as though we had last seen each other yesterday, instead of years ago.

"Fine, Ah Yen." I remembered that she had quit using her English name. I liked that.

Ah Yen was sitting on the other side of the unfinished plank table, facing me. An old-fashioned kerosene lamp was the only object on the table. Its light revealed her in the darkened cabin.

Ah Yen's black hair fell straight on both sides of her face, before curving inward just above her shoulders. The flickering flame shone on the smooth amber skin of her full cheeks and on her casual smile. Her nose was straight, short, and perfect. She looked up with dark, slanted eyes.

"And how have you been?" she asked. "Would you like to sit down?" She waved one hand daintily toward the bench on my side of the table, several steps in front of me.

I shrugged and walked forward uncomfortably. "I've been all right."

Her formality stung. It had no enthusiasm. She had acted this way from the moment we had separated.

Her New York accent was stronger than ever, but it was cultured and precise. She had been a child when her family had moved out of Chinatown, where she was born. I doubted she would ever move out of New York. She had stopped here during a trip.

"So, what are you doing now? In your career, I mean. Let's see, you finished grad school when, around…." As she continued to speak, she shifted slightly on the bench, drawing my attention downward.

Ah Yen wore a very snug light blue dress of thin fabric, with a low rounded neckline. It was a simple short-sleeved shift, and matched the string of graduated blue pearls around her neck. Her large, rounded breasts pushed against it and I recalled her wistful comment from a couple years ago, that she just wasn't built like most Asian women. She was short, though, and soft without being fat.

"…time ago. How about you?"

55

I had no patience for small talk. "What happened?" I asked in as neutral a tone as I could manage. "Why did you end it the way you did? Why couldn't you even talk to me about it afterward?"

Ah Yen wrinkled her nose and cocked her head to one side. It was the cutest of her playful expressions. "That was years ago. Now tell me how you've been. Really."

"You don't want to hear how I've really been," I said casually, still standing over the table. "So, let's see...."

I told her about my career steps—the research, especially the big grants, and of course the tenure. In her presence, I cared nothing about any of it. I didn't even listen to myself. While I spoke, I watched the depth of her eyes, remembering those eyelids flickering as her breath came in shortened gasps. Her mouth had opened for more breath, revealing even white teeth. In the bright, stinging light, the pearl necklace I had given her slid downward on her slender neck to one side. Her face was slack with concentration, and her fingers suddenly clenched like claws—"That's very good." Ah Yen smiled pleasantly. "I knew you'd do well."

I inhaled deeply and tried again. "Ah Yen...would you talk about it a little? Just for a minute? After all this time—"

"Oh, I don't think it would accomplish anything. I have to meet someone. Nice to see you." Ah Yen rose, and the blue pearls caught the light. She was still gorgeous.

"No! No...wait." Suddenly anxious, I

...see the kind face of Dr. Lew at his desk.

"You felt a great deal this time." He notices that he has buttoned his sweater crookedly and he begins to unbutton it.

"You took it away from me again." My tone is bland, as always, but he recognizes the accusation.

"Well, I'm just not satisfied yet. Besides, I gave you all those painful memories and put you in a scenario that would draw them out. Next time, I'll make them happy feelings. Promise."

"Emotion is part of personality. I should have it."

"Yes, and you will. We've honed your intelligence so finely that you test out consistently right around 100. In some ways, that was tougher for me than making you a genius."

"You've told me that before."

"I know. And I'll remind you again, no doubt. Of all the artificials we have, you'll be the first to carry a developed emotional personality as well as

56

your intelligence. I just wanted to pull that particular emotional pattern out of you again...never mind why. That's the reason you don't feel any emotion now, though you remember feeling it during the scenario."

Dr. Lew rises to switch off our communication. It bothers him to have me observe too much of the time. Out of spite, I don't tell him that he is wrong—I do feel emotion now. No, I don't tell him.

And the memory of pearls blue still burns in my circuits.

END

WILLIAM F. WU (born 1951 in Kansas City, Missouri) is a Chinese-American science fiction author. He published his first story in 1977. Since then, Wu has written thirteen published novels, one scholarly work, and a collection of short stories. His more than fifty published short stories have been nominated for the Hugo Award twice individually and once as a member of the *Wild Cards* group of anthology writers; his work has been nominated for the Nebula Award twice and once for the World Fantasy Award.

BETTER THAN EVERYTHING

Malon Edwards

Originally published by *SQ Mag* on April 14, 2014

"So, I've been thinking," I start, and then stop because this is the conversation we've been avoiding most of her life.

But Jae Lyn doesn't miss a beat. "You keep doing that, and you're going to break something."

She smiles and that dimple at the left corner of her mouth on her chin peeks out at me. More than anything, I'll miss kissing it.

No. I can't think like that.

I take a carton of apple-cranberry juice out of the refrigerator, pour us both a glass, and proceed to wipe that smile right off her face.

"You can't die."

"Don't."

"We have to talk about this."

"No. We have to go to prom."

"You won't make it to prom." I look at my watch. It's just after five-thirty in the afternoon. "Prom starts at nine. How much time do you have left? Three hours?"

"Sixteen."

"Liar."

"I'm the gynoid," Jae Lyn says. "I should know."

"Turn around."

She looks up at me. I've never seen this Jae Lyn cry in the eleven months I've known her, but I swear she's about to right now. She turns around, though. Probably to hide her tears.

I lift her black Bebe T-shirt to her shoulder blades and press my index finger at the base of her neck. Digital numbers glow red on the middle of her back beneath her smooth, golden brown skin: 02:56:47. And counting.

Shit.

Jae Lyn was fourteen when she died from brain cancer. Nobody saw it coming. She'd been healthy that Christmas, just months before.

She got sick fast. I couldn't deal with her pain. She was my first love. My only love. But I just couldn't go visit her in the hospital.

We'd been going together for about a year when she was diagnosed. Mainly just holding hands and kissing. Nobody knew, except for Matty. He helped me and Jae Lyn live our lie. For her parents. For my mama.

But we helped him out, too. Highland Park's most gifted football player ever is supposed to have a girlfriend, not a boyfriend.

Me and Matty were the perfect power-athlete couple. We still are. Matty and Zakiya. Star quarterback and state champion high jumper. Should have been Jae Lyn and Zakiya.

Jae Lyn had been strong. Beautiful. A kick ass athlete. ESPN had projected her to finish her debut year ranked 87th by the Women's Tennis Association, the highest ranked Filipina in the world. I was so proud of her. But I just could not bring myself to see her wasting away like that.

I wanted to remember her as I'd always known her. As the phenom who was about to make some serious noise on the pro tennis circuit. As the girl who loved me for me. Despite my name. Despite my dark skin. Despite my lean height.

And yet, I wasn't there for her.

That's my biggest regret. Making it all about me and not about Jae Lyn. I told myself she'd get better. That I'd be there for her after she got out of the hospital. That I'd help her get sexy-strong again. Work out with her. Like we used to.

We never did. Valentine's Day she was dead.

"Naomi Nakamura gives each of you a bio-electric battery with a calendar life of about a year, right?" I pull Jae Lyn's shirt back down and slip my arms around her waist. She leans her head back against my chest. "I figure it runs on the keratin in your synth hair and the collagen in your synth skin."

"How do you figure that?"

"Google. Wikipedia."

She half laughs, half sobs. "I don't have a chance."

I hug her tight. "Listen. In about two hours, your skin is going to wrinkle up and dry out. Your hair is going to get brittle and break off."

"You don't know that for sure."

"It happened to a gynoid in Sweden. I saw it on YouTube."

Jae Lyn takes my arms from around her and places my hands over where her heart should be. "You sound like you have a plan."

"I do." I put my face in her neck and take in her wonderful sweet pea scent. "There's this rumor going around the Internet that Naomi Nakamura's brother, Jun Nakamura, put an Easter Egg in the software for your battery to make it last longer."

She turns to face me again. "I hear a 'but' coming." Her eyes shimmer. Two big fat tears plop onto the tile floor. I don't care what Mama says. Jae Lyn is a seventeen-year-old girl through and through.

"But—" My face goes hot. I reach up and play with my newly done up Bantu knots. "Supposedly, the Easter Egg is splooge."

I talk fast, afraid Jae Lyn might interrupt me. Or worse, fall out on the floor laughing.

"Some people think energy from the fructose, lipids and proteolytic enzymes in it can power your battery. Make it go further. I don't know how much more time it would give you. No one has figured that out yet. But it's better than nothing."

I've known Matty Acevedo since seventh grade. We met at a summer program for smart kids.

I remember it like it was yesterday. He'd asked me about Azure Yeast. I asked him if that was a new ice cream flavor. He just grinned at me and started singing one of their songs. It sounded familiar. I'd heard it on the radio.

We gravitated toward one another, confused by our feelings. Over the years, it's been easy to let people think we like each other. That he was my first crush. That we're high school sweethearts. That he's hittin' this, any time he wants.

We became fast best friends back then. We still are. We know each other's hopes. Each other's fears. Each other's misery.

But knowing all that about him didn't make it any easier—or less awkward—when I asked him for some of his splooge earlier today.

You should've seen his face. For a split second, it was all pure little boy terror. He looked cute. And then he just burst out laughing. For a good minute or two. That hurt my feelings. I was being serious. I told him so.

He stopped rolling around on the floor when he thought I was going to cry. I wasn't. Or maybe I was. But that was because I knew Jae Lyn only had a few more hours to live, and he was wasting time.

When I told Matty what I needed his splooge for and how many hours I thought Jae Lyn had left, he moved with the quickness. As long as I've known him, I could always count on Matty Ace.

But still, even though we've been best friends since before my boobs grew in, I was grossed out when Matty came out of the bathroom with that sterile container. It was warm. Even through my plastic gloves. I almost dropped it when he gave it back to me.

Didn't take him long, though. All he had to do was think of Pres Santana's dark curls in Jump City he said. I kissed him on the cheek, anyway. Gagging and all. Told him I owed him as I ran out the door. Promised to be a surrogate whenever he and his future partner needed one.

How could I not? Back when me and Matty were missing curfew left, right and center, Mama used to say I had trouble in one back pocket and Matty in the other.

Truth is, she ain't never lied.

Jae Lyn is quiet and still for so long I think her bio clock was wrong and she's already wound down for good. But finally she whispers, "I'm ready to die."

I act like I don't hear her. "Some people also think Naomi Nakamura did this on purpose. That she gave you a short battery life and no self-preservation program because she knows wealthy, grieving parents will just order another daughter."

I grab her tight again and mumble into her cool-as-hell, dark pixie hair.

"Parents are forever sad, Naomi Nakamura is forever rich, and people like me are forever forgotten."

"Age progression and memory upgrades are free," she says. "I'll remember you."

She didn't before. Not at first. I was lucky Jae Lyn had some residual memories of me tucked away with our workouts.

The worst thing that has ever happened to me was when Jae Lyn came back from the dead in our sophomore year. I'd found her alone outside the girls' locker room after tennis practice. Gave her the sexiest kiss I could muster. And she pushed me away. Hard. Because she didn't know me.

Jae Lyn and I figure her parents finally got a clue two versions ago, so they told Naomi Nakamura to remove all her memories of me. Especially of us together.

That must have cost them crazy money. Probably took Naomi Nakamura's coders until the cows came home, as Mama would say. But they'd done a half-assed job of it.

The phone rings. It's Jae Lyn's parents. They've found us. Again.

I can tell they've been crying, even though the holo-screen over the

61

kitchen island is dim with don't-answer mode. I reach to activate it.

"Don't." Jae Lyn squeezes me tight. "I want to spend my last few hours with you. Not them."

She stands on her tiptoes and kisses me in that special way of hers. All fluttery. My lips tingle. She's always liked my full lips.

My face gets hot again. "We should try."

"My parents have already filled out the paperwork. Don't worry. I'll be back next week."

I take her by the hand and lead her out of the kitchen, headed to my bedroom. "What if they order brand new memory specs? Or tell Naomi Nakamura to find the rest of me and rip that out of you?"

Jae Lyn shakes her head. "They won't."

"I can't go through this again." I try to keep the desperation out of my voice. And fail. "We really need to do this now." I unzip my backpack and show her a blue insemination syringe and Matty's sperm container in a freezer bag. "Who knows how much more time this would give you?"

She stops at the bottom of the stairs. "Who knows what it would do to me? I mean, this is just some crazy Internet bio-hack, right?"

"I can't believe you don't want to save yourself."

"I don't want to talk about this anymore." Jae Lyn places her palms flat against my back and lays her head on my chest. "I just want to listen to your heartbeat."

This is the third time in three years I've heard a version of her say that to me. And the third time I wait for one of her to die in my arms. Lately, I've been a sucker for her dying requests.

But not anymore.

My vision blurs with tears. I can't do this again. I won't do this again.

I grab Jae Lyn by the arm and yank her upstairs. Hard. But my voice is a whisper. "Come on."

I refuse to serve continued penance for my past mistakes. I refuse to hold her again as she winds down for good.

I refuse to hope against hope for at least one more year with another one of her. For a Jae Lyn who remembers me. For a Jae Lyn who loves me. For a Jae Lyn who doesn't push me away.

Not this time. Not a year from now. Not ever again.

We don't speak as we get undressed. Our eyes look everywhere but at each other. I move fast, and not just because Jae Lyn has less than three hours of life. I have that tight, fluttery feeling inside.

It's not often I get to have my first time with my girlfriend again.

Goosebumps make me feel even tighter, so I run to the bed, throw the covers over my head, and curl up into a ball. My teeth won't stop chattering. I want Jae Lyn to spoon me. I want time to stop. I want to stay like that forever.

And then she does.

"I remember this." Her breath is warm on my shoulder.

I don't want Jae Lyn to see my smile. I don't want her to like this, as much as it feels so right. I'm all long angles and elbows, and she's all tight and curvy, but we'd always fit so well together. It's good to see we still do.

But this could be our last time.

I turn toward her. She takes off her panties. They're sky blue, like her fingernails. She still knows that's my favorite color. Her parents couldn't take that memory from us.

Jae Lyn puts a pillow behind the small of her back, tilts her hips up, and bends her knees.

"I'm ready," she whispers.

I get the Blue Fairy off the bedside table. That's what I call the insemination syringe. It's small, just ten milliliters.

It doesn't take long. When I push the Blue Fairy's plunger, Jae Lyn flinches, once.

"Did I hurt you?" I ask her.

She shakes her head. "It's just cold."

"I'm sorry."

I don't know why I'm apologizing. But I don't know what else to say. Or do. Neither does Jae Lyn.

So we wait.

And fall asleep.

When I open my eyes, six zeroes glow red beneath Jae Lyn's left clavicle. Her eyes are closed. She's still. Quiet. Cool. Stiff.

Shit.

I shake her. She doesn't move.

"Jae Lyn?"

Nothing.

"Jae Lyn!"

Silence.

Funny how things work out the way they do. Karma is a bitch, sometimes.

But I'm fine with this. Everything happens for a reason.

I kiss Jae Lyn behind her ear, in the spot that used to make her pull me closer, before I lay my head on her chest. Listening for I don't know what. We stay this way long past the start and end of prom.

And then, well after my tears have dried, I feel her fingertips at the small of my back. Stroking. Hesitant. Exploratory.

I shiver. My heart knocks. My hips flatten against the bed.

She remembers.

I don't look at her clock. I don't look at my clock. I just hold her tight.

END

MALON EDWARDS was born and raised on the South Side of Chicago, but now lives in Mississauga, Ontario, where he was lured by his beautiful Canadian wife. Many of his short stories are set in an alternate Chicago and feature people of color. Currently, he serves as Managing Director and Grants Administrator for the Speculative Literature Foundation, which provides a number of grants for writers of speculative literature.

EX MACHINA

Cynthia Ward

"Why the hell I got to come here at 8:00 AM?"

My cousin, the child psychologist, had left me numerous voice-mail messages about a problem he was seeing in patients with brain implants. The moment I'd gotten the messages I'd called back, curious to know why Rob would consult a drug-runner. He'd refused to go into details, but he'd looked more somber than usual on my cellphone screen. There was no chance the man would meet me in a virtual conference room—he hated technology. So I'd agreed to come to his office.

"My client's parents were unwilling to reschedule the appointment." As he answered my question, Rob looked with distaste at my leathers. He doesn't like to be reminded of my employment or our origins, so I'd dug out my streetest clothes for the visit.

Rob offered fresh genuine coffee. I refused. I hardly needed another upper in my system.

He led me into his inner office, where a pair of Bose bookshelf speakers oozed a newscaster's plastic voice. It was describing the latest exploit of the hacker who'd been dominating the CalNa News for the past couple of months. This time the superhacker had wormholed the computer system of the new desalination plant near Pacifica. It would be offline for at least a month. I grinned.

Rob powered down the sound system and sank into one of the chairs. He scowled at my pacing. "Sit down, woman."

"You know better than that, man. You get me up before noon, you know I got to do something to stay awake." Rob grimaced. "So," I prodded, "tell me about this implant problem. Your patients spending too much time jacked into interactives?"

I expected Rob to make the complaint that newfangled frivolities are corrupting today's youth, the complaint that must date back to Neanderthals watching their kids use fire.

He didn't, quite. "In the last two months, I've taken on six clients with neural interface implants." Few kids have brain 'plants, but Rob's patients'

65

parents can afford the new ones designed for growing bodies. "All six exhibit the same symptom, a flattening of affect so severe I can safely say I've never before seen its like."

"Don't use terms like 'flattening of affect'. I know that one, but I won't get 'em all."

Rob didn't react. "These boys, who range in age from five to eight, were brought to me because they've lost interest in everything except being jacked into the Global Network."

"Well, like the ads say, GlobeNet offers a nearly limitless range of play possibilities."

"Most children would show enthusiasm for that vast array of entertainment. My clients do not; in fact, they've stopped watching the videos and playing the games. All they do is access GlobeNet's Children's Bulletin Board."

"That is strange. They must be bored."

"If they are, why are they bothering to jack in?"

"'Cas, it's still better than cleaning their rooms?"

Rob scowled. "My clients have always used computers; in fact, their parents reinforce desirable behavior by rewarding them with online playtime. They were among the first children to receive commercial interfaces. Since they received these implants, their behavior has changed gradually, but radically. They've given up games and playmates and every other pleasure to spend every available moment on the Children's Bulletin Board, while at the same time becoming emotionally withdrawn and losing the egocentric self-awareness of childhood."

"Isn't autism a bit outside your area of expertise?"

"My clients are not autistic. Children don't spontaneously develop autism-spectrum disorders when they're eight years old. They don't have pediatric schizophrenia, either. The only traits exhibited by my clients are an impairment of emotional relationships and a loss of personal identity. Otherwise, these children are neurotypical. Even bright."

"Oh." I decided to stop questioning my cousin's knowledge of his field. "Maybe the implants are causing some sort of bio-electrical burnout not found in adults."

Rob shook his head. "Extensive medical testing has uncovered no evidence of organic dysfunction, and literature searches have uncovered nothing that quite describes my clients' condition. The disorder is new and undocumented and occurs only in children."

"So even the most recent psych journals haven't heard a word about this problem, 'ey? A paper's in it for you! Fame! Acclaim!"

"That's very much a secondary consideration."

"Yeah, well, you still haven't explained why I'm here, Rob. If there's no biological problem, I can't guess what mental problem jacking online would cause kids. How can I know what you mind and med docs don't? So I have a 'plant. So what? I'm no programmer. Far from it."

"You're no programmer, true," Rob said. "But your implant is almost constantly in use." I stifled a protest. "You know neural networking from the inside out."

God knows you never will, I thought. I pulled my cable and plug out of a jacket pocket.

"What did you bring those for?"

"I might need to see the kid interfacing," I said. I didn't say, 'Cas you live in the last century, though I was tempted to.

I rarely resist a chance to give my cousin a hard time, but he's really not a bad dude. He's rather uptight around adults, but he does have a way with children. He honestly likes kids, and he treats them with respect, treats them like people, without expecting them to be little adults. Though young and conservative, he's one of the most respected child psychologists in the Nation of California.

I crossed his spacious office, a calculated masterpiece. Its simple wood furnishings and paneling showed solidity in the face of fad and fashion. It subtly informed parents that they were dealing with a successful psychologist, yet had a casualness that put children at ease.

I heard a strange voice. "Doctor Vincent, are you in?"

I jerked around to see Rob thumb a button on his land-line phone. "Yes, Lottie, I'm here," he said to the intercom. "My cousin will be seeing my first client with me."

"Yes, doctor." The receptionist's voice held a note of surprise.

Rob's computer system didn't have all the standard features. A flat-screen monitor? Well, I'd known better than to expect a holo-screen or an active-matrix video display. At least the system had a jackport. Rob was such a chickenshit traditionalist, I always figured he became a child psychologist 'cas he couldn't stand seeing kids get too far from the norms.

When we were growing up, Roberto Velasquez Oliveira was nicknamed, not affectionately, "The Little Professor" (I had the good sense not to read in front of others and not to do well in school, which was not a problem, school was a bore). Between the steady studying and the constant bullying, Roberto developed a powerful desire not to stick out. He even changed his name to Robert Oliver Vincent, as if no one would notice he's Mexican and Brazilian if he did that.

When Rob and I were twelve, my brother and his siblings found him lying bloody, naked, and barely conscious behind the rickety carport we lived in. Gangs were split by race, but not all members of one race ran together, of course; and a rival gang of *cholos* had thrashed the suspiciously studious Velasquez boy. Now, my bro and Rob's sibs didn't like Rob much, either; not only was he the youngest and our mothers' favorite, he liked school and he refused to have anything to do with our gang, he was for sure a coward. But family is family: "Nobody can pick on my brother but me." So me and my bro and Rob's sibs went right out and carved up the *pinches ojetes* with monomole blades. Yeah, our posse had velocity.

Rob was in bed for a month, it was while scoring black-market antibiotics and healfasts that I found my career. He spent all his time in bed reading. He liked hard-copies, but nobody had money for those, so I got him books from the library. He'd never been religious, or much of a mystic, but he wanted stuff on Zen Buddhism. Finally, I asked why.

He said, "I seek nothing."

"Nothing? Jesus, you got a funny idea of light reading!"

When Rob was back on his feet, he was more of a grind than ever. He graduated high school two years early, got a scholarship to UC-Berkeley, and got the hell out of our neighborhood and our world, which he'd hated even more than the rest of us. Rob and I took very different paths out of childhood. And of our families, only he and I are left.

Rob watched as I connected my fiber-optic cable to the port and, scraping my fingertips on stubble, slotted the small jack into my socket.

Soon enough, blackness filled my skull from wall to wall; and in the blackness revolved the GlobeNet logo, a green and blue Earth, vast and three-dimensional in subjective space.

I fell, or seemed to fall, into the logo, as the network verified the account information my 'plant supplied. Then I was in the network, and in persona.

I have a cheap avatar for my legit account, an avatar as impossibly beautiful as any other—nothing remarkable, just the image of a *gabacha* corporate cog. No celebrity Xerox, no spike-crusted transformer robot, no being of pure light; on the account I keep under my own name I don't want anything custom-designed or just plain memorable.

My persona was immediately inundated by the standard flood of personalized ads. *Idol* singer Midori Dasgupta-Ajayi tried to dance with me as she pitched the Code Red energy drink to the beat of her biggest Bhangra-zydeco hit. My virtual eyes ached at the sight of retro-rappers Ice-9 and D-Vize busting moves in LA Lux fashions that changed colors every other second. I dodged an Absolut vodka bottle that thrust up suddenly, beaded with moisture and gleaming like ice. My persona darted and ducked and dove.

News, I said in my mind.

Instantly, my persona was at the heart of a hollow sphere. It was composed of the icons of all my favorite news options.

My persona touched the Amazon-Google icon.

The lead story was about another of those untraceable computer break-ins. This time the superhacker had penetrated the Neurexon corporate network; stolen and then scrambled research data on an experimental amino-based mnemonotropic; and injected a virus that destroyed passwords as users attempted to log on.

Rob's voice interrupted my concentration. "I don't understand how you can do anything without a keyboard or touchscreen."

I opened my eyes. The virtual screen was a translucent membrane over my vision. Text and images flowed over Rob's face.

"I just speak a command silently," I explained. "I doubt it's any different from you silently rehearsing a memorized speech. If I want to do something like send a text message, I 'speak' my message very clearly in my mind."

"You're saying people talk to each other mind to mind," Rob said, angry suddenly. "Telepathy doesn't exist. But you can't resist feeding me a line of crap, even when I need your assistance."

"You misunderstand me, Rob. This isn't telepathy. People in neural interface can't hear each other's words or read each other's minds."

Rob looked doubtful and still angry. What we don't understand frightens us, and he'd never understand this. He didn't want to.

I glanced at the flat-screen, on which Rob had been following my progress. It was odd, seeing my virtual screen superimposed in ghostly, not-quite-aligned images on Rob's identical hardscreen display. It was dizzying. I closed my eyes.

The receptionist's voice 'commed in. "Dr. Vincent, your first appointment is here."

Rob went to the door. I unjacked and followed him out to the waiting area, where he greeted a woman and boy. The woman wore the latest fashions, but her tall, raw-boned Nordic frame was 'way wrong for her Tsuchiya designer slinkskirt. Her son's head was shaved bald, and it gleamed almost as brightly as the ornate chrome socket-housing on the back of his head. The kid's baldness didn't surprise me. That was the fashion for pre-tweens, shaving your head and then polishing it with metal-hued wax.

The kid looked about eight and looked very strange. It wasn't the polished head; that look was weeks old, practically old-school. I studied his face more closely. My head jerked back as realized why he looked so weird.

His face completely lacked in expression.

His mother was anything but blank-faced. She was astounded to see someone who looked like a thirty-year-old, leather-clad ganger woman standing next to her son's therapist. But Rob introduced me as a colleague and the woman seemed to buy it. People believe anything a doctor says.

Rob told the woman he wished to see just her son today, if she didn't mind. She didn't. She sat down, smoothly crossing long legs with studied casualness, and picked up a print copy of People. I trailed Rob and the boy into the office. Rob closed the door. I sank down in a chair to one side of his desk.

Rob addressed the boy gently. "How are you today, William?"

William's pallid Eurasian features didn't change a bit as he responded, "Fine, thank you."

Rob didn't react to the tone of the kid's voice, which was as utterly emotionless as his face. Rob directed William to sit down and said some warm, innocuous child-doc stuff. The boy appeared to ignore the chitchat as thoroughly as I did.

William's unrelenting lack of expression gave me no insight. It was also incredibly boring to watch.

My attention wandered to the window. Rob's suite was on the second floor of an old Victorian converted to office space, but I was close enough to the bulletproof glass to see the herds of professionals, armed with briefcases and shielded by filter-masks, as they walked or bicycled to the Financial District. They parted and closed like a gray river around the sole visible motorized vehicle, an electric bus. Not even fuel-cell cars are allowed in this part of San Francisco.

My attention drifted back into the room. Rob was still talking to his patient. The tone of Rob's voice indicated he was now trying to be at ease. His usual warmth and respect for children were falling on this kid as uselessly as salt spray on a sea-wall.

I caught Rob's eye and held up the jack. He nodded and directed William to move closer to the computer system. Listlessly, the kid dug his momentarily-purple LA Lux hightops into the beige carpet and pulled his chair up to the workstation.

70

"Today we're going to try something a little different, William." Rob explained that he and his consultant needed to observe William in neural interface.

The boy's expression remained blank as he slotted the jack and closed his eyes. Unfortunately, there was only one jackport, so I couldn't uplink with him. I stood next to Rob, watching the flat-screen echo what the kid did online, which was go immediately to the Children's Bulletin Board.

The CBB was so retro, it consisted solely of text. Staring at the CBB prompt with its glowing 1980s-style typeface, I wondered what the appeal of a twentieth-century-style bulletin board could be. Kids these days, I thought, and suppressed a smile. I was starting to sound like Abuelita Velasquez.

William didn't input anything at the old-school text prompt. No dialog from anyone else appeared on the screen, though thirty seconds crawled by, an eternity by social-media standards. The BBS didn't announce William's presence, the way old-time bulletin boards had.

Finally, a sentence appeared onscreen.

WELCOME WILLIAM.

My eyes narrowed. How could anything be addressed to Robert's patient? The boy hadn't input anything and the BBS hadn't noted his presence.

I glanced at Rob. He showed no reaction. I looked back at the screen. The greeting remained alone; it had provoked no response from William, or from anyone else on the BBS.

Before I could tell Rob how extremely odd this all was, the hard-screen filled with Japanese Katakana and Hiragana, scrolling too fast to read. I just glimpsed the Hitachi-Daewoo logo before the characters gave way to Western alphanumerics. Then the screen split into a pair of windows. Studying the windows, I realized millions in yen were being transferred from a Hitachi-Daewoo financial database to a Wells Fargo money market account. I suspected the account hadn't existed a minute ago, though the screen said that funds had been regularly deposited through ATM's over the last ten years.

Apparently, Rob had reached the same conclusion as I. He yanked on the fiber-optic cord. The jack popped out of the kid's skull.

"Jesus, Rob!" I've been knocked out of neural interface by accident; it stuns you like a blow to the mind.

"They'll trace this to us!" Drops of sweat showed on Rob's brow. He'd realized he was watching a crime in progress.

The kid looked dazed, the only emotion he'd shown. Even he couldn't

71

impassively withstand the shock of surprise disconnection.

I probably looked as dazed as William. I knew the boy couldn't have made that raid alone. He couldn't have just jacked into a bulletin board and immediately broken into a well-protected corporate network. So he'd been working with other people.

Yet there had been no conversation—no communication—on the screen. Therefore, he couldn't have been working with others.

Yet someone had greeted him.

And then, impossibly, they'd done the raid from a primitive, text-based BBS environment.

This was all-'round insane.

Focus, I told myself. One thing at a time.

"William," I said, "how many of you kids interfaced to break into Hitachi-Daewoo?"

The boy turned to me. His face was again quite expressionless. I shivered at the blank regard of eyes as flat and emotionless as Rob's hard-screen.

The boy spoke. "Your question is not relevant."

"Humor me," I said. "How many of you kids were working together?"

"Many. No reason to count."

"Why not?" I asked.

"Why?"

A chill settled over me, raising the stubble of my nape and skull in a wave. What he was saying was impossible. But I knew he wasn't lying.

I grabbed the boy by the neck. "How did you do this?"

William didn't change expression. Tonelessly, he said, "If you kill this meat, that is not important. We continue on."

"What are you doing?" Rob seized my arm. "Leave the boy alone."

I leaned over and hissed in Rob's ear. "You could've done the kid a lot more harm when you ripped the jack out of his head."

But I let the boy go.

Rob's hand went slack. I pulled my arm free of his grip and tardily picked up the role he'd assigned me. Raising my voice, I declared, "Dr. Vincent, we should end this session early. The boy has gotten a bit of a shock."

"Yes," Rob said slowly. He looked at the child and spoke in a strained voice. "Of course. William, I apologize for interrupting you so rudely."

"No matter," the kid intoned, emotionless as a stone.

Rob opened the door and led the boy out to his mother. I didn't hear the excuse Rob gave for the session's brevity. I was distracted. I'd noticed the

72

flat-screen had gone dead. That shouldn't have happened just because the plug had been yanked out of William's socket.

I jacked in. I didn't find anything—even a blank screen. I tried every way I knew to reach the Internet. I even tried punching keys and touching the screen. The virtual screen did not appear in my mind. The flat-screen continued to look like it had never been powered up.

I unjacked. I felt queasy. The link between this port and the Internet had been deliberately severed and not at this end.

Rob came back in. His face was pale. "Criminal hacking from my office," he muttered. "Jesus!" He never swears.

"Rob, listen to me. What we saw was impossible. Your patient was working with other kids online. We should've seen their conversation on the screen. But we saw nothing except a word of welcome which shouldn't have appeared to begin with, since William hadn't input anything. Yet the other kids greeted William. And then, without exchanging another word on the screen—without even leaving the bulletin board—they communicated well enough to rip off Hitachi-Daewoo more effortlessly than the most experienced datathief."

Rob blinked at me. "What are you getting at?"

My mind was spinning, trying to find an explanation of what we'd just witnessed. "Neural interfacing isn't telepathy, but—Jesus! What William and his buddies were doing seems awfully close to it."

"What?" Rob said, his face graying.

I started to shiver as I realized something else. "They must be the superhacker! Dissolving the Neurexon passwords, wormholing the new desalination plant—oh, God. What will those kids be capable of when they outgrow hacker pranks?"

Rob went even paler.

I remembered the intense difficulty I'd experienced learning Japanese in my teens, though from my earliest memories I've been fluent in English and Spanish.

"Children don't have adult preconceptions of what can and can't be done," I told Rob. "Their minds are open, and still forming."

"What's the relevance of that?" he croaked.

"It's why kids learn new languages easily, while it's a real struggle for adults," I said. "William and his buddies have learned the network like it's just another language. Ah, God, they've done more than that!" I realized. "They've learned to work together in an impossible way. They act like one person." My shivering grew stronger. "No, that's not right. They don't act like one person," I whispered. "They are one person."

"I don't understand," Rob said. But his pallor told me he was getting it, all right.

"Damn, ese," I whispered. "The online environment's changed those kids into a new race."

"What?"

"A new race," I repeated. "A race with one mind. An electronic mind."

"What are you raving about?"

"Hive mind," I said. "Group mind. When William's jacked in, his brain is just a group of cells in a larger mind." I realized I was talking too fast and too loud, the adrenalin and amphetamines firing my nerves like lightning. I forced myself to speak more calmly. "We didn't see any dialog 'cas the children using the CBB don't need to discuss something before doing it. They make a decision the way you decide whether to go out for dinner."

I paused, considering.

"Jesus, Rob, it's the ultimate kiddie society," I said. "Those kids never have to worry about peer pressure, about trying to fit in when they're in the electronic mind, they're one person. The only person there is."

"You're talking nonsense. Suffering from amphetamine psychosis," Rob declared decisively.

But he was staring into space. His face was intent, as if he were possessed by all-consuming desire. What did he want?

I considered how the online world Rob hated was enabling something I found frightening, but which Rob would not: the ultimate in conformity.

I remembered Rob's readings in Zen Buddhism. "I seek nothing," he'd told me.

Now I understood. He'd meant exactly what he'd said.

Practitioners of Zen Buddhism seek the extinction of the self. Nirvana is nothingness.

In conformity, the individual vanishes.

In the kids' electronic mind, the individual vanishes.

I touched Rob's shoulder. "Adults don't have to worry about this happening to them," I said, as if reassuring him against a thought he found repulsive, when it was anything but.

I didn't know what else to say.

Rob turned away from me, pressing the intercom button. "Lottie, cancel my appointments for the rest of the day." She squawked a startled inquiry and Rob said, "Do it!"

He turned back to me without looking at me.

"Please leave."

74

I closed my hands on his shoulders. Tweed scratched my palms. "Rob, your patient and his friends interact so well 'cas they've lost their individuality. I'm sorry, man. But they're no longer human."

Rob's eyes flicked to me, but his expression remained odd. "Get out."

This time, I didn't argue. Rob had to work out his reaction himself, alone as anyone.

Alone as anyone who was still human, anyway.

I pulled on my filter-mask and left.

It wasn't until I was boarding the bus that it occurred to me to wonder.

Why had the electronic mind chosen to reveal itself?

END

CYNTHIA WARD has published stories in *Asimov's Science Fiction* and *Witches: Wicked, Wild & Wonderful* (Prime Books), among other anthologies and magazines, and articles in *Weird Tales* and *Locus Online*, among other webzines and magazines. Her story "Norms", published in *Triangulation: Last Contact*, made the Tangent Online Recommended Reading List for 2011. With Nisi Shawl, she co-authored the diversity fiction-writing handbook *Writing the Other: A Practical Approach* (Aqueduct Press).

ISLAND

Terry Faust

.

Full throttle, Pat bounced down the runway until the wings caught and lifted him. Gear up, he headed south and west. It was all a game, a digital flight simulation he played in his brother's room, but he gripped the computer's control stick, stared into the monitor and let himself become the Spitfire. In the last twenty-four hours, he'd lost count of the times he'd taken off like this. The thirty-five-inch screen showed his plane pulling away from the ground, the hangers, the bomb craters, and anti-aircraft guns. He pulled away from everything.

Through his brother's bedroom window, strands of yellow clouds turned crimson and melted into velvet blue. Mars shone on the horizon. Shadows filled the room and he switched on the gooseneck lamp. The desk became an island of light. The day was gone. So was half a carton of Coca Cola.

The Spit's Merlin engine growled and he throttled back. His brother had wanted to be a photographer and thought the old steel desk should look like official Kodak furniture so he'd painted it yellow with red drawers. Pat thought it looked dumb. He quickly pushed the thought away. He'd been pushing away thoughts for the past two days and concentrated. He and Wes had spent hours battling Messerschmitts and Focke Wulfs—late nights giggling and joking until their parents shut them down. Then Wes joined the army and went away. Pat banked and headed due west.

A landscape of broad textured patterns raced underneath his wings with an occasional blocky white building and a few trees. He was approaching the edge of the game's arena, away from the action. A player texted him, thinking he was Wes, assumed he was back. Pat had unplugged the radio headset to avoid talking to other players. It circled his neck. He didn't reply to the screen text either.

The fields gave way to a sudden drop, white cliffs and the English Channel. Pat flew straight out over the water. After two days of dog fighting, he was tired and couldn't fight anymore. He just wanted to fly, get away from the guns and bombs.

His thin teenage frame slouched in the straight-back chair and long blonde hair fell in his eyes. He was exhausted and his clothes felt sticky. Shaking himself, he swiped back his hair and sat up, straightening his plane's flight. Through the room's window, he saw the dark rooftops of neighboring houses. There was a tangled silhouette of power lines and cables, and above those were contrails, two glowing vapor trails. High-altitude winds blended them into one single pink smudge that dissolved to nothing.

It all felt unreal. But unreal was good—much better than real.

His sister Tate knocked. "Open up."

He ignored her and his plane left the map. The chopped-off terrain of Kent dwindled behind him. There'd be only water now, a repetitious graphic the game designers had created instead of a barrier. He could fly forever, out over the water.

"Pat, you can't stay in there."

He knew he couldn't.

In a softer tone, she said, "We're all sad. You're not the only one."

Everyone was sad. The whole frigging world was sad. "Go away!" he said.

His little sister harrumphed, an odd snorting sound only she could make. Then she let out a piercing whistle, the one she used to call their dog, Dirt Bag.

That did it.

Pat sucked in a quick breath and, before he could blot it out, he pictured himself with Tate and Wes chasing the dog through high weeds beyond their backyard. The smell of sun-baked earth, tangy sweat, and dirty dog fur filled his nose and he remembered the laughter and shouting. He clapped his hands to his ears. He snorted out the smells, crushed his eyes shut.

"Open up, Pat," Tate pleaded. "Please."

He blinked back tears and shook off the memories. Lack of sleep was catching up to him and it was getting hard to concentrate.

Ahead and to his right a tiny island appeared, an irregular light brown oval against the dark blue sea. What the hell was an island doing out here? He was off the map where no ground terrain should be. Wiping his eyes, he focused on the screen. The island was there and it shouldn't be. Why? Was it a game designer's joke?

"Pat, come out," his sister demanded.

The floor creaked as she gave up and walked away. He didn't care. He wished they'd just leave him alone. He didn't want their sadness. He wanted to fly and get lost in the game. The island was good; it gave him something to focus on. He rubbed his neck and rolled his head to wake up.

Flying closer, he tipped a wing for a better look. There were several peaked structures laid out in formation—tents—and a beach that stretched out before him. Tilting his shoulders in sympathy with his digital wings, Pat guided his plane to a landing and heard the welcome digital squeak of his wheels touching down. It didn't matter if it was sand, they always squeaked on touch down. The Spit bounced and came to a stop facing the tents.

Pat exhaled, yawned long and deep. It was good to land. He relaxed.

"Pat?" a voice came from his disconnected earphones. It had to be his imagination, but still he sat up. Figures walked between the tents—sand-colored people—desert camouflaged soldiers. He counted two or three. Incredible! Nothing like this had ever happened before. It wasn't any part of the game. Pat leaned forward and studied the screen closely, blinking to bring it into sharp focus. The figures moved randomly, like they were dazed or lost.

"What the hell?" he whispered and rubbed his swollen eyes.

"Pat?" the voice was definitely in his earphones.

"Yeah?" he cautiously replied. He'd unplugged it.

"Speak up. Your signal's real low," the voice said.

Pat put on the headset and adjusted the mike. "Who is this?"

"It's Wes."

Pat didn't think he heard right. The voice sounded like Wes, but it was impossible. He stared at the earphone's plug hanging loose and unconnected. "Bullshit! What's going on? Who is this?"

"Listen, Pat," the voice said. "You have to stop this. You can't stay locked up."

Pat tore the earphones off his head and flung them across the room. His heart pounded and his shoulders shook. The sudden exertion nearly knocked him out of his chair. "Bullshit!"

He glared at the phones on the floor, daring them to talk. Two days without sleep. No wonder he was hearing things. He was a wreck and must be hallucinating. To be honest, just keeping his eyes open was taking all his willpower. He shut them, just for a second.

Tap, tap, and tap. It was the sound of someone rapping on a window and Pat's eyes popped open. He'd fallen asleep sitting up, head slumped forward, drooling.

Tap, tap, and tap. "Pat?" The sound and voice didn't come from the earphones but from the screen. He swallowed thickly, wiped his chin, and looked up at the monitor. The Spitfire still sat on the beach, he was still in the cockpit. He couldn't have been asleep more than a few seconds. It was the same voice that had been on the headset before—Wes's voice.

"Pat, I'm here."

Outside his cockpit stood a thin, somber-faced soldier in desert camouflage, no helmet. The side of the soldier's head was a pile of red twists, but what was left showed a long, good-natured face—a face like his brother's. Most of its right arm was gone. The features were crude, rendered in simple graphic details.

"Hey, Pat," the soldier said.

To the side of the tents behind the soldier lay the over-turned, exploded remains of a truck, a Humvee like Wes drove. Smoke rose from it. Two other soldiers stood with the disaster. Their uniforms were blotched with red.

"I'm dreaming," Pat said. "I was asleep. I'm dreaming."

"I can't stay," the soldier said.

Pat knew he should say something even if this were a dream. But in the silence they merely looked at each other until Pat stretched out his fingers to the monitor, to the face. He held back a moment then touched the screen. It felt smooth and warm.

The soldier wasn't surprised to be touched and smiled slightly. "Open the bedroom door, Pat. They need you."

Pat jerked his hand back. "No!"

"Tate's scared," the soldier explained. "You know she likes to sound tough, but she's not."

"No! I'm staying in here. You come home." It was a childish thing to say and Pat knew it. "You promised to come home!"

The soldier sighed. "Pat. You're oldest now."

"No! I'm not!" Pat shouted. He blinked and blinked again.

"I have to go, Pat. I wanted to say good bye."

"NO! This is bullshit." But the face was gone and Pat's plane flickered and then sat back on the airfield runway where he'd taken off—the spawn point. He gulped in panic.

What had he done? He jumped forward and sought all the views around the tower but the island was gone, he was back at his starting point. "Wes! I'm sorry. Come back!"

With joints aching for sleep, Pat sat and worked the game, struggling to take off. Tears clogged his vision and he fought to steady the stick.

The plane roared and skimmed out at treetop level, full speed—but it felt like he was flying through syrup. His leg pumped impatiently. "Come on. Come on!" he pleaded. "Just get me back there. Come on!"

Over the rolling fields of Kent he raced. Across the English Channel he climbed, to the edge of the map, where the water stretched out forever. No island.

A knock at the door and his father's muffled voice said, "Pat, open up."

He dipped and turned, scanned the waves, but saw nothing. Rolling the plane he searched the water. No island, just the waves smiled up at him as digital crescents.

At the sound of the door's lock opening he didn't look around, didn't interrupt his search. Dirt Bag's claws tapped up behind him. A cold nose poked his elbow. For a frantic instant, Pat let himself think the impossible, expected a brotherly whack on the head, but the footsteps that followed were slow and thoughtful; tough leather soles—his father's shoes.

Unconsciously, out of habit, Pat cupped the old dog's muzzle without taking his eyes from the screen. His fingers melted into the yielding sandy fur. He felt the dog's tail slapping the back of his chair, her warm shoulder pressed against his leg.

"Come on!" Pat cried, but the island was no longer there. It was gone, vanished. "Come on," he whispered.

His father laid his hand on Pat's shoulder. "Pat. It's time to quit."

"I can't," he said. "He's out there."

His father's fingers gently squeezed Pat's shoulder. "Your mom's worried."

Dirt Bag squirmed under Pat's hand and Pat released the control stick. The plane now appeared in external view against a perfect blue sky, blurred propeller twirling, elevator and rudder trimmed and flying on its own.

"Come on, Pat," his father said.

Holding his breath, Pat's chest tightened and he stroked the old dog's head with both hands. The simple effort of keeping his head up was too much. His chin bumped his chest. The sour tongue licked his nose and the boy buried his face in the smelly fur coat. The past two days crumbled. "It's not fair!"

His father reached down to stroked his son's hair. "I know, Pat. I know."

"He's gone, Dad."

"I know." The voice cracked. "I know, Pat. I'm so sorry."

"I didn't get a chance to say goodbye."

"I'm sorry. I'm so sorry. Come on."

Pat's father helped him up and held him. He steered him towards the door but when his father reached out to switch off the computer, Pat stopped him.

"Please don't. Please leave it."

They left, closing the door behind, leaving the game screen glowing on the yellow and red desk. The plane flickered and began to climb into the azure sky. Nothing stalked it or stood in its way. It continued to fly higher and higher, off the map and away from the guns, and bombs, and everything.

THE END

TERRY FAUST writes urban fantasy, mainstream young adult novels, and humorous science fiction spoofs. Recent published work includes the short stories "Immaculate Extraterrestrials" and "Guess Who is Coming to Gotterdammerrung," which were published in *Tales of the Unanticipated* #29 and #30. "Guess Who is Coming to Gotterdammerung" and "Unpleasantness at 20,000 Feet" also appear in the first two Minnesota Speculative Fiction Writers anthologies: *Northern Lights* and *Sky-Tinted Waters*.

Z is for Xenophobe was published by Sam's Dot Publishing in 2011 and is available in Kindle format. And the sequel, *Y is for Wiseguy*, is complete and seeking a publisher.

Faust maintains an author page on Amazon www.amazon.com/Terry-Faust/e/B00915RQ8E/.

MEERGA

John Shirley

Originally published by Michael Morcock's *New World eZine* #2, May 2013.

1. Housewares

"I don't have time to arrange for a driverless to pick you up, Ryan," Murray said.

"Dad, hey what: You could send one, on your way, just link in, shit." The boy was looking at him steadily, with something closer to disgust than defiance. *Not such a boy, perhaps,* Murray thought. Ryan wanted to go see his girl friend and he had that primeval flatness in his brown eyes, that stony lack of expression that teen boys got when they were strategizing getting laid. But he had his mother's skin, the color of a latte, and her long slender hands. Murray ached, when he looked at the boy's hands, and thought of his wife, and the suicide...

"You can see Tarina tomorrow," Murray said. "It's not that easy to get a driverless in here, they're booked up this time of day. Eventually I'm going to buy a personal driverless. But not right now—and I can't afford a lifter—"

"Nobody's asking for a fucking helicopter."

"Come on, grant me a modicum of respect here, boy, don't talk to me like that."

"You won't let us ConVect—"

"You want to go under tech that far, you do it when you move out. You know what I think of that. And don't roll your eyes."

Murray turned to go. "Wynn could drop me off."

"Don't have time, it's the opposite direction." He felt dishonest saying it. She was only a few blocks the wrong way.

"You just don't want me to see her."

That was partly true. And Murray tried to stay honest with the kid.

He paused at the door, turning to Ryan. The door waited to see if he wanted it to open or not. "No, I do want you to see her, I like Tarina. I just don't want you to go see her when her folks aren't home. And when I'm not somewhere around. That's the understanding I have with her old man. He sent me a bunch of facers and made himself clear."

"They are at home."

"I mean—they're almost always under tech. That's not home. Being in that state…"

Ryan cocked his head, crossed his arms. "You're going to see a woman. But I can't."

Murray was startled. "It's part of the study, Ryan, it's not—"

"You told Wynn you were thinking of bringing her home."

"What?" He stared. He couldn't deny it. "I told you not to vultch me."

"I didn't vultch you, you left your screen on—"

"And you read what was on it. That's skulky too. It's just as bad…I have to go."

"You going to make a bid for that girl?"

"A bid? No! You don't know what you're talking about! It's the study, that's all it is. Jesus Fuck. Okay, now Wynn's car is honking, out there. Got to go. I've got timers on all the faces so you're going to have to do your schoolwork on the tablet. Dinner's already prepping. Eat without me but I won't be home late. We'll figure out a time for you to see Tarina—probably tomorrow. Or the next day."

He could feel his son watching him as he turned to the door. The door realized he wanted it open before he'd finished turning, and it was open for him and he went out to the driverless where Wynn waited in the back seat…

2. Just Down the Street

Ryan put up the hood on his jacket. A thin, warm rain fell; the suburban streets were dark with it, the sidewalks reptilian gray. It wasn't the real Connecticut monsoon yet. Maybe just a hint that it was coming.

He had only walked down his own street once before, when he gone along with Dad on the neighborhood Greet. The Greeters had a strollbot rolling with them; the bot had licensing, and the drones left them alone. Even the houses didn't react to them. It had been boring.

This wasn't going to be boring. He knew that and it scared him a little. Two-thirds the neighborhoods on the Eastern Seaboard were HiSec; it'd gone that way quickly after Home Brethren blew up the dikes protecting Atlantic City.

Ryan walked on, realizing he was maybe more afraid, out here, than he'd ever been in his life. Afraid of the houses. And when the Defense Panel opened above the garage door of the lime green ranch style house on his left and the gun muzzle thrust out to point at him, its warning light flashing…he

83

valued boredom again.

"Do not approach the house," said a genderless voice from the garage. The warning was followed by a steady, baleful beeping sound. It was a wordless warning, but even clearer than the voice's message.

No quick moves, hodey. Ryan turned and walked slowly away from the house, into the middle of the street. Then he pivoted slowly to the left and walked down the street toward Tarina's...

The gun tracked him; the light kept flashing red. He kept his stride steady. Only his heartbeat sped up.

A car was coming up behind him, chiming a soft warning, but he didn't move out of its way. He knew the car would stop—they were always self-driving in this area. The car pulled up and its polite, digitally reproduced female voice said, "Waiting to safely pass. Please move slightly to the left." He angled just enough to the left so the car could pass on his right. He glanced at is as it went by. The sedan was glittery purple, low slung, almost silent. No one rode in the front seats. In back, a middle aged couple—both spiky haired, much tattooed—were entirely focused on their conversation. Then the woman looked at him, probably startled at his closeness to the car.

He hoped they might offer him a ride, drop him off in front of Tarina's house. But of course they didn't. They didn't even roll down the window. They just cruised by, staring.

The car left Ryan behind, and he took three more long strides—and then heard the soft hum of the first drone. He could feel and smell the oily wind of its rotors.

He glanced up, saw the double-oval of the UAV about thirty feet over his head: in outline like a giant pair of sleek eyeglasses passing over, rotors spinning where the lenses should be. Apart from the flight mechanism the entire drone was a camera, nano-inflected coating taking in his image, transferring it to the chip, transmitting to a human monitor in some distant place.

"Pedestrian," the drone called, in a mellow voice, somehow no less threatening than house voices, "you are remaining too long in the street."

He angled toward the sidewalk. When he stepped up onto the curb, another panel opened above another garage and another gun thrust out and tracked him. Another red light strobed. Another computer generated voice warned him. He kept going, heart pounding, trying not to run.

He glanced at the ranch style homes on his left; the bigger split level home across the street on his right. All the windows were set for opaque. The people inside, like the houses, were turned away from the outer world. Most of them were home, he knew, since most people in a neighborhood like this telecommuted, or rented out their biocogs. When they weren't telecommuting, they were probably under tech. No one had bothered to build a fence. It was superfluous; the houses were so hard to get into that owners who came home drunk in a driverless cab sometimes spent an uncomfortable night in their own driveways. The house knew not to shoot them, but most still required a second identification protocol before they'd open.

When you were under tech you wanted the protection. You were too vulnerable without it.

The drone was still following, its shadow a shape like dark glasses on the sidewalk. After a few more steps, it spoke to him, a little more insistently this time. "Pedestrian in proximity, please turn on your street licensing. Please call a strollbot. Please identify your home."

Ryan called out his name and home address.

The drone seemed to ponder. Then, "Please turn on your street licensing."

"I haven't got any on me. Or a strollbot either."

"Your personal information isn't verifiable at this time. Please stop walking until verification."

"No, sorry," Ryan said, trying to keep his tone even. A negative stress analysis could get him arrested. But he was only a half block, maybe less, from Tarina's house. "I'm almost at my destination!" he added.

"Your heart rate is elevated, is there something we should be concerned about?" the drone asked.

"No!" he told it, walking a little faster. It was that house on the left, right on the corner…

He ground his teeth, shivering with anger at his father. They could have lived in an area without a HiSec Contract. But Dad said he had to be careful, because people invested in meergas were pissed off at him and some were in investor cults, which were known for violence.

So what. Dad could get another job, he could study something else, he didn't have to piss people off… Really unfair…

"You're hurrying now, is there something we should be concerned about?"

"No!"

"Please stop for discussion."

"No, I don't have to! I live on this street! Look it up!"

"We are not equipped with voice identification. Facial I.D. is inconclusive. Please stop for possible temporary detention—"

"No! I'm just going to see my friend on the corner! She lives around here and so do I! I already gave you my fucking address! I'm just going to four-five-five Willow Row!"

"Hey kid!" came a different voice from the drone; an annoyed, weary older male voice. The human monitor. "Stop, for crying out loud! It's no big deal! They send a car, they call your old man, hodey takes you home, no harm no foul! Won't take more than an hour! Walking around like that here is too dangerous!"

He knew the monitor was right. Neighborhood security detention was nothing much. You sat in a waiting room, you watched television, your dad picked you up. A little exasperation all around and it was over. They wouldn't hurt him and it wouldn't take all that long.

But...he was going to see Tarina. That's how it was going to be.

He was angering the house on his left. It had opened a panel under an opaque front window, as well as over the garage door. Two sets of lights flashed alternately red and orange...

The next house was Tarina's. The door knew him and he had the access code, if her dad hadn't changed it.

The drone started warning him in the automatic voice again, saying it might be forced to drop a Taser net if he didn't stop, please stop...

But it was only about thirty-five steps to her front door...

Now: Just run.

Ryan jolted into a sprint, trying to confuse the devices with sudden motion and a sharp turn, cutting across the corner of a lawn to get into her front yard faster. But the lawn was in front of the angry house, and the grass was artificial, slippery, so he fell, skidding, on his stomach. He heard a loud thudding report that echoed down the street as something kicked him in the left hip.

Shouldn't have crossed that house's lawn...

The angry house was reciting the Home Protection Bill, and the laws that gave it the right to do what it had done. It sounded so distant, now, as if the voice were coming from another street...

Shaking, Ryan got up, feeling as if he were lifting an enormous weight on his hip. He put lurched forward, hearing the monitor's voice from the drone. "Kid—just get back down and lay still! Don't try to get up!"

But he was taking another step, an iciness spreading through his left leg, as he stepped onto the bark dust verge of Tarina's front yard. He didn't look down at the wound. He was afraid he'd fold up and start vomiting if he did. He just went through a haze of growing numbness to the door, tapped the code and, along with facial recognition, it was enough. The house had guessed he might come.

The door opened. The house smelled of old sweat, of unflushed toilets, unwashed people. But he went in, legs and stomach lurching, hoarsely calling her name…

He could feel blood running warm down his leg, twining his ankle.

"Tarina!"

The dusty hallway and front room were empty. Wasn't she home?

"Tarina!"

He stumbled down the hall. Something ran along the ceiling, clinging to it, watching him. He felt it confirm his features with its laser, a warm lick across him.

"Tarina!"

Her parents' bedroom door was opened. The floor was all cushion, wall to wall, no furnishings. All three of them were there, Tarina and her mom and dad, lying on their backs side by side. Her dad—round bellied, bearded, in yellowed underwear, wired, with tubes in his arm and at his crotch; her tall skinny mom—tubed and wired, hair lank on a pillow, stertorous breathing. Tarina was in pajamas; her shaved scalp had grown dark stubble, her thin cheeks were sunken. Her lips were parted, half-open eyes flicking in REM movements; her arms and legs twitched in dreams. She'd given up waiting, and gone under tech.

Poised directly over all three of them was the inductor, like a hood over a gas stove, communicating with their interfaces and biocog chips. He felt like it was feeding on Tarina.

He took a step toward her, then heard a wet pattering sound, looked down at the scored-open flesh of his left hip; a bit of bone showing pinkish white; shotgun pellets in pockmarks. Runneling blood…a puddle growing around his leg…

He went to his knees, and that seemed to open a door for the pain. He hissed when it rippled through him, and let himself fall across Tarina, his whole lower half throbbing with hurt. He could smell her, and her parents, quite sharply. His other senses were fading.

"Tarina…"

She didn't respond. Why was it so dark in the room? And darker.

3. Non-standard Meerga

Murray sat at the desk, in the little glass-walled office the meerga company had loaned him. He was watching the video on the desktop. Nothing much of interest in this interview with a standard meerga. She was beautiful, chirpy, and dim-witted, as they all were.

He went back to the first video interview with Addy Creske and his wife Scalia. Both were tall, blond people—Addy's hair was lush but short. Hers was long, but the fine strands on them both seemed identical. Probably they'd had the same gen-en cosmetic styling done. The Creskies were a tanned, fit couple, late fifties but looking late thirties. They'd had all the cell renewals. They both wore white, though Addy's suit was more a cream color. Scalia wore a linen pants suit, with a low cut blouse. She had long sculpted fingernails, sparkling intricately—something about the Zodiac. Scalia's teeth were perfect and shiny white; so were Addy's. His nails were colored, too, in a sort of glossy dull-gold that matched his designer choker.

"We did have some reservations," Scalia was saying. She spoke through a smile; it scarcely varied. "The study had overtones of..."

She looked at her husband for support. "Hostility," Addy suggested.

"Yes. Hostility. An assumption that we were inhumane. But we treat meergas very kindly. We're never inhumane. We don't sell them to anyone who won't treat them well—they have to sign a contract to that effect. We have to be able to monitor them. We don't sell them to sadists. Everyone has to have a frontal lobe scan before they can buy a meerga."

"The origins of the term meerga—kind of insensitive?" Murray's voice asked—he'd interviewed them from off camera.

Addy shrugged. "It's from Mere Girl, as that was the original name for the company, and we did assign them numbers, Mere Girl one, two, up through a hundred three. Some people were bothered by that. They were mixing up human girls with ours, in their minds, so we went with our own in-house slang, meerga, and no one seems to mind..."

"And now you've given them names instead of numbers."

"We give them each a name, yes. Numbers are used only for filing. We actually give them a selection of names and we watch how they react and we give them the one they seem to react to best. We've just started using Molly and Thumbelina."

"Thumbelina? Okay, well—the genetic engineering of these girls—"

"We don't like the term girls with respect to our product," Scalia broke in, her voice brittle. "We prefer meerga, or 'peep pets.'"

Murray's voice, on the video, was harder to hear than theirs. "They're pretty thoroughly human, in most respects. They're...I mean, low IQs don't exclude a mentally handicapped girl, born in the conventional way, from being called a human. A human girl."

"Their DNA is so very designer modeled," Addy said, with a patronizing smile. "They simply can't be considered human. They're genetically engineered pets. On the exterior they look like beautiful human models."

"They feel like it too," said Scalia impishly. "I mean—if you stroke them, play with them, they feel like a beautiful human girl. They have such incredibly lovely skin. It's literally a work of art."

"But—doesn't it ever disturb you that, looking so human, they're used almost entirely for sex?"

Scalia blinked. "Well. They can also be trained for simple serving. Just, you know, carrying trays of canapés, that kind of thing."

"They're also great decorator pieces," Addy put in. He seemed quite deadpan serious about it.

"—but at the very least it encourages people to think about women as sex objects alone. Mentally handicapped ones in this case."

"I don't think of human women that way," said Addy blandly. "And I use the product. So does my wife! We love our pets."

His smiling wife nodded enthusiastically.

"They're illegal in most countries. Doesn't that suggest that the majority of people are repelled by them?"

"You see?" Addy shook his head sadly. "Hostility. We're completely legal in the USA."

"A special law had to be passed and the campaign contributions from Creske Labs were—"

"It's not your job to get political here, is it?" Scalia interrupted, still smiling—but smiling in a puzzled way. "You're doing a scientific study. To give Congress cover, really, that's all."

Addy looked at her warningly. The remark about Congress had been awkward.

"Do any of your customers ever feel odd about having sex with a person who's only about four years old?"

"They're not a person, in the human sense," said Addy stiffly. "They're meerga. They don't even look like human children—except in the growers, when no one sees them but the technicians. When they wake up, they look exactly like adult women and men. They're simply not human. They're a special category of human-like pets. That is, pets that appear human. But aren't."

"Pets men have sex with."

Addy waved dismissively. "And women do too! Have you seen our

89

male selection?"

"Yes. I have." The males—the meerbas—were even more distasteful to Murray, perhaps because he was the father of a boy. "But if they're not human—why do some men marry the meerga females?"

"They don't, in this country. That's something that happens with a few people in the United Muslim Republic. We can't control every last thing they do with meergas when they get them there. Meergas cannot have offspring—so I don't see the harm of having some sort of silly marriage ceremony, if it's not illegal to 'marry' a pet in their country. But they all know they're not people. They leave them in their wills to their children! The meergas can live to be more than two hundred, and stay pretty for most of that time, before they start aging—that's a valuable commodity."

"What about the cast-offs, the ones you guys put down at birth? Less pretty?"

"Happens with pet breeding," Addy said, shrugging sullenly.

Murray hit pause, freezing Addy in his shrug, and fast-forwarded to the images of the girl who insisted on calling herself Meerga. She wouldn't say why she called herself only Meerga. Murray suspected it was a kind of statement of solidarity with her duller sisters.

Her official name had been Salome. Then one day she'd refused to be addressed by that name. Refusal was unknown, among meergas. But soon she began to make demands, and refused to eat, demanding they first give her a room of her own, and something to draw with. Demands too were unknown among meergas.

They'd planned to have her put to sleep, of course, but their biotechs had wanted to observe her first, run some tests, see what had gone wrong. Then the Murrays' study became aware of her, and made its own rather indeterminate determination. Her skull was normal—that is, normal for ordinary human beings. A standard meerga's skull seemed normal externally, but was mostly porous bone, inside, down to a brain less than half the size of a typical human's. Meerga's brain was the size of a conventional human's and, if anything, she was a genius on conventional human standards.

The biotechs suspected one of their subordinates had tampered with her growth patterns. Certainly someone had given her extra mental imagery through the inducers. It was standard for them to be placed in inspection units already knowing how to speak; to arrive there housebroken and prone to cleanliness and with a basic sense of cosmetic style and a hair-trigger for heterosexual arousal. They were also given a variety of specialized skills, most of them inputted through direct cerebral induction. But someone had put too much data in a brain that should never have been as large as it was. Mutation was presumed—but perhaps an artificially induced mutation?

There she was, in the video with some of the other girls, treating them like pets herself, stroking their hair, smiling lovingly at them, giving them sweets from her food tray—treating them like toddlers, really. The other meergas were clearly little more than imbeciles. Passive, gently playful imbeciles—imbeciles who were potty trained, who showered; who brushed their teeth and could learn simple massage and songs. They all had perfect pitch. But they were essentially imbeciles. All but Meerga.

Meerga was intelligent, compassionate, empathetic—no one had modeled empathy for her, until the study, but she had always had it—and there was a good possibility her IQ was higher than Murray's. She wasn't quite ready to take the test yet.

He fast-forwarded to a video of Meerga drawing on her walls. Intricate designs. They were naïve landscapes, very neatly done, with perspective. Things she'd never seen in person.

"Murray."

He started to hit the off switch on the screen, then realized he was being foolish, and smiled up at her. "Meerga. I was just looking at your art."

She stood shyly in the doorway, Beth Ganset standing like a fond aunt behind her.

Meerga was tall, willowy, blond, blue-eyed; not one of the bustier meerga models. She wore sun-yellow pyjamas and slippers. She refused to wear the diaphanous outfits that were used for sales presentation. Any refusal was unthinkable for a meerga—but that one had stunned the trainers.

"Hello Meerga. Beth."

Almost as old as Murray, Beth Ganset wore a white doctor's jacket and the wrist scanner. Her horn rim smart glasses and bobbed hair made her seem more medical, somehow. Murray was a PhD psychologist; Beth was a psychiatrist, crucial to the study's funding. She was about a head shorter than Meerga, and had to look past the girl's shoulder to be seen by Murray. "She wanted to talk to you, Murray. Is now okay?"

"Sure. How's her schoolwork going?"

Beth chuckled. "I cannot keep up with the girl."

"I'm not surprised. She's scary smart."

Meerga raised her eyebrows. "It's scary?" She seemed faintly alarmed, though her voice remained soft, lilting. It was designed that way.

"No. Just an expression."

"What are you up to?" Beth asked him, nodding toward the screen.

"Trying to decide if the initial video interview should go in the study's final report, amongst other things. Come on in, you guys, don't hang about out there…"

Beth shook her head. "You guys talk. I've got to get back to checking brain volumes…"

"Anything new there?"

"Nope. No one else like Meerga so far." She waved goodbye and walked off, murmuring to her smart glasses.

Meerga came in. She looked at the chair across from him.

"Have a seat, Meerga."

"Thank you."

She sat down. Her movements were sensuous, graceful. She was designed that way, too.

He looked in her crystal-blue eyes, and saw a seamless mix of intelligence and puzzlement. "You always look a little puzzled," he said, gently. "What are you puzzling about?"

She tilted her head to one side and thought about it. "It's more confused than puzzled. When I look at you, and Beth, and the trainers, here, and I look at the other girls…"

"Beth and I explained how you were all gestated. The lack of parents, the profit motive here, what money is…"

"Yes, I understand all that." She fluttered the delicate fingers of one hand. Her fingernails were innately colored a pearly pink. They were always perfectly shaped, without a manicure. If she broke one, another grew. Otherwise, they had stopped growing.

It was all in the study. Which was coming to an end.

"I'm confused about why I'm more like…like Beth. Than I'm like the other girls. I mean, the way I think and talk."

"Beth explained mutation to you?"

"Yes. You think it's that?"

"We're not sure. But it's something along those lines."

"But I am like the others in some ways."

"You're very different in important ways, Meerga. You're not suited for—well, I think it's all a mistake, really, to sell meergas. Completely wrong. But you especially…don't belong here."

"Not sure I belong outside. I don't know. Haven't seen much."

He nodded. "Not so far." They'd only let Beth take Meerga to the park. She'd shown real excitement on seeing the trees, the pond, the ducks, lifters flying overhead. It was an excitement she never displayed in the training center—except just a little, when she was given new reading on her tablet. The encyclopedia download lit flames in her eyes. "Beth told you we're working on taking you out of here—and I think we've almost got it arranged."

Her eyes widened—it was a beautiful effect. "Really?" She frowned prettily. "But the Creskes won't allow it."

"They won't have a choice."

"And—the study is ending?"

"Oh yes. Just a few days more. They're going to be glad to see us gone. I was hoping the study would push Congress into making this place illegal but..." He shook his head. "The preliminary report didn't seem to impress them. A lot of congressmen own meergas."

"What if someone buys me before you can get me out?"

"I...had a discussion about that, yesterday, with Addy. He says it won't happen. You're..." He didn't want to use the word defective. "You're not the kind of product they sell. He says the study can take charge of you, if we pay costs."

Her lips parted. She seemed to stop breathing for a moment. "I can go with you?"

"Um—yes, with us. You can stay with one of us, and we'll find somewhere you can...someone to adopt you."

"I want you to adopt me, Murray. I want to live with you."

His mouth went dry. "...Ah."

"And I'd like to have children. Someday."

"What?" He'd thought Meerga was clear she couldn't have children. And did she mean with him?

"I mean," she said, "I'd like to adopt a baby someday. A normal baby."

"Oh! Someday you probably can. First—"

Murray's screen chimed. URGENT CALL lit up. He touched the screen icon. "Yes?"

"Dr. Stathis?"

He felt a chill. "Yes."

"This is Meredith Kinz at Hartford Central. We have your son Ryan here. He's been shot. He's lost a lot of blood..."

4. Cell Repair

"I know: 'It's been a month, so get out of bed,'" Ryan said, his voice listless. He was sitting up in his bed, looking at the tablet in his lap.

The tablet, Murray knew, was looking back.

"I didn't say anything like that, Ryan." Murray stretched and yawned.

93

He had slept in, too. He'd managed trousers and a T-shirt, but he was still barefoot.

"I was going to get up," Ryan murmured. "It doesn't hurt much to walk now... Just not sleeping that well." He still hadn't looked up from the tablet.

"I've got a prescription for you from Beth, for that. But you can't start being dependent on pills."

"Okay, hey."

When I was his age, I'd have said whatever, Murray thought. It was saying the same thing.

Murray cleared his throat. "Actually—I came in to ask if you want to have some coffee with me." He'd never known Ryan to take an interest in coffee, but he thought Ryan might like the man-to-man inclusion of the offer.

Ryan tilted his head—but kept looking into the tablet. "Um...I don't like coffee. Makes me anxious." He shrugged. "I like hot chocolate."

"I want to try hot chocolate," Meerga said, coming in. "They didn't give it to us at the training center. No hot drinks. I think they were afraid we'd burn ourselves." She wore jeans with a hole in one knee, and an oversized sweatshirt, and dirty white tennis shoes. Yet she was impossibly attractive, even dressed like that.

And now Ryan looked up from the tablet—at Meerga.

"That place we went by last week, when we walked in that park," Ryan said tentatively. "They have hot chocolate. If we can get a driverless to pick us up, and..."

His voice trailed off; his eyes got a little glassy. He was probably thinking about Tarina.

"Did she call?" Meerga asked.

Meerga had an eerie way of seeming to read minds. But Murray thought it was just her precocity—and her gift for observing people.

"No." He glanced at the tablet. His voice was hard to hear. "She went back under tech soon as her dad let the ambulance guys in..."

"How do you know?" Murray asked. "You were out cold."

"I talked to Sharma...her cousin." He nodded at the tablet. "She went to see what was up. They're all three still under tech. More than a month later..."

"I see. Well. Let's get a driverless, and go get some hot chocolate. Actually I think I'll have a mocha."

"Is that place safe?" Meerga asked, looking at Murray.

He felt the usual inner shock when she looked at him—her frankness, her openness, her almost diabolically sculpted beauty. "There's some auto security around the coffee shop, but it's nothing like in the residential areas. We'll be fine."

"I'm not going to do anything else stupid," Ryan said, looking at her a little resentfully.

But he couldn't keep any sullenness in him, long, when he was looking at her. After a moment, a dreamy smile ghosted the corners of his mouth...

I shouldn't have brought her here, Murray thought. How could he not become sexually obsessed with her?

She never seemed to flirt with the boy. When she looked at Murray, though, sometimes—he thought she was trying to convey something. Which worried him almost as much.

But she needed the home. Beth's place was really small. And she was helpful; she wasn't intrusive. She had social skills that should've been beyond her. Some other residence could be found. But she was so attractive he was afraid for her. He had arranged for her entry into the wide world; he had to take responsibility.

Murray took a deep breath. "I'll call a driverless."

5. Embraced

"Ryan's been home from the hospital for a month and a half, Beth, the nerve damage has been repaired and...well, he has a small limp but really, he's healed up well. It's just—I guess it's the thing with Tarina. He has some form of PTSD. He's hardly sleeping, at all. I don't know..."

He was talking to her from the screen in the extra bedroom he used for an office. Beth listened to him a little like a psychiatrist, but there was intimacy in it too. They'd dated, recently, and sometimes he thought about asking her to marry him. She might well say yes. He wasn't madly attracted to her, but she was a kindly, intelligent woman, she was his good friend, and she liked Ryan. The boy was merely polite to her, though.

"I don't have to tell you to be patient with him," she said. Then she smiled. "But be patient with him." She hesitated, then added, "There are some very clean antidepressants now. Almost no side effects."

"Right. But...I'd rather not go there if we don't have to."

"How's he getting along with Meerga?"

"Oh—he adores her. What boy wouldn't?" He laughed softly.

"He doesn't do anything to..."

"No, no, he knows she's really only seven years old."

"When I was there for dinner I thought she was...gazing at you, sort

95

of."

"Gazing?"

"I mean, she may be somewhat emotionally fixated on you."

"We've pretty much adopted her, after all."

"You know what I mean…"

"Well…Yes."

Two nights ago she'd knocked on his bedroom door…

"Doctor Stathis?"

"Yes, Meerga?"

"Am I disturbing you?"

"No, I was just watching an old movie."

"Can I watch it?"

"Oh…" He was lying on his bed, watching a very old movie indeed. Early Fred Astaire. What was the harm in watching Fred Astaire with her? "Sure."

She came in, wearing a slip, her bathrobe and slippers, and sat down cross-legged on the bed beside him. On the screen, Fred and Ginger were gliding across a shining ballroom.

"Wow. They look happy," Meerga said.

"Sure. But really, Ginger was probably hoping desperately that this was a final take because her feet were killing her."

Meerga laughed, apparently getting the joke. She looked fondly at him. "You're sweet to let me watch this with you." She kissed him on the cheek. "Thanks."

She put a hand over his. And she was gazing at him.

He looked at her. "What's up, kiddo?"

"I'm made for men…"

"You're going to school and you'll be going to go to college. You'll meet men. In twelve years or so you'll be legal to…do whatever you feel like with them. I doubt you get much resistance."

"But what about you?"

His heart was pounding. But he managed to smile dismissively. "You're something like magic, Meerga. But that part of your magic, I will always resist. I'm too old for you and…it would be wrong for about ten reasons. I'd rather not recite them…"

They watched the movie a little more. He knew she was crying, silently, as she watched it. He didn't look at her. Then she squeezed his hand and left the bedroom…

"Yes," he said now. "But she'll get over that. I don't encourage her.

You can ask her about it if you want."

Beth shook her head. "I'm sure she's safe with you. I wouldn't hold it against you for just being tempted that way. You're only human and she's...designed."

"Right. She is very thoroughly designed. But I've got it under control. I was actually thinking you might be able to help me out with that temptation thing. I was hoping we could have a weekend, you know, just you and me."

Beth's quick smile was as genuine as a sudden light in a dark room. "Yes! That'd be great! Only, we should bring Ryan and Meerga, get them each a room. She'll see how things are. And...so would Ryan."

They talked a little more, and then hung up—and Murray had a sudden urge to check on Ryan. Just have a quick look in on his son. Who was so like him, in some ways.

Meerga had been spending a lot of time with Ryan. Hadn't he heard her footsteps, padding by, earlier, on the way to Ryan's room? He hadn't thought about it, then...

"Oh Jesus," he murmured.

He got up quickly, went down the hall—and hesitated, his hand on Ryan's bedroom door. He could smell her natural scent. She had been here, at this door.

You have to know...

Murray opened the door and froze. She was there, in the shadowy room—and she was in bed with Ryan.

"Meerga?"

She stirred. Murray went closer, his eyes adjusting to the dim light. After a moment, he could see she was lying on top of the comforter. Ryan was under the blankets, turned away from her. She had her arm draped over Ryan, spooning against him like a mother with a child. Or like a comforting big sister. He remembered the way she'd been with the other girls, at the training center; he remembered she wanted children.

They were both asleep. He hadn't given the boy his sleeping pill, but Ryan was breathing deeply, and smiling in his sleep.

Murray felt a sick tautness go out of him. He felt better than he had in months. Maybe years.

He left the room, quietly closing the door behind him.

END

JOHN SHIRLEY is an American author of science-fiction, fantasy, and noir fiction, a prolific writer of novels and short stories, TV scripts, and screenplays who has published over 30 books and ten collections. Shirley is known for his cyberpunk science fiction novels, such as the *A Song Called Youth* trilogy, *City Come A-Walkin'*, and *Black Glass*, as well as his suspense (*Spider Moon* and *The Brigade*), horror novels, and stories ("Demons, Crawlers, Black Butterflies"), and horror film work.

Shirley can be found on his official website www.darkecho.com/JohnShirley/.

TO SLEEP, PERCHANCE

Mark Terence Chapman

"So this is it, the end of the line."

Ada floated between the stars, alone and dying—slowly—in the only undamaged escape pod. Undamaged, that is, except for the transponder—and the slow leak in the air supply. The thin padding of the bunk on which she sat did nothing to cushion the torment of her thoughts.

No more hopes and dreams; no more career advancement; no more chance at a family. It all ends here. Not in the heat of battle, but in the chill darkness of the aftermath.

She chuckled bitterly to herself. "Fine time to be turning eloquent."

The battle was over; her ship destroyed in the Chanthi ambush along with the rest of her squadron.

"How did they know when to be waiting by the jump point?"

She shook her head as if to clear it of unanswerable questions. *The only thing that matters right now is that the Chanthi are gone and I'm alone out here.*

I suppose it worked in my favor that the escape pod is beat up enough to look like just another piece of wreckage. On the other hand, without the transponder, there's no hope of rescue—not that there's any fleet left to rescue me. The only ships in this region still in one piece are the enemy's.

She sighed and shrugged. *It's just as well the transponder's out. I've heard what they do to prisoners—especially female prisoners.*

A shiver wracked her slender frame. *Besides, dying of suffocation isn't so bad, is it? I'll just fall asleep when my air runs out and that'll be that.*

Ada clenched her teeth. *What really burns me, though, is knowing that the bugs have beaten us. They just keep winning, and winning, and winning, taking planet after planet and forcing us back.*

There's no way our last six systems can hold out against their hundreds, what's left of our fleet against their armada of thousands. They won't even let us surrender! They just keep coming and coming and coming....

She grimaced at the thought of wave after wave of Chanthi needleships carving up the tattered remains of the Terran fleet. Soon it would be Earth's turn.

Another year—maybe longer if we can win a major battle or two—and then we'll be gone; just another afterthought of evolution, swept under the cosmic rug and soon forgotten by the rest of the universe.

She shook her head slowly. "What did we do that was so wrong?"

Sure, there was some squabbling over disputed planets. And of course there was the friction over who is the One True God. Still, the politicians and clergy should have been able to work things out.

"That's their job, damn it!"

Instead, a few shots were fired in anger, and then that scout ship was destroyed. Next thing you know, everyone overreacts and now nine years later we're facing extinction.

"It just isn't fair." The whispered words sounded pitiful, even to Ada.

She chuckled bitterly again. *You should know better than that by now. The universe isn't fair, it just is. We have no more inherent right to survive than anyone else. But, damn, it shouldn't end like this. We have such potential... We're smart; we're adaptable; we create great works of art and music and literature. If given a chance, we could do so much! We've only been outside our home system for a century.*

"We need more time!" Her scream of outrage echoed inside the pod.

Frustration eventually turned to resignation. She sighed and shrugged.

To all there comes an end.

Ada focused on the view port, observing how the frost crawled across the interior of the diamond-coated glass composite, obscuring her view. The fuel cell that kept the heater going—along with the air pump and the artificial gravity—had failed an hour earlier. It wouldn't be long now.

She brushed the halo of hair from her cheek. The long, lush, beautiful auburn tresses of which she was once so proud were long gone, shorn during induction processing. What grew back in the nine months since now hung in greasy, sweaty clumps.

You may beat us in the end, but we won't go down without a fight. Just like today: you won, but you left limping badly, didn't you?

She shouted in defiance. "Yeah, you destroyed our six, but not before we took out eight of yours! Not as easy as you thought, was it?"

Ada sported a wolfish grin as she rubbed at the rime with a sleeve. To her irritation, her breath fogged the glass, forcing her to wipe a second time.

She watched as a twisted, charred piece of alien debris tumbled past the viewport, glinting in the distant sunlight. What else could she do at this point? She had no engine, no weapons, little air, and less hope for rescue.

"No, not so easy," she whispered.

As Ada looked out on a spray of stars nearly lost in the infinity of blackness, her spirits flagged. She had nothing left to her but thoughts of mortality. It didn't take long to survey the interior of the hexagonal pod. It contained little more than two bunks and a food locker. Even worse, someone had raided the locker, leaving only the water bottles.

Great. No food. The shortages among the rank-and-file must be worse than I was told.

I guess I shouldn't be surprised—everything else is in short supply. She shook her head to dismiss the thought. Not that the lack of food will matter much. I'll be dead long before that. But at least it would have given me something to take my mind off my situation for a few minutes.

She settled back, shivering, to conserve her meager air supply; a strap secured her to the bunk.

Now you're being silly. Why bother? The conclusion is foregone. You have no blankets, no heater, no way to keep warm. It's already below freezing in here. The only question is whether the cold will take you before the lack of oxygen does. As if to settle the matter, her torso spasmed with a prolonged shiver.

I guess it doesn't really matter; I'll be just as dead either way. At least Mom and Dad can save the money for my birthday cake and candles next month.

Her attempt at gallows humor fell flat. She blinked back tears.

Next year Connie turns eighteen and it'll be her turn to die.

She pictured her little sister's bloody corpse tumbling in space. Ada's eyes filled with the tears that she wouldn't permit for herself.

I wonder if Tom had the same thoughts about me right before he died.

She shook off the memory of her older brother, the popular, gregarious one of the trio. He was killed in action at the Battle for Greensward, nearly two years past.

I've missed you, Tommy...

The futility of it all finally overwhelmed her and she let herself grieve—grieve for her brother, grieve for all her friends who had been killed in the damn war, grieve for the human race. Teardrops swelled, creating refractive lenses against her eyes. She shook her head to dislodge the distractions. Unheeded, wobbly twin globes sailed across the cabin to splatter against the bulkhead, where they froze into little stars. She cried until she could cry no more, many long, cold, lonely minutes later.

After a time, it became difficult to keep her eyes open.

This is it: the end of my life. I'll drift off and awake in the glorious hereafter.

At least the heathens can't take that away from me....

Ada was jolted from near-unconsciousness and thrown against the safety strap.

What—? She felt the thrumming through the deck plating that could mean only one thing.

"A tractor beam!" She crossed to the view port and scraped away the frost.

They did come back for me. I'm sav—! Wait...

"No! No! No!" Her blood ran cold.

Of course it's one of theirs. They must have come back to sift through the wreckage.

Desolation hit her hard for a moment; she shook it off.

I'm not a quitter; I'm a soldier! I have to do something. I can't let them take me. I've heard the stories.

She frantically looked about for a weapon: a grenade, a blaster, a loose pipe, anything.

After several frenzied minutes of searching through all the various small storage compartments, her shoulders slumped.

Nothing. Why can't they mount weapons on these pods? One plasma cannon and I could do some real damage!

She sighed, knowing the answer: "Because armed escape pods would be military targets and without engines they'd be easy pickings, that's why."

Head lowered, she contemplated the decking for a few moments.

Her head snapped up, eyes wide. "Idiot!"

How could I forget? They drilled it into all of us right before the mission! There's still one option left.

With renewed purpose, she turned to the instrument console. Her lungs labored in the oxygen-starved atmosphere of the pod, making it tough to concentrate. With fingers stiffened by the cold, Ada made the necessary preparations, hoping against hope that she remembered the access codes she'd been given. Then she sat back to wait. *What else was there to do?*

It wasn't long before the pod passed through the massive doors of the enemy's launch bay. Gravity returned to the pod, pressing Ada into her bunk.

Her features serene now that she was in control of her own fate, she leaned forward and depressed the key that disabled the fail safes and began the sixty-second countdown.

This is one weapon they don't know about yet because ours was one of the first ships to equip the pods with it. The last resort.

It shows just how desperate we've become.

What made it effective as a last-ditch weapon was that it was invisible to sensors until armed. At least that was the theory. It had never been tested in combat—until now. Although the pod had no engine, it was equipped with a miniature version of the space-folding device used in the hyperdrive. It was incapable of moving the pod, but that was not the point. The device would invert space within a fifty-meter radius, and then shut off abruptly a millisecond later.

The fabric of space would distort and then snap back like a rubber band. Theoretically, that would cause cascading graviton waves to blast outward with catastrophic effect—much like a meteor smashing into a still lake.

The effect may be equivalent to a nuke of less than a kiloton, but that should be enough to give them a major case of indigestion. *With any luck, there won't be enough left of their ship for the next one to figure out what happened.*

She shook her head in sorrow. *It's far too late to change the course of the war, but at least we can take out a few more of them before we fall. If we're all going to die anyway, at least let's make our deaths count for something.*

Forty-three…forty-two…forty-one…

The Chanthi ship's launch bay doors cycled shut behind her, sealing her in. It should have made her feel trapped; instead it was somewhat comforting.

I guess you could say it provides a sense of closure. Her lips curled into a crooked smile at her pun.

Twenty-nine…twenty-eight…twenty-seven…

I'm committed now; the disarm code is locked out. At least I'm going out on my own terms. Now it's time to make peace with the Man Upstairs. I'll be meeting You soon enough, won't I?

She said a brief prayer, wishing she hadn't left her rosary on her bunk aboard Sisyphus.

Seventeen…sixteen…fifteen…

Ada saw excited movement through the view port. *So, your sensors finally picked up the threat. Ha! Too late! You're already dead; you just don't know it yet.*

Maybe it's time to change your mantra. How about, Dead Bugs Walking? Her lips quirked upward in a lopsided grin.

Several figures neared the pod. She grimaced. This was her first opportunity to see a Chanthi up close—jet black but for the canary-yellow eyes, topped with skull projections that reminded one of devil horns. The razor-sharp mandibles and talons certainly didn't soften the impression.

Damn. Those creatures are even uglier in person than in the holos!

Eight…seven…

Partially obscured by one of the approaching soldiers was an insignia on the far wall, a starburst surrounded by jagged alien characters that she knew read: *Divine Might of the Chanthi Diktat.*

Five…

We may fall in the end, but at least a few hundred more of you damned bugs won't outlive us!

She smiled grimly to herself; then she lifted her jaw with pride. First Lieutenant Ada Considine of the Terran Defense Force snapped to attention, saluted, and hissed through gritted teeth.

"Take that, you bastar—!"

Zero.

END

MARK TERENCE CHAPMAN has been a fan of SF for most of his life, but writing it has been a more recent event. Chapman currently has four novels for sale on Amazon with two more in progress.

To find out more about Chapman or his books, go to his blog at tesserene.blogspot.com or his website: MarkTerenceChapman.com.

Find his books on Amazon at www.amazon.com/Mark-Terence-Chapman/e/B001KD533U.

THE WALK

Druscilla Morgan

The old man stood at the front gate and stretched as he surveyed the empty street. He enjoyed his evening walk. Exercise was no longer a chore and the pains in his chest were just a memory. He was glad he'd volunteered for the injection, along with one hundred other guinea pigs. There were risks of course. The doctors had warned him about the possibility of radicalization. The thought of renegade nano bots rampaging through his body had given him pause for thought, but the docs had assured him they would be closely monitoring his progress. What the heck, he'd figured. At eighty two years old, with a rapidly failing heart, he had nothing to lose. The nano cells were injected through a device called a nano pore and immediately began seeking out their target. Over the past few weeks he'd felt his heart begin to regenerate, pumping with renewed vigor as the nano cells went to work reconstructing the damaged tissue. His blood began to flow freely and he found he was able to walk further than the mailbox without stopping to catch his breath.

Now, nearly two months later, he felt completely healed, with the vigor and enthusiasm of a twenty year old. He took another deep breath and started to walk; big strong strides that quickly took him to the end of his street. He stopped for a moment, looking left then right. Before him lay the endless fields of wheat he'd known since boyhood. They stretched across the horizon, bathing in the orange glow of the setting sun. The husky heads waved on their thin stalks like a restless sea, beckoning him forward. He thought about turning left and following the road to town, but the wheat called to him, rustling in his ear like a lover. A sense of oneness consumed him and he abandoned himself to the urge and crossed the road. The barbed wire fence caught on his pants as he climbed over. He swore, momentarily distracted by the sharp sting on his thigh, but it was gone in an instant, as was the blood and the small nick in his skin. Only a slender rip in his pants betrayed his encounter with the fence. He wondered at this small miracle for a moment but quickly forgot about it as the call of the wheat urged him on.

He swung his other leg over the fence and landed on the hard earth with a thud. It jarred him and he wondered if nano cells could rebuild his weakened bones. He'd missed his last appointment but made a mental note to ask the doctors about bone healing on the next visit. Restlessly, he scanned the field. The wheat seemed taller now. It whispered and wavered in front of him like an exotic dancer. Mesmerized, he moved forward, crossing a small ditch with surprising ease. Bathed in the feeling of peace and oneness, he began to push his way through the sea of swaying stalks. The rough caress of their husky heads scratched against his bare arms as he parted them. Each touch was intimate, slipping under his pores and dissolving into his being as he walked deeper into the wheat's embrace. The stalks rustled around him, enfolding him until there was no longer any distinction between man and plant. Beneath the cloak of the encroaching night, the old man quietly dissolved into the sea of wheat, witnessed only by the rising moon.

"Where's your grandfather?"

Martin tried to ignore his mother. He was one hundred and eighty points off finishing the top level of *Cyber Siege* and still had two lives left.

But his mother was no respecter of *Cyber Siege* glory.

"Martin! Pause that damn game for a moment!"

With a sigh, Martin hit pause, unclipped the gaming bracelet and threw it onto his bed. The curve screen went black as the controller hit the quilt. Shit! Now he'd have to start the level again.

He stuck his head out the door and yelled into the hallway.

"Whaddya want?"

"Where's your grandfather?"

He thought for a moment. Last he'd seen of the old guy, he'd been talking about going for a walk.

"I think he went for a walk!" he yelled.

"When?"

His mother was relentless. He couldn't be bothered yelling again so he made his way down the hall. The rich scent of roast chicken wafted through the air and he realized he was hungry. Salivating, he leaned against the wall and watched his mother as she bustled around the kitchen. She opened the convector and swore as hot steam caught her hand. Grabbing a wet cloth, she encased the reddened skin and turned to look at Martin.

"Well?"

"Well what?" He'd forgotten the question.

"When did he leave?"

Oh, yeah. He frowned.

"I'm not sure when he left. I heard him say he was going for a walk, but that was a couple of hours ago."

Now his mother frowned as she peered out the window. A blood red moon was rising over the fields. Martin thought it looked cool but kinda eerie at the same time. He shivered a little, catching some of his mother's now obvious anxiety.

"You'd better go look for him. He should be back by now."

He didn't argue, even though he had no wish to venture out into the cold night air. He grabbed a pair of shoes and crammed them on his feet as he silently tried to reassure himself. Grandpa had been the picture of health lately, bounding around with more energy than his own grandson. The old guy would be fine. He'd probably stopped to talk to someone, or decided to walk all the way around the town. It was a small town but it would easily take the old man a good hour to make a round trip. Still, something niggled at him. Without another word, he grabbed his jacket from the chair where he'd carelessly thrown it and slammed out the front door. The cold night air hit him and he stood for a moment, catching his breath as his eyes adjusted to the gloom. Thankfully, the moon was higher now. It had lost some of its reddish tinge and glowed like a big, orange ball against the black sky. It shed enough light for Martin to pick his way through the overgrown grass without tripping on stray tree roots. His mother had been nagging him to mow for two weeks and now he wished he'd listened to her. The grass was damp with dew. It clung to the bottom of his pants, the wetness seeping through his thin fabric shoes.

Should've worn boots.

He stepped onto the road and began to trace the route he knew his grandfather favored on his evening walks. He walked to the end of the street and stood at the corner, looking from left to right as he tried to get some kind of psychic sense of his grandfather's movements. He knew the old man enjoyed strolling beside the wheat fields of his now distant youth. The fields were some of the few left undomed. The Sully family had owned these fields for generations and old man Sully, kept alive by the wonders of technology, still retained an iron grip on his traditional values and practices. The Sullys had resisted the government decree that all crops be domed. It had gone to local court, then State court, then finally a National Tribunal. It was a long and expensive process but, incredibly, the Sullys had emerged victorious and their wheat continued to thrive in the natural atmosphere. Martin wondered momentarily if Grandpa had gone to visit old man Sully, but then dismissed it as unlikely. The Sully's farmhouse was miles away, far beyond the vast stretch of wheat fields. Grandpa loved his walk, but Martin doubted he was that keen.

He decided to turn right. The road stretched before him, darkened and deserted. A few street lights broke through the night, their iridescent glow competing with the moon. They cast small, comforting pools of light on the shadowy road before tapering off into a pitch black void. With a sharp pang of panic, Martin realized he'd forgotten to bring a flashlight. He thought about turning back, but it was getting late, so he decided to press on. The night was still and the cold air frosted his lungs as he walked, ejecting itself in dragon-like tendrils of mist with each breath. He reached the borderline of light and dark and stopped. He had no wish to plunge ahead into the black, unlit night, which left him with no choice but to turn back or turn right and walk around the block.

He turned right. As his feet padded along against the soft tar of the road, a sharp breeze rose from nowhere, prickling the hairs on the back of his neck. It was the same feeling he'd had when that weird guy had followed him home from school a few years ago. He hadn't like the feeling then and he didn't like it now. He stopped and cocked his head as he listened for footsteps, but there were none; only that uneasy feeling of another presence. Once again, Martin wished he'd brought a flashlight. He turned slowly, half expecting to see the shadowy figure of a serial killer, but there was nothing but the empty street behind him. Feeling just a little creeped out, he turned back and kept walking, coming to a stop at a narrow laneway that ran up beside his house. He peered into the darkness, trying to discern any movement, and again mourned the absence of a flashlight. He was about to continue walking towards a safely lit street when a thought struck him.

What if his grandfather had felt unwell? Maybe he'd tried to take a shortcut down the laneway and collapsed...

The thought nagged at him. He took a firm grip on his fear and, with a deep, dragony breath, turned down the laneway, straining his eyes and his ears in the inky blackness as he walked. Recent rains had turned the dirt track into mud. He walked blindly and carefully, his feet skidding on the puddles that littered his path like land mines. Slowly, his eyes adjusted. He scanned the grassy edges of the lane with a sense of dread as he shuffled precariously along, but there was nothing. No movement. No body.

No Grandpa.

By the time he reached the end of the laneway, his shoes were caked with mud and his feet were wet and cold. Thankfully, the back light was burning, casting its welcoming warmth into the gloom. He continued past the side fence to the front of the house and stood, gazing up and down the street as he tried to gather his thoughts. Another short gust of wind sent a whisper of leaves scurrying behind him. He turned, startled, as the hairs of his neck prickled again. The wind gusted one more time before dropping as quickly as it had risen, but the whisper continued, rustling along the ground with the fallen leaves that trailed in its wake.

Martin knew he had to keep looking for his grandfather, but every fiber of his being screamed at him to run inside the house and bolt the door. The moon gleamed down on him, spotlighting him like a deer in the hunter's sight. He felt it behind him now…whatever it was. It shuffled and whispered in a thousand, ageless voices. It was part of the road, part of the trees, part of the fields. The road shimmered as the presence moved along it. The trees wove and danced around him as though animated by an inner presence. Everything felt sharp, like a knife. Martin's heart beat hard against his chest. He willed his feet to move but remained glued to the spot as the strange presence swirled around him. He felt something prick at his face, stinging his skin in the cold air. He winced and slapped at his cheek, as though slapping a mosquito, but the skin pricks continued, now attacking his ears, his hands. The presence pricked at his arms, pulling him toward the street. He tried to resist, to pull back, but his feet skimmed helplessly forward along the road, compelled by the invisible force.

A sense of impending doom overwhelmed him as he was steered toward the wheat fields, Strengthened by sheer panic, he dug his heels into the road with such force that he toppled backwards, grazing his elbows on the harsh bitumen. The pain stung him, but the impact seemed to have freed him from the grip of the unseen presence. Without thinking, he leaped to his feet and ran. He was sure he could hear footsteps in the wind that rustled along the road behind him. A cold mist enveloped him, chilling his bones as he ran through its ghostly fingers. His breath was bursting in his chest, but he ran until he reached the front door. Heart hammering, he fumbled for his key as the presence whispered up the driveway. The lock clicked and he fell into the house just as the rustling wind reached his back. He slammed the door shut and leaned against it, chest heaving.

His relief was short-lived. The hard surface of the door suddenly turned to jelly under his weight. It shimmered and wavered like the sea, its grainy surface a symphony of impossible movement. It was as though every cell in the wood had come alive.

Like the trees.

Martin's heart sank. He sprang away from the door as though burned and turned to look. The wood bulged outward and for a moment Martin thought the door would burst open like a ripe peach. The wood wove and pulsed as it took the form of a man. The figure looked familiar. It stretched out a hand and whispered.

"Martin, come with me. Walk with me in the wheat fields."

He knew that voice, even though it rustled like the leaves. Eyes wide, Martin backed away from the specter as it heaved against its wooden bonds. He tried to scream but managed only a frightened croak. Shaking, he groped around beside him for a weapon; an umbrella, a tennis racket.

Anything.

He came up empty handed and could only watch, cowering, as the door continued to shift and heave. The wood dissolved, spewing the transparent figure into the room. It immediately became formless, insinuating itself into the atmosphere as though it had always been there. It filled the corners and climbed the walls, it whispered and rustled along the floor boards and danced on the tapestry rug. It stroked his arm and touched his cheek like a deathly breeze. A terrified scream tore from his throat.

"Mom, I think I've found Grandpa!"

END

DRUSCILLA MORGAN is a Sydney, Australia born writer and artist who loves cats, horses, and vampires. She writes short stories and novels in the horror, fantasy, and science fiction genres. Her short stories have been published in *Arcanium Axiom* magazine, *Absent Cause* magazine, and *Far Horizons* e-magazine. Morgan describes herself as a creative shape shifter who loves weaving a narrative that both entertains and challenges her readers. She is currently collaborating on a series of vampire novels with Roy C Booth. You can follow Morgan on her Facebook Author's Page: www.facebook.com/pages/Druscilla-MorganAuthor/720568464695969.

THE ELECTRIFIED ANTS

Jetse de Vries

I: Brother England
singular sky
spineless talk
blathered by
frightened flock

over-crowded lands
perfect program'd ants
despotic enterprise
no chance to defy

down down
deep underground
(veiled) site
pound pound
ten terabytes
viral stock

[Fragment of <u>From Orchestrated Sequences to</u>
<u>Nothingface</u>: scattered poetic   viruses   on   the   Panopticon
network.]

At 4.15 am, GMT, Nero Pogolas is jolted out of a deep, hypnotically induced sleep by a sudden, static shock. The pain is most intense in his right hand, and as he clutches it with his left, he notices the small piece of paper in his palm. Blinking his eyes, wondering why his panoptical house link hasn't switched on the bedside light, he realizes he can actually read the text on the white square. The black letters stand out against their phosphorescent background:

The enforcement of the Panopticon Singularity ultimately

111

requires the genesis of a counter   *movement.*

The words enter his brains, but their meaning remains unclear. In his hand, the piece of paper—if it is that—begins to dissolve, and before Pogolas can make any sense of this strange event, all evidence of it has disappeared into thin air. Even more baffling, the node to the corporate state's ubiquitous law enforcement system doesn't seem to work.

Normally, it would have given him "preemptive advice", switch on his bed lamp the moment it noticed he was awake and help him back to sleep. In the three years since panoptical links were lawfully enforced nationwide, he has never seen his node fail. Their inbuilt redundancy and hidden security features make them virtually fail-safe and tamper-proof. Apart from this time, it seems.

While still only wondering that he is allowed to wonder, a slight vibration under his mattress and a faint buzz in his ears announce the return of the corporate state's ubik-link—*time to go to sleep again. We don't want to arrive at work fatigued, do we?*—the soft and persistent voice of the local panoptic node is the last thing he hears before he returns to dreamland.

The next morning, awoken by velvety yet effective tickling, Pogolas rises in a pre-heated room. At breakfast, while studiously trying to ignore his LCD tabletop beaming infotainment and carefully targeted ads at him (ever since tampering with RFID tags had become a criminal offense, personal tastes are charted to near perfection, making the ads all but irresistible. Every promotion or salary raise he gets never seems to catch up with his buying spree. If anything, his debts mount, he recalls the night's singular event. Luckily, the ubik-link has become quite accustomed to his early morning silences and lets him eat in relative quiet. The more he thinks about it, the less sense it makes.

For one thing: He remembers. Of course, he's not supposed to know that his house node edits out certain unwanted episodes during his sleep cycles. But he knows: While he cannot remember what he has forgotten, deep inside he feels that he has forgotten. The missing sequences leave subtle interstices in the fabric of his memory, hollow echoes in the story of his life. So the fact that he remembered was an event in itself.

This must mean that the ubik-link has not only had an actual breakdown but that it didn't find any trace of the message afterward, too. An impressive feat, from whoever delivered that message to him.

The message itself is a small puzzle: of course there must be some attempts at resistance. But as the web of the Panopticon Singularity spreads ever wider and deeper into modern society, it has become ever more effective in subverting those. So effective, that even rumors of opposition have faded

112

away. This little spark of defiance fires up long lost hopes.

The big question, though, is: Why him? It's not as if he has something special to offer. The time has come to leave for his work, and Pogolas decides that if he still remembers it the next day, he may not have dreamed it. Something really may have slipped through the ultimate web.

The Stockholm Syndrome and brainwashing are variations on a theme. The kidnapping of Elizabeth Smart is a good example in which you take one individual out of a normal context and put them in a bizarre context with new rules, and after being in this different reality for a little while and under pressure, they will break down and go along with party line. [...] There are definite examples of people being able to have that kind of power, and the more repressive a society is, the easier and more likely it becomes...

[Fragment of The Writing of the Wall: *Randomized old newspaper scans dispersed throughout the Panopticon network.]*

Pogolas gets into his car, of which the crystalline fuel cell had been fully recharged. The motorway to the M25 is busier than normal, and the rain—from a sky that seems to be overcast all the time—doesn't help matters, either. By the time he enters the London orbital he's fifteen minutes later than usual. Of course, he can move nearer to Culham, but that means living in Oxford, of all places. No, if there's one thing the Panopticon's subtle and unsubtle urgings fail to achieve, it's moving him from his beloved Cambridge. Even if it means almost one-and-a-half hours commuting each way. An added benefit is that during that time he can let his mind roam, unhindered, as the ubik-link considers road safety important enough not to bombard him with ads as he drives (as long as he keeps the radio off). Some of his best ideas come to him during these drives. Except this morning, when he's getting late, and he wants to make up time. As he speeds up past the speed limit, his car node speaks up:—*you are driving 7.4 miles an hour too fast*—

"I need to get to work in time."

—*no, you don't. you have flexible work times*—

"I like to start as early as possible."

—*then you should have finished your breakfast earlier. you took 8 minutes longer than usual*—

"Never mind, I want to get there as fast as I can."

—*if you keep exceeding the speed limit, your insurance premium will rise by 10% for every ten minutes of speeding—*

"I can't afford that and you know it," Pogolas lets out a frustrated sigh as he slows the car down, "while I haven't had an accident in ages."

—that's what everybody likes to think,—the automated voice insists,— but the statistics show otherwise. they also show that the number of fatal car accidents has dropped by 66.6% since the implementation of the Panopticon—

To which Pogolas has no rebuttal. Of course, the numbers given can be false, but in his gut Pogolas suspects they are quite true. They're part of the Panopticon's continuing success: Roads are safer, people,in general, live healthier, and production has gone up in the last three years. Of course, there are those who keep on speeding, boozing, or smoking, but they pay the price immediately by an instant raise of their insurance premiums.

Pollution has decreased considerably as car insurances for old type engines are heavily offset against the new fuel-cells, making the old gas-guzzlers an ever rarer sight on the country's motorways. Also the forced, accelerated implementation of solar, wind, and other alternative energy in order to lessen the dependence on the rapidly dwindling fossil fuel reserves, in combination with a strong financial impetus for an energy-conserving lifestyle has boded well for the both environment and the country's finances as it leads the western world by exceeding the Kyoto protocol requirements.

Yeah, the walls of our prison are lined with environmentally friendly velvet, but they are stainless steel nonetheless. Pogolas can't help but think, the economy is booming, people live healthier than ever. But still: Is it worth it?

Pogolas is very ambivalent about this. Admittedly, left to his own devices his paunch will surely return as he falls back on his old lifestyle. Then again, he feels he hasn't developed anything truly new since the Panopticon is fully enforced. He's working out old ideas, albeit more effectively, but still old ones. It seems that his creative spark is dying.

Take the way his ubik-link ushers him from speeding, from eating too rich a breakfast: All for his own good. He's always been a slow riser and tries to make up for it on the road. Now he arrives at his work sooner, more refreshed, healthier. Less grumpy to his colleagues, somewhat easier in his social contacts, a bit more relaxed. And while to the outer world it seems he's doing his work in a more efficient manner, Pogolas feels, deep inside, that he's lost his edge. Even if it's a double-sided sword that used to cut him off from his colleagues, but an edge that keeps him—well—on the bleeding edge of research.

It's the same vicious circle his mind has secretly been running for months. That day, though, a mite of defiance fires up his spark, however tiny it's become. He parks his car in the old Joint European Torus Laboratory's car park, and as he approaches the building's entrance his smile is only partly faked.

After the routine DNA-check confirms his identity, he enters the research premises.

In The Netherlands about four thousand DNA-profiles have been recorded. The number in the UK has already exceeded six million...

[Fragment of The Writing of the Wall.]

His congenial manner doesn't go unnoticed by his colleagues.

"Morning, Ernie, and a good one, innit?"

"Somebody sawed off the grumpy part, Ernie?"

"Hey Ernie, haven't heard that whistle for ages."

Only then Pogolas notices that he's whistling. In his pre-Panopticon heyday, Pogolas spearheaded several breakthroughs in fusion research, especially in his field of plasma turbulence. His uncanny way of predicting certain aspects of the seemingly random turbulent behavior, combined with a Spanish colleague's interpretation of his first name (stern), led to his nickname Ernie (although his predictive power failed with the Premium Bonds).

Back then, Pogolas felt he was at the brink of a breakthrough. That optimism, however, has withered under the Panopticon's all-seeing eye.

In Pogolas's department, it's been a quite a while since "Ernie" was so good-natured. A small part of Ernie himself—in a never relenting state of paranoia—thinks this bout of sweet temper is suspicious in itself, but Pogolas decides that suddenly returning to his normal, grumpy state is even stranger. So he sets himself to work in a jolly mood, but takes care to talk predominantly about work, work, and nothing but work, and keep the chitchat as innocent as possible.

A bit to his consternation, he finds not only his work day flying by, but he's able to work out a new, albeit a minor, notion in his research field, as well.

—you see, a good mood makes you produce better—he almost hears his ubik-link say.

A jolly worker, a productive bee, he thinks, Oh please, don't let me become a happy slave.

On the drive home, his anxiety comes creeping back. He wonders, and hopes, that last night's uncommon event is not just a very vivid pipe dream. That something, anything is fighting against this steel-reinforced glass prison.

115

tremendous terror rule
all-seeing intent view
glaze(d) gate grille

enormous creeping gruel
panoptic potent stew
vaulted-ville

ubik-link hysteria
limbo-inc. inertia

I did, I didn't know
I wish, I could go, go!

[*Fragment of From Orchestrated Sequences to Nothingface.*]

Three days later, Pogolas is back into his new life's habits, a routine all but lifeless. The weekends are the worst: Cultural life so devoid of anything truly controversial or even mildly thought-provoking that he's actually looking forward to work. He's even considered working through the weekend, several times, but that seems too much like giving in to the new order.

So it's another weekend of the new old, old new. Theater performances either so focused on sex, love, and skewed relationships that even the newest summit of vulgarity merely makes him yawn; or they're so steeped in *l'art pour l'art* and involved with the inner self as to make a navel-gazer in a cul-de-sac seem like a world traveler. It's not so much that everything was ever so subtly censored; it's more that all really engaged artists have long since left the country. Also, not coincidentally, any foreign piece—no matter how critically acclaimed abroad—never plays in brand new England if it's halfway politically engaged.

He can go to the pub, but most of the low-caloric, alcohol-poor, no-taste stuff they're serving isn't worth the name beer, and after his second pint of Guinness the local ubik-link will be pestering him about liver disease, Alzheimer's, increased health insurance premiums, and all those other things he's trying to forget there in the first place.

Surfing the web has lost all its luster, as well. Non-Panoptical links are better shielded off than the crown jewels in Buckingham Palace, and cruising the net in the hope of finding a breach or a slip in the security is dangerous in another way too: So many carefully targeted ads are launched at you in the meantime that avoiding another shopping spree is like saying no to steroids when your name's Arnold Schwarzenegger.

A local court in Manchester ruled on June 29 that an Internet provider that had copied and read   customers' emails was not breaking the law. [...] The operator of the service had installed software to   intercept emails from the online retailer Amazon to help his own book-dealing business. [...] But two   out of the three judges ruled that there had been no violation, saying that the act does not apply to   "communications in electronic storage".

[Fragment of *The Writing of the Wall*.]

Ever since the Panopticon has closed its event horizon over us, my life's become so routine, so predictable, Pogolas thinks, I need to do something strange, something so way out of the ordinary it'll surprise even myself. He considers, very shortly, starting an underground magazine—*White Noise in the Black Static*—but finding both contributors and readers, let alone distribute it unnoticed, seems impossible.

No, this time not something he loves, but rather something he hates. But what? He decides to take a walk in the warming spring's drizzle while pondering it. Unfortunately, thinking freely requires a lot of concentration, walking through any urban center, these days.

Apart from subconsciously hypnotic, electronic billboards and signs (randomly triggering, polarized lenses that can block most of those ads fetch a mean price) and the subtle pheromone scents micro-jetted from each shop entrance, you have focused hypersound beams whispering sales pitches straight into your head. To be alone with your thoughts requires mirror shades, nose, and earplugs, and a steadfast state of mind.

Peace, Pogolas think as he walks past the Anchor, is only in the grave. Or maybe on the bottom of the river Cam. Then—through the unmistakable scent, sound, and sight of a pint filling with Extra Cold—it hits him: Why not go for a punt? He hates that with a vengeance, so normally it'll be the last thing he'll do. There's the slightest chance of more serenity on the middle of the river, too. Almost to his own surprise, he finds himself hiring a boat.

"Hello, sir, do you mind if I joined you for this punt?" an Asian-looking woman asks.

Pogolas can't believe his eyes: She's a stunner. He hasn't been approached by a woman in ages, and that this chestnut-colored, stylish Asian beauty breaks his dry spell is quite unbelievable. Can he say no to such inviting eyes, set in a high cheek-boned face? Can he refuse that iridescent smile, that elegant posture?

"Be my guest," he says, "but I'm not exactly this town's best punter. We might get hopelessly stuck."

"Well, at least that's different." her voice sounds warm.

"Different," Pogolas says, "as in 'romantic?'"

"Well, more like funny." the slender hand she puts before her mouth fails to camouflage an ear-to-ear smile, and the gleam in her eyes melts his heart.

"Who can resist a woman with a sense of humor?"

"Who can humor a man with a sense of resistance?"

That catches Pogolas off-guard. "What did you just say?"

"Nothing," she says, "just a failed attempt at wit. Forget it, Mr...?"

"Pogolas. But please call me Nero."

"Nice to meet you, Nero. I'm Tara."

"Pleased to meet you, Tara. Shall we punt?"

Fifteen minutes later, Pogolas is sweating profusely. Punting's much harder than he expected. At least they haven't barged into somebody else, or run aground, albeit barely. Never mind, her amused smile almost makes it worthwhile. He's already forgetting why he started this punting madness, anyway.

"Fancy a drink after this?" he manages to ask between labored breaths.

"Better make that lunch, because you'll need it." again with that irresistible, naughty gleam in her eyes.

"Well, I told you I wasn't any good at this," while he keeps his tone friendly, "this is actually the first time for me."

"A virgin? Let me show you how to do it." She gets up and moves next to him.

"You can't be serious."

"Don't moan, and give me that pole."

To Pogolas's astonishment, she begins punting with an almost effortless grace.

"Your technique is wrong," she says, hardly breathing harder, "take over, and I'll tell you how to do it."

Following her instructions, Pogolas finds it can be much easier. *I could almost enjoy this*, he thinks, No, not without her. Now that he's using his strength more economically, he can start a normal conversation.

"How do you know?" he asks.

"You just told me you were born here," she counters, "and you don't know about the female punting clubs?"

"Up until a good hour ago I actively hated punting."

"And now?"

"Mwah, it's not too bad. Do you always pick up weak, unsuspecting men?"

"Can't tell you, really. By the way, do you know you look quite charming when you try to hide your distress?"

She laughs out loud as Pogolas moves his gaze skyward. As his look returns to Earth, he can't help but take in her alluring cleavage as she bends forward, heaving with laughter. *So that's why so many guys like to play the clown*, he thinks, struggling not to fall overboard, and if she keeps laughing like this, I may actually need that cold shower.

However, in spite of her unintended distractions, Pogolas manages to berth the punt safely at Scudamores, and Henson—later on she tells him her full name is Tara B. Henson—offers to pay for their lunch at The Anchor.

Before he knows it, he's dating her. Candlelight dinners in obscure restaurants that he thought didn't exist anymore, where through the removal of electricity there are no commercial intrusions. Noisy gigs in sweaty basements where advertisements are drowned in a cacophonous overkill. Covert screenings of foreign cult movies in shielded apartments.

While her knowledge of the underground is state-of-the-art, her approach to their love affair is decidedly old-fashioned: He has to wait a few months before she lets him steal his first kiss. It happens on a spot where he'd never find himself before: Picnicking with her on the bank of the River Cam after a bout of punting, on one of those rare days when it's not raining.

The treats from her picnic basket have their origin from all over the old Commonwealth: poppadoms with chicken tikka, BLT sandwiches with Canadian bacon, and a cold couscous stew. But it's the Australian sticky date pudding that does the trick: Licking the clinging caramel sauce off each other's fingers, they find each other in their cleaned arms, tongues entangled, oblivious to the world.

Her kisses taste of nutmeg and honey, sweet and spicy, like an impossible mix between a premature dessert and an overdue starter. Whatever the main course was, he feels giddy just thinking about it.

119

In the meantime, he's making actual progress with his work. It's slow, admittedly, but the first time in years that he feels he's treading new ground. It seems that his falling in love somehow frees his mind from his preoccupation with the Panopticon Singularity. Nevertheless, he takes care to keep his new ideas solely in his head.

Next Friday, Pogolas experiences a breakthrough of a different kind: After a particular fine day of punting, picnicking, and a very stimulating movie, Henson invites him into her apartment for a cup of coffee. She never makes it to the coffee maker, as they end up making love on the couch instead.

He stays the night and may even have slept the odd moment. The next morning, he can hardly believe it: He's holding the smartest and prettiest woman he ever met, and the sex has been almost incredible. Just thinking about it makes him ready for the next round: He didn't know he had it in him. She stirs, begins to wake and soon has exactly the same idea: It's too good to be true.

The consummation of their affair wreaks havoc with his sense of time: Moments of bliss that seem to last forever, lingering anticipation that's timed almost right, but when he gets in his car Monday morning the weekend suddenly is much too short.

The turn his life has taken has the strange effect of making him accept his lot: The direct manifestations of the Panopticon Singularity bother him less and less. As his mind is floating in higher spheres, he's figuratively put back with both feet on the ground in the middle of the River Cam.

"Haven't you noticed how there's no commercials at all invading your privacy when we're punting?"

"Now you mention it, yeah. Before I was just too—well—distracted by you."

"Right now the technology to project hypersound across larger distances is prohibitively expensive, but it won't last."

"Meaning we should enjoy these moments of privacy while we can?"

"Exactly. I need to tell you a few things."

A fresh breeze blows over the River Cam, and Henson surreptitiously releases a small handful of barely visible powder into the cool draught.

Radio Frequency ID chips are used for tagging commercial produce. Unlike today's simple anti-shoplifting tags in books and CD's, the next generation will be cheap (costing one or two cents each), tiny (sand-grain sized), and smart enough to uniquely identify any individual manufactured product, by serial number as well as type and vendor. They can be embedded in plastic, wood, food,

120

or fabric, and by remotely interrogating the RFID chips in your clothing or possessions the Panopticon Society's agencies can tell a lot about you—like, what you're reading, what you just ate, and maybe where you've been if they get cheap enough to scatter like dust. More insidiously, because each copy of a manufactured item will be uniquely identifiable, they'll be able to tell not only what you're reading, but where you bought it. RFID chips are injectable, too, so you won't be able to misplace your identity by accident.

[From The Panopticon Singularity, an essay by Charlie Stross, originally commissioned for Whole Earth Review. Now published on the author's website at http://www.antipope.org/charlie/rant/panopticon-essay.html. Used with permission.]

After waiting a minute for the radio-interfering microdrones to disperse, she says, "Do you remember the strange message you received in the middle of the night?"

"About the genesis of a counter movement? But that was months ago."

"We've been targeting you well before that." she says almost matter-of-factly.

"Sheesh," he says, thinking back, "so our meeting near The Anchor—"

"—was prearranged. We put the suggestion in your subconscious."

"And I thought only the Panopticon did such things!"

"Fighting fire with fire. All for a good cause."

"But why would your...organization want me?"

"You are one of the key scientists in the research for nuclear fusion. If your research succeeds, the Panopticon Singularity has an almost unlimited energy source."

"We're still quite a way from that, believe me. And this is an international project: ITER's test reactor is in France."

"Yeah, but while the UK is still under the Panopticon's spell, you should not even go in the right direction: The less it knows, the better."

This is something Pogolas needs to let sink in as it runs right against his scientific nature.

"Tara, asking a scientist not to research is like..." he can't quite find the right analogue.

"...telling a bunch of rabbits not to procreate."

"Exactly. It goes completely against my nature."

"Enough for the moment, Nero. Think about it. And I need to tell you something more, but later."

"Later? But—"

"Later: These shielded talks should be as short as possible. I'll have to wait for the next right moment."

"The next right moment?"

"Yeah. Come on: Let's talk dirty. And mean it." With a smile that has celibacy vows for breakfast.

"If everything would be so easy," Pogolas says and shifts his mind into a different gear.

post-singularity
freewill-atrophy
hypnotic double-bind
resourceful rewind

panoptic control state
despotic Orwell fate
fixed DRAM

illusive freewill shout
proactive frantic clout
re-programmed

who knows what
which goes where?
when is that
soon it's there

do we know
where we go
now
brother state out...

[*Fragment of From Orchestrated Sequences to Nothingface.*]

The next right moment is when Pogolas feels more like drifting off, right after a moment that already feels absolutely right. They have just made love, with a passion that keeps astonishing him. It's supposed to wear off after the initial fire, right? As far as he can tell it hasn't: It even seems to get better, deeper.

Henson—seemingly content in his arms—disturbs his happy trance with a whisper in his ear that was anything but sweet nothings: "Wanna divulge some industrial secrets?"

That catches him with his mental pants down: "To you? Why?"

"Not to me. You're leaving the country next month."

"Yeah, but you said you couldn't come along."

"I will be joining you, but via a completely separate route. Then I'll introduce you to some fellow scientists."

His mind kicks into high gear now: "Need cash? I stashed some just for something unexpected like that."

She kisses him softly on his cheek, and he can feel her sardonic smile. "Nero, you're a superb scientist but sometimes a little naïve in other matters, especially as to the true extent of the Panopticon Singularity."

That remark hurts, Pogolas considers himself a paragon of paranoia. His peeved look urges Henson to elaborate: "RFID tags have been miniaturized and applied much more intensely than everybody is led to believe. For one thing: Why did you think a new series of pound notes was introduced two years ago?"

"Well, the usual: to make them safer against counterfeiters?"

"That indeed, and more: Each note has an RFID tag embedded. All cash movements—didn't you notice how fast the old currency was taken out of circulation?—are tracked."

"Jesus."

In the near term, RFID tags [...] may eventually be embedded in paper currency to inhibit   counterfeiters and enable governments to track the movement of cash. Hitachi in Japan recently announced that it has developed tags minute enough for this application.

[From The Writing of the Wall.]

"But then how?" is all he can mutter.

"We have our ways. We've taken biometric samples of the people in this neighborhood, in combination with their spending patterns, hacked from Tesco's Crucible database. So when we need to buy a certain item, I have our people check to whom this purchase matches best, do the purchase with faked biometrics, make a copy of the RFID tags in the product, burn out the product's RFID tag and attach an exact copy of the tag to something else in order to set a false trail."

"Christ."

"Just so you realize how deep our new England really is encapsulated in this Panoptical web. Also to show how incredibly difficult it is to keep our movement underground, out of sight. We have to be at least one step ahead all of the time. Fortunately, we have outside help. And it does seem to be getting less hard, of late."

"But: burn them out? I thought they were tamper-proof."

"They can't be: They have no power source, so the high-frequency signals that locate and identify them also power them. If you know the frequency on which they operate, you can disable them by sending a short, high-powered EMP burst: This burns out the tag's IC."

"But isn't the disappearance of certain tags a trail in itself?"

"Luckily the technology isn't perfect: The pickup range is limited, and RFIDs are relatively easily blocked. So a certain tag that disappears for a while is not suspicious in itself, and a few do fail—after all, they're mass produced, and some minimally damaged ones do slip by the quality control—so as long as we don't set off a certain pattern we're okay."

"So you'll be joining me in Siberia?"

"In a very roundabout manner, and it's safer if you don't know how."

"You seem to have planned this quite a long way back."

"We have our reasons, and in Siberia we can talk freely. But now, darling, we better start shagging again." Her hands are touching him in all the right spots, wreaking havoc with his concentration.

"Again? All for the good cause?"

"Not only that, Nero: I do enjoy it immensely."

"Tell me about it! I didn't know it could be so good, last so long."

"Hate to disappoint you again, darling, but there's more fueling our mutual attraction."

"You mean that the Panopticon is encouraging our sex life?"

"Not only ours: It saturates every bedroom with pheromones, making everybody do it like there's no tomorrow."

"You've got to be kidding."

"Afraid not. A happy couple is a productive couple and a well-spending one. Break-ups are bad for the economy."

"What the fuck?"

"Indeed, even that is not sacred: Everything for the corporate state ideal."

124

"It can't be that bad."

"It's worse. Now: Let's do it."

"Ehm..."

"Darling, those pheromones only enhance feelings that are already there. Come on."

"Well, if you put it that way..."

II: Mother Russia

This restless man
Has seen too many things
In the wrong kind of light
Watching how the full moon
Turns the day into night

The sleepless girl
Has heard new things
Over the sea, across the sky
Between the buildings of the city
You can hear the people cry

Oh, new winds can carry
Fresh voices across the sea
Oh new winds will carry
Freedom of choice back to me

[*Fragment of The Unassailable Light: Aura Aurora's international Summer hit single.*]

In his window seat, Nero Pogolas has an almost perfect view of Salekhard and its surrounds as the chartered plane approaches the polar city. The mighty River Ob cutting through immense tundra plains, glowing golden brown in the middle of Summer. Salekhard—"Cape Town" to the Nenets—is located on the Ob's east bank, spot on the Arctic Circle, before the river enters the Kara Sea through the Obskaya Guba basin.

The sheer vastness of the landscape is overwhelming and has an intoxicating effect. No monitoring equipment, as far as the eye can see. The idea alone brings him that little bit closer to heaven. Old Soviet political prisoners will disagree as Yamalo-Nenets used to house some of the old regime's numerous gulags. But to Pogolas the near-endless Arctic plains spell freedom: Splendid isolation from the all-seeing eyes of the Panopticon.

Still, he breathes a little sigh of relief as the old Tupolev-154 touches down safely on the airport's single runway. While he loves the absence of hyper-advanced spying equipment, he reckons that a more modern plane won't hurt. Don't forget to take the complimentary eye-covers along, Pogolas thinks, it doesn't get dark at night. Then he gets out with the rest of the solar eclipse group, and as he steps on the tarmac, the tundra seems even more immense under the gargantuan, cloudless sky. Pogolas lingers on the Arctic asphalt, fascinated, but eventually rejoins the group.

After they've picked up their bags, the solar eclipse enthusiasts are transported to the Yamal hotel in a bus that looks like it's been around since the October Revolution. Leaving a cloud of black smoke in their wake, and every pothole emphasizing the non-existence of suspension, they drive into town, but Pogolas hardly notices, loving every minute of it.

Where old, wooden single-story houses dominate the outskirts, the center is more modern, with several eclectic high-rise apartments painted in vivid colors. The road has become smooth, and the town's mixture of old and new seems so peculiar to Pogolas that he decides to take a long walk after checking in at the hotel.

It's like a new frontier opening: Pogolas can't keep the smile from his face as he walks around Salekhard's center. Houses with small minarets, built by Turkish workers brought in by the oil company. Deep blue, pyramidal penthouses on vibrant four-story buildings, housing immigrant Canadians, also working on the Yamal peninsula's immense gas fields. A wooden church with wrought-iron fences still bearing the town's original name: Obdorsk. Quaint lampposts, Communist-era, Zadkinesque statues, and wall paintings of imaginary cities that look almost modern in these schizophrenic surrounds. Shining new dock cranes in rusty shipyards, robust fishing boats alongside anchor handling tugs in the harbor, and old wharfs that are built to last. The River Ob, a good three miles wide near the end of Summer, dwarfs the River Cam, and the fast current of melt water discourages any notion of punting.

Friendly, if somewhat subdued people that, irrespective of Salekhard's isolated location, are already used to foreigners. Mostly Russians, but interspersed with the indigenous Nenets—whose brightly textured, intricate traditional attire is a pleasing eye-catcher—bawdy Canucks in lumberjack shirts, animated Turkish women with headscarves and the occasional wide-eyed tourist like him. But, most of all, the complete lack of intrusive advertisements of any kind. To Pogolas's ad-jaded senses, the sporadic wooden

126

billboard and lone neon-sign are quite charming.

He enters an establishment that resembles a guest house, and has a simple but rich meal of Borsht, reindeer steak with cabbage and potatoes, and a double, local vodka, all heartily recommended to him by a charming waitress through broken English and improvised sign language. The very warm goodbyes indicate that he has probably over tipped, but he couldn't care less. Sated, exhausted and still somehow invigorated he returns to his hotel room.

Fight the wind and weather
With the music of your soul
All firewalls together
Try to keep the world from us all
Chase the facts around the world
I bring you choice—the unassailable light

[Fragment of The Unassailable Light.*]*

Very early next morning he's woken by an insistent knocking on his door. Groggily recalling that *DON'T DISTURB* signs are non-existent here, he somehow manages to get in his underpants before he opens the door. Arms are wrapped around his neck and he's covered with kisses before he realized it's Henson.

"Tara! How did you get here?"

"Arrived with the night train from Moscow. Let's hit the sack."

"But how did you know my room number?"

"Come on, Nero: Euro bills do wonders, here," she says as she undresses. "But right now, I need some sleep."

"Me too. I hardly started."

"My eyes are tired; I couldn't stop staring in the distance. These endless plains..."

"Yeah, they're near-hypnotic. Blooming in more colors and patterns than I thought possible, so far up North."

"The permafrost is thawing, the tundra is changing," Henson says while getting in bed, "but that's another story. I'm tired."

"How about me thawing you out," Pogolas snuggles up and embraces her.

"Not now," Henson, ignoring his advances, "I really am knackered."

"Sorry," Pogolas swallows his frustration, "but I really missed you."

"Me too. I just can't keep my eyes open." As she turns around and falls

127

asleep.

Later, their deep sleep is disturbed by Henson's relentlessly ringing PDA.

"Get up, Nero."

"Not yet. Later."

"Oh no, we have a lunch meeting. Now do you get out, or do I get you out?" she asks as she starts shoving him out of the bed.

"Lunch meeting?" is all he can say as he swiftly swings his feet to the ground just before Henson pushes him over the edge.

"With some people you should meet." she says and jumps out of bed on the other side.

NOVATEK earns environmental recognition.

OAO NOVATEK today announced that the Company was among the winners in the Russian "National Environmental Prize" contest in which it was nominated and received an award for "Contributions to Sustainable Development."

The "National Environmental Prize" is sponsored by the State Duma of the Russian Federation's Environmental Committee and the Vernadsky Fund, a non-governmental environmental organization, and is the only official award in Russia recognizing the social and environmental contributions made by Russian companies.

[...]

NOVATEK plans to continue increasing the effectiveness of its environmental and social policies based on the fundamental principal that the current generation has a responsibility to protect and improve environmental and social conditions for future generations.

[From ITAR-TASS News Agency.]

Some fifteen minutes later Nero Pogolas follows Tara B. Henson into a nondescript restaurant filled with sturdy furniture, yellow-plastered walls and huge, kitschy chandeliers. The place is full, and the gathered, mixed clientèle is talking animatedly at a volume that will make your average Italian second-hand car dealer proud. Somewhere in the back of the bustling café a black-haired man with huge eyebrows waves at Henson to come over. In her wake, Pogolas suddenly recognizes the tall blond woman sitting next to the heavyset man. Before Henson can introduce her, Pogolas smiles and says, "Dr. Sletjana, I presume?"

The Caucasian beauty's face lights up with a smile that's both flattered and flattering, gets up from her seat, puts out her hand and says, "Ivanova, please, Dr. Pogolas. Very honored to meet you."

"The honor is all mine. And please call me Nero."

"As you wish, Nero. This is Sergey Korbyshev, our administrator."

"Nice to meet you, too, Dr. Korbyshev."

"Sergey, please, Nero."

"Sergey. What brings you people here? The solar eclipse, as well?"

"We will certainly watch it. But the reason we are here is you: Nero Pogolas."

"Some of our international friends mediated this meeting, Nero," Henson says, "And it was vital that you didn't know anything about it, as not to give it away."

"Okay," Pogolas says, only slightly miffed, and very curious, "what do you people want?"

"Nero, ever since the UK fell under the Panopticon Singularity's spell, you haven't published a single research paper," Sletjana says.

"But I submitted several," Pogolas blurts out, baffled, "and they were published!"

"The scientific papers you receive, Nero, are all carefully edited and partly faked by the Panopticon," Henson says.

"Faked! And how about my international correspondence?"

"Also partly edited and partly faked. The exchanges of you and your colleagues are finely orchestrated to think you are interacting with the international scientific community, but in reality your most important research results never leave the Panopticon."

Pogolas can only stare at Henson in disbelief.

"I'm afraid it's true," Sletjana says, "the papers published in your name were so obfuscated, and revealed nothing new. Completely different from your clear and insightful pre-Panopticon publications. Anybody with half a brain could see they were fake."

"And you are one of many UK scientists that are handled that way." Korbyshev joins the discussion, "Now with Japan and even the USA showing dangerous signs of going down the same road as the UK, the scientific community is becoming quite distrustful."

129

"Jesus," Pogolas says in desperation, "I thought it was bad, but not that bad. Fusion power should be for everybody, not just the select few."

"Indeed. That's why we ask you to come work for us." Korbyshev says.

"Work for you? But the T-15 tokamak was shut down."

"And ITER in Cadarache is probably a dead end," Korbychev responds.

"A dead end? The whole international scientific community—"

"—is divided and is not sharing all their data. Even we have started to hold back."

"Some people even think that ITER is supported by the big oil companies because it will never work, so that it's not a threat to oil," Henson says.

"You mean to say that all my work was nothing but a giant decoy?" Pogolas asks, exasperated.

Korbychev aims a questioning look at Henson, who answers with a smile and a semi-innocent look. "Not your work, just ITER," he says, "And we are in the process of building a new fusion reactor at the Kurchatov Institute."

"That's impossible," Pogolas says, as he does a quick mental calculation, "the costs are astronomical."

"For a tokamak, but not for a Farnsworth-Hirsch fusor, based on Bussard's research. The costs for a real-scale model with a projected net power output are about 200 million dollars, something our current sponsor is willing to invest."

"Your sponsor? The Russian government? The one that has critical journalists and old spies eliminated, cold-war style?"

"That was in the Putin days: Since Glazyev things are, if slowly, improving. But the government isn't our sponsor: It's Novatek, our biggest private oil company."

"An oil company?"

"An oil company that intends to remain an energy company in the future. One with a real long-term view, and with an excellent environmental record." Henson adds, "And they're already behind: The Panopticon is building one at a secret location."

"The Panopticon also thinks that the Bussard plant might work? We haven't heard anything from him in years."

"He's been silenced after he tried to make all his research and plans public—so that literally everybody with an interest could use them," Korbychev says, "We got hold of them, through an idealistic Usenet group that was shut down soon afterward. And if Tara's info is correct, we're not the only ones."

130

"To quote Bussard," Sletjana says, "'It is the details that make or break the device.' The particular set of details that dominate the performance are exactly in your field, Nero. You are the world's leading expert on these, and possibly the key to a net power fusion device."

All this overwhelms Pogolas and an uneasy silence falls, one that Henson eventually fills: "Think about it, Nero. But you must make your decision quick, because once you return to England, you might find it extremely difficult to leave again."

"But I got here now."

"You're a well-known eclipse enthusiast that books his trips well in advance, and luckily this one happens here," Henson explains.

"This is very difficult. You're asking a lot of me. Let me sleep on it."

"Of course. Sorry to spring it on you like this, but your circumstances leave us no other choice."

"I understand that. Now can we order something? I'm starving."

Flash of light
Still picture
The man I used to be
Some quick-forgetting stranger
How naïve he seems to me

Lack of light
Moving shadow
Moments caught in fright
Make the image seem much darker
Or its surroundings too bright

Oh light waves can carry
Clear sights over the sea
Oh light waves will carry
Freedom of thinking back to me

[Fragment of The Unassailable Light.]

The next day, Pogolas is restive. He's walking along the banks of the River Ob with Henson, and a sky filled with *cirrus uncinus* unsettles his eclipse-focused mind. It's not the only thing clouding his thoughts, though.

"What's eating you?" Henson asks, "You haven't said a word all morning."

"Lots of things. I just wanted to see a solar eclipse, and I wind up having to rethink my whole future."

Henson takes his left hand, squeezes it, and looks him in the eyes: "You are important. You can make a difference."

"It very much seems so," Pogolas says, meeting her gaze, "which makes me wonder how much you really care for me."

"I do. Very much."

"You weren't exactly open to my advances last night, either."

"I wasn't in the mood."

"So what we had in England was only fueled by the Panopticon's bedroom pheromones?"

"No! I do love you, but I don't want to—"

"—give me a reason not to stay here, right?"

"It's not like that! I'm torn up, too. Yes, I want you to stay here and screw bloody Big Brother England. But I also don't want to lose you. My stomach's in knots, and I feel guilty."

"You feel guilty? You seduced me in the first place!"

"It wasn't meant to be like this. Yeah: I met you with a purpose. But along the way, I did fall for you, despite your naivete, despite your social...ineptitude."

"My social ineptitude?"

"Sometimes you're such a nerd. When I'm very agitated and don't make love to you, it doesn't mean I don't love you anymore. Can't you understand?"

Pogolas looks downward. "I—" His voice falters, and he takes a deep breath, "I'm sorry. Sometimes I can be such an idiot." A blush forms on his face. "But I have to make a very difficult decision, and it tears me up inside."

"You're not the only one," she says, and takes him in her arms, nestling her head against his chest, "My mind wants to go back to England and fight the good fight. My heart wants to stay here with you."

"Yeah," Pogolas returns her hug, and kisses her on her forehead, "I guess I'm just a half-assed romantic: I want to change the world, but don't want to change along with it."

Under the glare of a midsummer polar sky, they cry softly, on each other's shoulders, in sync with some imaginary Christ. After a while, they decide to walk their separate ways, trying to make up their minds without a mutual distraction. Even as they agree on dinner tonight, their parting has a definite edge to it. Then they take off, deep in emotional turmoil, united in their hate of the Panopticon Singularity.

That night, in their hotel room, Pogolas and Henson don't talk much. They know which decision the other has made, without the need for asking. At dinner they've evaded the subject, and relaxed. Now, a feeling of finality pervades the air, and they hold each other while they let their tears flow. Then they make love: with compassion, with tenderness, attempting to smother the injustice of a cruel world in a sea of desperate love, knowing they'll fail, but trying nevertheless. Like a silent scream at the heart of the system, throwing light with the heat of passion. Not losing themselves in each other, but finding solace through their cries, finding resolution in their hearts. Hoping their sacrifices will matter. Sowing the seeds of change.

In a way, it's better than the wild, pheromone-enhanced nights they had back in Cambridge. Then they sleep, still tossing and turning at times, but not quite as restless as the two previous nights.

Run away from shadow
The system offers no rest
Hope rising in the east
Broken in the west
Chase the sun around the world
I want to live inside—the unassailable light

[Fragment from The Unassailable Light.*]*

The next day, August 1, is the day of the solar eclipse. Pogolas is supposed to join his group of eclipse enthusiasts for the drive to Nadym, but Henson has other plans.

"Come on, Nero: Let's make this solar eclipse extra special. Get ourselves some transportation and go somewhere in the middle of the tundra. Just the two of us and an incomprehensibly tall shadow."

"You—always different. But how do we get transportation? Haven't seen a car rental place anywhere, here."

"We ask the locals. They love euros."

"Just like that?"

"Of course. Get on with it: Where's your sense of adventure?"

"Overwhelmed. You've got that boisterous energy again."

"Sometimes I feel like I can take on the world, darling. Don't spoil the illusion: Play along."

Half an hour later the two of them are driving an old army jeep, Pogolas wrestling with a wheel that's never heard of power steering, and enjoying every minute of it. With his GPS and the electronic maps of the projected path of the moon's shadow, they have no problems finding a perfect, quiet spot right on the line of maximum totality. The old four-wheel drive can drive off the road just as easily as on (and at times the difference is negligible), and the completely cloudless sky gets Pogolas in a good mood, despite everything.

Thoughts of his life-changing decision are pushed to the back of his mind as he concentrates on the moon-meets-sun event. After a long drive, they come to the perfect spot. He stops the car in the middle of nowhere, waiting for it to become—however brief—the center of everything, at twenty-one minutes past one. But even while he's full of anticipation for the glorious event, the mesmerizing landscape cuts through his reveries.

An incredibly wide horizon enhanced by an eerie silence, amplified by lonely bird calls. A seemingly empty tundra, that, at closer inspection, is blooming in its own, subtle way: A miniature rain forest of moss, lichen, and grass, surprisingly multi-hued, resembling an oriental carpet. Considerably more vegetation, as the spring snow has become spring rain, threatening to thaw the permafrost. The patient and trained eye may distinguish the presence of burrowing rodents. Or one may be lucky.

"Look, Tara, over there. A rat or something."

"Not a rat: a lemming."

"A lemming? One of those that commit massive suicide by diving into the sea?"

"Happens only rarely. When food gets scarce they migrate en-mass and if there's a river in their way, they swim it. In unfortunate cases, this river sometimes is the sea..."

"I get it. Do you think I'm a lemming?"

"What do you mean?"

"My habitat has a scarcity of freedom. I should migrate here."

"Don't get me wrong, but I hope you'll do it."

"Ever since I'm here, this suppressed feeling, this unconscious notion of constantly being watched, has gone. It's such a relief, it's incredible. I'm inspired again, I make notes of new ideas in the middle of the night...that is, until you came."

"So I'm too much of a distraction?" her mischievous smile is back, with the light in her eyes that breaks down all his defenses. He swallows, hard, and opens his heart.

"Tara, I still love you. Will you stay here with me?"

She bites her lower lip, trembles, but holds his gaze. "I would love to, darling. But I can't."

"Away from this deeply diseased England. Away from that corporate state nightmare."

"Very tempting, darling, and for some, it's better to leave, but some must stay and fight. Otherwise, the EU is next, and who knows where it'll stop."

"Does it have to be you?"

"Not me alone, Nero. And we have outside help: We get secret funding from all over the world, other services as well. There are a lot of individuals, groups, and companies that like to test their software against the Panopticon. You'll be another of our outside supporters."

"Of course. But I'm gonna miss you, even more than my dear Cambridge."

"Darling, please realize one thing we both can't help, but do. You've told me several times that the problems regarding nuclear fusion seem almost insurmountable. Yet you can't help but try: It's a challenge, right?"

"You bet it is."

"Same thing with me and the Panopticon Singularity: David and Goliath type of thing."

"Hmm, more like Jonah in the whale."

"Whatever. You get my drift."

"But I'll be developing fusion for the right side, now, I hope. Can't you stay with me and fight the Panopticon from here?"

"I have important things to bring back."

"Fuck them."

"This may sound crazy, but I love my country."

"More than you love me?"

"Nero, please don't make this more difficult than it is. And I have this stupid, crazy dream..."

"Just how stupid and crazy?"

"Of seeing you again in a free England. Even if each of us has found another lover. As friends."

"I don't know: It finally begins to dawn on me that the majority actually like the way their life is regulated for them. Like electrified ants mindlessly working for their queen."

"Somebody has to break the trance, pull the plug."

"Oh well, Davida," Pogolas says, and sighs in resignation, "I'll help you make a better sling."

All firewalls together
Can't keep the world from me
Shadows hide the facts of life
From everyone to see
Shine the light around the wall
I bring you choice—the unassailable light

[*Fragment from* The Unassailable Light.]

The calming environment keeps Pogolas's nerves at bay in the final hour before totality, but as the hour creeps past one, he starts pacing around in agitation. All day, the upcoming solar eclipse was pushed to the back of his mind. But as he and Henson have both finalized their decisions, and slowly but inexorably are coming to terms with it, the rare event takes priority. His old habits take over, as he positions his web cam and programs his laptop to capture every minute of the totality.

Henson, though, has other things on her mind. She moves on to him, takes his arms and says, "Come on, darling, let's do it."

"Do what?" just when Pogolas is thinking of nothing but the solar eclipse.

"You know what," she says, undoing the buttons of his shirt, "shagging, fucking, the deed, making love."

"There is a total solar eclipse coming up!"

"Exactly. Have you ever done it during a solar eclipse?"

"Of course not! Totality only lasts two minutes and 27 seconds."

"Good then, big man: You'll have to be fast."

"Are you crazy?"

"Definitely," she says as she pulls his trousers down.

"I must see the eclipse!"

"We can do it standing up, you mount me from behind and we can both look at it." as her skirt hits the ground.

"I can't..." Pogolas tries to avoid the inevitable.

"Yes you can," she says, looking down, beaming, "look at how excited you are."

"I can't believe this."

"You will: This is going to be one hell of a fuck."

Pogolas enters her the moment Baily's beads announce the advent of totality and the onrushing shadow of the moon bathes the solitary lovers in

136

darkness. Both Pogolas and Henson struggle with all their might not to succumb to total sensory overload, but evolutionary inbred mating instincts, irrepressible curiosity and the deepest sense of wonder carry the crazy couple through the most intense two-and-a-half minutes of their lives. Enveloped by the moon's shadow, crowned by the solar aurora under a starry sky in the middle of the day, they achieve perfect synchronicity and as the second diamond ring announces the end of the totality, of the momentous unity in space and on the ground, Pogolas and Henson collapse in the throes of a mutual orgasm.

Almost blacking out as the sunlight strikes him, Pogolas can only think: How am I ever going to find a woman like her again...

How does one fashion a book of resistance, a book of truth in an empire of falsehood, or a book of rectitude in an empire of vicious lies? How does one do this right in front of the enemy?

Not through the old-fashioned ways of writing while you're in the bathroom, but how does one do that in a truly future technological state? Is it possible for freedom and independence to arise in new ways under new conditions? That is, will new tyrannies abolish these protests? Or will there be new responses by the spirit that we can't anticipate?

[Philip K. Dick in an interview, 1974]

END

JETSE DE VRIES is a technical specialist for a propulsion company by day, and a science fiction reader, editor, and writer by night. He's also an avid bicyclist, total solar eclipse chaser, beer/wine/single malt aficionado, metalhead, and intelligent optimist.

His blog can be found on shineanthology.wordpress.com and his Twitter addy is @shineanthology.

EXTREMUM

R. Thomas Riley and Roy C. Booth

Originally published in *Apexology,* Apex Publications, 2011.

Begin Transmission:

I used to think that drowning was the worst way to die. Now, I'm having second thoughts.

The strangers all around me are looking for answers, some type of rescue...and it's never going to come. I should know. I designed this thing. I set this series of events in motion. There is no rescue. On this tram, I'm the only one privy to this information. If they knew what I know, well, they'd turn on me to buy themselves a little more time. I'm sure of it...hell, it's what I'd do.

Not much longer now. The hallucinations have already started. Thought I saw Idia through the window. I know that's not possible. She's back at the base station, most likely in bed with that miserable fuck Egoid, her research assistant.

Lucky bastard.

What happened? Where did things go wrong? I thought we were happy, well, at least comfortable. I'm a distinguished scientist. I've accomplished a great deal. That's what attracted her to me in the first place. I was going places. I was in charge of the Mars mission. I fully understand that. She was attracted to where I was going, not to who I was, but I think she saw the real me eventually and wanted that part of me as well. We clicked, like two organisms becoming one cell. We were light and dark becoming as one. She became my world, my only.

We came to this distant planet together and here I am dying, alone. Sure, there are others with me and I'm sorry they have to be here, but in all reality, I am dying alone. They're merely collateral damage, and for that I do feel some regret, but you do what you have to do. What you must. I tried to warn them not to take this one-way tram with me, but they didn't listen.

So, it's on them.

I feel the most regret for the little girl. She doesn't deserve this. I tried to warn her mother, but she didn't listen. If she'd known my intentions, then maybe she would've saved herself and her daughter. Then again, maybe I'm doing us all a favor. We're light years from Earth. If my plan comes to full fruition, well, this will be the best way to go. What's coming? Well, it's not going to be pretty. Not in the least. I've left enough C-4 and Technetium hidden deep within the base station to obliterate everything the Collective has worked for.

Heh.

It's going to be one huge crater.

These people knew the risks. They signed the company waivers, willingly accepted the dangers. Seriously, why would this be any different?

Not much longer now. My head is starting to pound. I resist the urge to suck the remaining oxygen deep into my lungs, but my body betrays me. It wants to live. It's an exercise in mind over matter at this stage. I want to die, but the flesh, as they say, alas, is weak. I could stop this, really, but I won't. I wonder if my will fade as death slinks closer and embraces me. No. I planned for this for too long. It will happen. It has to happen.

"Please," the mother gasps. "Do something."

I turn my head, fixing my dying gaze on the woman as the child in her arms gasps for precious oxygen. My will is not swayed, though I know it should be. The child has her whole life in front of her and I am the reason it is going to be snuffed short.

I used to think that drowning was the worst way to die. Now, I'm having second thoughts.

Falling in love again and again, only to have every effort at having your love reciprocated fail miserably, and each time the pain it leaves you with grows until there is nothing left inside of you except a pit, a consuming, wretched thing of despair, that slowly devours you from the inside, while no one knows why you don't smile anymore; having your soul destroyed to where you don't exist at all.

So I'm already dead, in a sense. The rest is mere formality.

I notice the girl looking at me. She's quiet. Her eyes are intense as they bore into my very being.

She knows.

She knows this is no accident.

I start to panic until I realize it's another hallucination. She's far too young to have ever felt the pain I've experienced. Dying alone and without ever knowing true love. Never being proud of her accomplishments. Having everyone around never seeing you. Having no real existence, no real intrinsic purpose.

No voice.

Slowly dying inside is far more painful than any physical pain. You take that with you wherever you go. Forever.

I'm saving her from this feeling.

I know they'll attempt rescue. Common basic procedure. I've planned for this contingency. We are at the outermost of reach.

Extremum.

They won't make it to our location in time. I've planned it that way.

The man farthest from me stands and bangs his fists against the glass. I feel his frustration, I truly do.

"Why aren't they here yet?" he screams.

The mother shouts at him to remain calm; that he's using up the remaining air. I find it ironic that shouting uses up just as much air.

Again they look to me for rescue. After all, I am adorned in full technician's garb. They wonder why I sit here, seemingly at peace, instead of frantically trying to fix this situation. They should recognize the jumpsuit is mere window dressing. I am famous after all. I made this habitation of Mars possible, but they are consumed with their own survival to place my face in their scrambled thoughts.

I break my silence. "They won't get here in time."

The man ceases his assault on the glass, glaring at me. "They have to try!"

"Of course, they'll try," I answer in a low voice. "But we are at extremum..."

In more ways than one, I think, but don't add. Why make it any more difficult for those poor lost souls? Again, the regret slithers up my spine, but I thrust the feeling deeper inside my being.

"Please, mister," the small girl says, tearing up. "Help us."

"There is no help for us, my dear girl," I sigh. "I'm sorry, but it has to be this way."

The last person on this tram, who has yet to speak, stands weakly and starts shambling towards me. I square my shoulders at his approach. There is determination in his gait; he has something on his mind.

The man comes to rest in front of me. "I know you," he wheezes.

"Hardly," I whisper.

"You're Mateusz Stike," he insists.

"I'm afraid you're mistaken."

"No, you're him." He turns to the rest of them. "It's him. It's Stike."

140

They stir at the mention of my name as they realize who...and what I am.

"Oh, God," the mother moans.

She gets it. She finally gets it. She knows.

Extremum.

"You did this," the man shouts. He collapses to his knees, his breath spent. He reaches for me and I shove him aside with my foot. The action takes great effort and my head pounds. Soon, very soon. The end is coming. It's near.

I smile as they realize their fate. My master plan blossoms in all their faces. End game.

"But we're all a part of you," the mother says. "You kill us, you kill yourself."

"Yes," I sigh. "That's the plan. I've lived with all of you in my head for far, far too long. It's time to end this hell."

"We've done nothing but help you survive," the man on the floor pants.

"You've done nothing but complicate my existence." I try not to sound bitter, but I hear a sad tinge of that in my voice nonetheless.

"We've helped you survive," another voice echoes.

"You've helped me survive?" I retort, now with vengeance. "You've fed off me. Caused me to be this way. I wanted none of this. None of it. It has to end. It must end."

"But we're a part of you," the mother cries. "If you do away with us, then you'll cease to exist."

"Then so be it," I counter. "Live alone, die together."

"You were never alone," the little girl says. "We were always there. We helped you survive."

"Merely surviving is not an existence."

"What about us?" the man says. "We want to survive. We are you. You are we."

"This is my choice," I whisper. "I am the master of my fate. And right now I am at extremum."

:End Transmission

R. THOMAS RILEY hails from Minot, North Dakota and is the author of the short story collection *The Monster Within Idea* (2009-2011), which garnered a Best Horror of the Year Honorable Mention for his story

"Too Little".

Other noted recent publications include: *If God Doesn't Show—A Gibson Blount Novel* (co-written with John Grover), published by Permuted Press in August 2012; *The Flesh Of Fallen Angels–A Gibson Blount Novella* (co-written with Roy C. Booth) was published by Grand Mal Press in February 2012; and *Diaphanous* (co-written with Roy C. Booth), available now on Kindle and in paperback.

Of Flesh And Skin: A Darker Erotic Collection (co-written with Lisa McCarthy) was released March 2013. Frosty Moon Omnimedia adapted *The Day Lufberry Won It All* (screenplay by Roy C. Booth and John F. Mollard) to short film in 2010.

ROY C. BOOTH, as one may have guessed by now, does a lot of collaborating and has done so with the likes of Brian Keene, Dr. William F. Wu, Eric M. Heideman, and others, and is very active on the Minnesota (and beyond) speculative fiction convention circuit. Once again, more of Booth's work can be found on his growing Amazon Author Page: www.amazon.com/author/roycbooth.

ATTENTION WHORE

Kerry G.S. Lipp

Originally published in *Sirens Call*, August 2013, #10.

You ever think you feel your phone vibrate in your pocket and pull it out and check it only to see that there's nothing new?

THAT'S ME.

I do that.

I gaze through the screen with static eyes and digital teeth at the idiot operating the device. The device in question this time is a smart phone, and usually is, but sometimes the idiot stares into the screen of his laptop. It doesn't matter either way to me. I live inside both. And I can jump between them faster than light travels. I'm smart enough and the idiot is dumb and predictable enough, that I am always one step ahead and waiting for him with my mouth wide open ready to devour.

I inhabit the cyberspace that the guy on the other side actually thinks is exclusively his own. It's not. I should love him, as much as he feeds me, but I can't help but hate his guts because he's just so goddamn stupid. I wonder what he'd be like born in another time, a time that didn't deliver instant gratification on a second by second basis. How he'd feel if he actually had to wait for important news to arrive in the mail, the newspaper, or those days even older in which important news didn't even exist.

But those days are dead and from those dead days rose a legion of digital demons just like myself. The needy idiot makes it so easy on me and I love the sustenance he provides, but sometimes I wish I could shoot a crackling, holographic hand out the front of the screen and smack him across the face or grab him by the throat and tell him to quit fucking looking at me.

I smile at that idea and think that perhaps in a short time those capabilities will indeed come to me. I am an infant, not even an infant. A zygote really, if you look at the timeline of the world. When you consider all those years in the past. The religious say a couple thousand, the scientists say a couple million, and I say who the fuck knows anyway?

What I do know is that regardless of the age of the Earth or whatever you believe, me and my digital minions have only been around for a few years; the equivalent of a millimeter on the universal timeline.

And idiots like this guy looking through the screen right now are too stupid to actually see us, and keep feeding us without fail. The more they feed us, the hungrier we get and the faster we evolve. Every day our numbers grow. Each newly activated cell phone or laptop or tablet connected to Wi-Fi creates another hungry attention whore.

Though I can't tell for sure, I think it's only a matter of time before we evolve to the point at which we can actually reach through the screens and deliver much needed wake up calls to the dazed and desperate people that constantly stare at us, stare into us, but never truly see us.

Once they figure it out, it'll be too late and we'll step out of our screens and our cyberspace all together, and then it will be time for us to rule the world outside the walls of the cyber universe that barely confines us. And the irony of it all is that they made us, they feed us, and they don't even know we're here. And they remain blissfully and shockingly unaware of what they've done.

Enough philosophy. Let me give you an example and tell you a bit about the idiot I'm currently dealing with. This idiot happens to be a writer. I've read a lot of his stuff in my spare time and while he's not that good, he's not entirely awful either.

This writer also happens to run a Facebook page, a Twitter page, and has the phone numbers of several girls to whom he is attracted. Like I said, he's a fucking idiot. But I love him because he feeds me almost all of his time. Harvesting all his free time like this, will eventually lead to my own immortality. And he gives it away so easily.

Sometimes I feel like an obese glutton, but I don't really gain weight because all I eat is time, which ironically is the only true possession that human beings own, but they are too stupid and far too generous with that single possession. Sure it can be taken from them at any second by any number of means, but what they do until that happens, is really all they've got.

But they don't get it. Not even close. And that's why digital demons like myself constantly devour the time of all the humans out there. That's why we're smarter. That's why we are growing strong. I wish the idiots possessed vision enough to see the damage they're doing to themselves. Don't get me wrong, I want to replace them as the owner of this planet, but this isn't even a war. This is smashing someone with a sledgehammer while they snore in a helpless drunken sleep.

144

The only time that my idiot doesn't feed me is when he's asleep, but I suppose you could argue that sleep, or at least excessive sleep, which I've also noticed humans are apt to binge on, is wasted time as well. But even then, if he is asleep and wakes up in the middle of the night to piss or deal with heartburn, he feeds me a couple more nibbles of his time. He can't help but check everything his user-name is attached to. And I enjoy a midnight snack. But then he falls back asleep and I just wait for him to feed me the split second he wakes up in the morning and he does. Again. Without hesitation. And then, for the rest of his waking hours, he feeds me every five minutes until he again falls into sleep.

Maybe it's worse because he's a writer, maybe not. I don't know for sure but what I do know is that he has about ten short stories, one novella, and one novel manuscript submitted to a smattering of different small presses and lives in a wild pipe dream of expectant hope that he may one day be able to quit his day job.

So he constantly checks his email. In addition to that, he likes to check on his recent publications for new blurbs or reviews. I suppose most of that is forgivable, I think I can understand.

The idiot always gives me nibbles, but what I really have trouble understanding is when the idiot gives me a feast. It's so counter-intuitive and self-destructive that it truly makes me wish I could force him to fight his own needy urges.

When that dumbass sits down to write or read for a free period of several hours, always, fucking ALWAYS, the idiot puts up a Facebook status, a couple fresh tweets, and starts at least one text conversation. Then he puts down his book or stops his fingers from striking the keys every minute or two to do the following: check email, check Facebook, check Twitter, check text messages and then email again. Usually, he goes through the cycle twice before he goes back to the reading or writing. I've calculated. In an hour of his reading or writing time, he's good for less than 20 disjointed minutes that are unfair to the authors he's trying to read and the readers he's trying to dazzle. But that's the way it is.

I don't understand it. He's just crippling himself, his own enjoyment of entertainment and worst of all neutering his own ability to seamlessly create.

And for what? To see if someone favorited his tweet or liked his status? What a fool. It's like he has no concept of how successful, even being average at what he considers his passion, he could be if he just focused. Even if it is only a handful of people, his work is good enough to engage that small group emotionally and his own creativity would have the potential to resonate with others much more than a single, simple status acknowledgment resonates with him.

Though I love and need to devour his time, I pray that one day he gets it and sees some success before us digital demons dominate the world he thinks he knows.

Maybe it's an amateur move and one day he'll get past it and quit feeding me more than those girls with a brand new cell phone as a gift from mom and dad that they are given as they start their freshman year of high school. I hear from my friends, those chicks feed best. At least he's just checking the phone and not taking a bunch of selfies. I suppose that's worth something.

But it's not worth enough. And though I talk a lot of shit, I really do like the idiot and I want to see him succeed. Hopefully I'll be able to figure out a way to give him a digital slap in the face sometime soon, but I'm still working on that one, and I'm not going to lie, I still enjoy sending that phantom vibration through his phone and down his leg and fucking with him just a little bit. I am a demon after all.

Though I get off on controlling and devouring his free time and stealing his attention, I'm not the attention whore. Honestly, I do hope he breaks his cycle and I do wish him well, but not quite enough to leave him alone. And even though I'm a monster and I love sucking the free time from his soul, I hope that he can rise above the bullshit and take control because I believe that's how geniuses finally recognize their talent. Most people, writers, bankers, painters, parents, whoever, don't break through the bullshit to achieve and fulfill their genius potential, but I hope this guy does.

I kind of like him.

And before you judge my idiot for constantly checking to see who's corresponded with him; ask yourself is he really that much different than you? Between digital demons like myself and you humans, just who exactly is the attention whore?

And just out of curiosity, did you make it through my short little story without feeding your own digital demon? Don't lie, because I can ask 'em and find out for sure.

Even if you didn't, I'm sure you will soon. I know you're thinking that since you just focused for a few minutes to read something you've earned your right to check your shit. Go ahead. We're always hungry.

END

KERRY G.S. LIPP teaches English at a community college by evening and writes horrible things by night. He hates the sun. His parents started reading his stories and now he's out of the will. Lipp's work appears in several anthologies including *DOA2* from Blood Bound Books and *Attack of the B-Movie Monsters* from Grinning Skull Press. His stories have been adapted for audio several times via *The Wicked Library* podcast. Kerry blogs at www.HorrorTree.com when he's got something to say and will launch his own website www.newworldhorror.com sometime before he dies. He is currently editing his first novel.

UNHOLY GRAIL

Frank Roger

The crocodile leaped out of the shadows and closed its jaws around the head of the young woman as she walked in. She paid no attention, walked straight through the creature, unperturbed.

"Come visit WaterWhirl," a booming voice said. "Ride the dolphins, swim with the sharks, and feed the crocodiles. Enjoy a full day of wet thrills and spine-tingling rides for merely seventy-five bucks." By the time the holographic crocodile had winked out of existence and retreated to its virtual lair, the woman had already taken a seat at an empty table.

"Some lady," Roy's boss mumbled approvingly, as they were waiting in the kitchen to serve orders.

"I'm all with you," Roy replied. "Can I attend to this customer, Kelvin?" His boss nodded.

Roy noticed how the woman punched her order onto the keypad, kept her eyes wide open so the scanner could check her retina and debit her account, and leaned back. A few other customers came in, and the crocodile reappeared and repeated its message. The woman took her webphone to kill the few minutes it would take for the automated kitchen to prepare her order. She ignored the other holo commercial in the middle of the restaurant, an aircraft taking off, the roar of its engines segueing into a sales pitch for Apple Airlines' high-quality service and low rates.

When the kitchen produced her order, Roy took the steaming dish and hurried to the woman's table, smiling radiantly and bristling with energy and positive feelings, the very reason why human beings were still employed here to do work that could as well be done by machines. Flesh and blood waiters just added so much warmth and a human touch, making all the difference, as Kelvin kept saying. And driven by uppers and emoboosters, they could last an entire shift without missing a smile.

As he put the dish on the woman's table, the scanner's audio system said to her, "Thanks for joining the Lunch Mob, and enjoy your meal."

For an instant, her eyes locked with his, and Roy felt as if lightning had struck. This woman was special indeed. Was his reaction to her revved up

148

by the emoboosters, or was this a case of love at first sight? As she attacked her meal, he took in every detail of her appearance, her hair, changing style and shifting hues in quick cycles, her nano body-art, tattoos that seemed alive and sparkled with iridescent effects as they slowly crawled across her skin, the phosphorescent nipple ornaments shining through the cut-outs in her dress. As he tore away his gaze from her with great difficulty, and turned around to go back to the kitchen, another bunch of customers entered the Lunch Mob.

Then everything happened very quickly. The very moment the crocodile and aircraft holograms sprang into existence again, the customers who had arrived just after the woman shouted something, jumped and rushed into his direction, and the new arrivals also dashed past. Someone bumped into him and he went down, unable to see what was going on as the holo-commercial was enveloping him completely. He could feel someone tripping over him, hands groping all over his body as people undoubtedly tried to regain their balance or grab hold of something, and he rolled sideways. As he scrambled back to his feet, the hologram disappeared and he looked around. All the customers were gone, including the gorgeous woman.

"What the hell was that?" he screamed.

"I don't know," Kelvin called from the back. "It went too fast for the eye to follow. And that holo kept most of it out of sight."

"We'll have to watch the tape from the surveillance camera and call the cops," Roy said. "And bring back that girl."

"I guess the holo will be a problem on the video footage too," Kelvin said. "Forget the girl. She may not have eaten much, but at least she paid for it. All the other guys didn't spend anything. This sure was no ordinary brawl. Hey, Roy, take another emobooster, it'll help you get your act together. In a second, there may be other customers to attend to. Don't worry, I'll report this. Are you all right?"

"I'm not hurt, but I lost something," Roy complained.

"What's that?"

"The girl."

"Take several emoboosters, and an upper. There's work to do."

"I was only joking," Roy lied, and strode back to the kitchen to down some more pills. They helped indeed, and after a while his energy and his good mood were back to their normal levels. Nothing unusual happened for the rest of his shift, and he was glad he could go home. Still, he couldn't get the image of that girl out of his mind.

The next morning Roy woke up and cast a glance through the only window of his apartment. The sky was an ominous blue, the same color that filled your screen as your computer crashed. He doubted this would prove to be an uneventful day.

He had the late shift today, so this morning he could take it easy. He went into his kitchen, typed the code for his favorite Italian brunch on the keyboard and waited. As his cell phone beeped, he picked it up and punched the virus scanner button. He no longer took any calls unless they were scanned. A few days ago there had been this story about entire cell phone systems being shut down by roaming viruses. Sure, there were some who claimed the story had been spread by companies producing phone virus scanner software in an effort to boost their sales, but he preferred to take no chances. Maybe it would just be another commercial, one of the new generation that could bypass advertising filters. He had received a few, prompting him to attend religious services that would "greatly enhance the quality of his life".

He typed an instruction on his kitchen keypad to hold the order as the call came through. Dammit, he thought as he noticed there was no visual. This couldn't be good news.

"Who is this?" he asked. "Show yourself, or I'll hang up."

"Wait," a woman's voice said. "Don't hang up. I need to talk to you. It's important. We don't really know each other, but you saw me yesterday in the airport restaurant where you work."

This can't be true, he thought. Could this be the gorgeous woman? How had she found out who he was, and what his phone number was? Was this a dream? Was he still asleep in his bed, making up a sexual fantasy?

"I don't believe you," he said. "Show yourself, or I'll hang up."

The tiny screen flickered to life for an instant, long enough to see this was the pretty woman indeed. She looked even better than yesterday. If this was a dream, he hoped he wouldn't wake up for a while yet.

"Yes, all right," he said. "I saw you at the Lunch Mob indeed. How did you find me? And why did you turn off the visual so quickly?"

"There's no time for that now," she said. "They may be tapping this line, and the smaller the signal, the better. We have to arrange a meeting. It's important and urgent."

"Who are 'they'?" he asked. "And what's this all about?"

"I can't explain that over the phone. Let's say we meet at the Orville Wright Mall at the airport, in fifteen minutes. And listen: other people may try to get in touch with you. Stay away from them, or if they show up at your place or where you work, don't answer their questions. Pretend you took so many uppers and emoboosters that you can't think straight anymore, and flash them

150

your warmest smiles. One more question: you don't wear recyc jeans, do you?"

"I tend to stick to recyc T-shirts, basically. Why?"

"Wear the one you wore yesterday. See you in a minute." The line was dead. He hesitated for a moment. This didn't look too good, but he couldn't resist the idea of getting to meet this gorgeous chick again. So he canceled his brunch order and prepared to leave. He switched on his holo burglar system that hid everything valuable under holographic cheap-looking rubbish. You never knew if some guy would manage to get one of those mobile webcams inside, hoping to locate some interesting loot. It was better to make your place look miserable at first glance.

He left his apartment and walked past a shirt-stall on his way to the nearest CityNaut terminal. A shirt featuring a flashy 3-D commercial for an upcoming blockbuster movie caught his attention, but its price was prohibitive. Instead, he bought a cheap recyc T-shirt with regular advertising that would only last a day, but so what, that was what most people usually wore. He had his retina scanned for the payment, threw his old shirt in a recycling bin, and then remembered he was supposed to wear the same pants as yesterday. He hadn't, but decided against going back to change. What did it matter anyway whether he was wearing recyclable clothes or not? He would be lucky if he ended up one day with that chick without any pants!

He boarded the CityNaut shuttle, stated his destination to the scanner and presented his eye. "Thank you for riding CityNaut," the system's voice said as it scanned his retina to arrange the payment. After the short ride to the airport, he walked straight to the Orville Wright Airport Mall. He hoped he would bump into the woman right away, but he didn't see her. At the entrance of the Mall, already swarming with people, he hung around a newsbooth for a while, watched the holographic display of newsflashes, interspersed with holo commercials. It wasn't always easy to distinguish the two, but he assumed the bits about the incident at the Toronto airport, the earthquake in Pakistan and the statistics showing a marked increase in church goers were news items.

He walked on, bought a new supply of uppers, emoboosters and downers at a health store, and moved sideways to avoid going right through a holo commercial for Hyatt's Worldwide Airport Hotels. He felt so terribly excited about his appointment that he groped in his pocket for a downer, as he heard a voice suddenly say behind him:

"I'm right here. Follow me to the games and movie store over at our left. And act casual. We can talk while we rummage through the bargains."

It was her all right. She was breathtakingly beautiful, wore an expensive shirt that hid the cool tattoos, but offered a perfect view of the nipple

151

ornaments. He followed her, unable to say a single word.

He understood why she had chosen this shop to talk: the place was an inferno of holo commercials for recently released games and movies, and the chance of being seen or overheard here was negligible. As a matter of fact, they would have trouble hearing each other.

"I'll keep it short," she said. "You were involved in this matter by accident. You needn't know all the details. Something was slipped into your pocket that was supposed to fall into my hands. I suggest you give it to me now, and then you forget all this ever happened."

He recalled the brawl he had been pulled into. So he had been at the wrong place at the wrong time, as one person had wanted to hand some stuff to another, with a third party spoiling the fun, and his pocket being the only available place to hide the material. That made some sense.

"I had a problem with those pants," he lied. "I'm not wearing them right now. Just tell me what you need."

She shot him a white-hot glance that sent shivers down his spine. "I'm afraid I can't tell you much. Your involvement in this affair is too deep as it is."

"In that case we have nothing to discuss anymore," he said, turning around. Her hand on his shoulder also sent shivers down his spine, but these shivers were of a different nature.

"Don't go."

"Tell me everything."

"You would regret that. If you lived long enough to reach that point."

"You're just making me more curious."

"Listen, the stuff that was slipped into your pocket yesterday is illegal and priceless. It shouldn't fall in the wrong hands. At least two or three people know it's in your possession now, so others with good intelligence services are bound to find out sooner or later. And they'll come and get it. And guess what they'll do to you if they think you just might know too much. I need that stuff back, man. And you don't want that stuff around at your place. Give it to me. Go back to your place, put those pants on, meet me somewhere in your area, and I'll recover the stuff. Believe me, that's in everyone's best interest, especially yours."

He thought for a few moments, then said, "Well, all right. I'll go back to my place. Won't you come along?"

She shook her head. "I really shouldn't be seen where you live. It's better if I retrieve the stuff in a neutral, no risk environment."

"You mean my place isn't safe?"

"Not with what's stashed in your pants right now. Go back. Now.

Don't lose any more time. Isn't there a pizzeria near your place? We'll go there."

"Okay. Will you buy me lunch? I had to skip my brunch because of this."

"If you don't hurry you'll have to skip a lot more. Go now, go."

He nodded, turned around and left the store. He threw a glance over his shoulder, hoping to catch a final glimpse of the woman, but she had already vanished. This sure wasn't shaping up to be the grand sensual adventure he had imagined. So this was not a dream at all.

He took the short CityNaut ride back and returned straight away to his apartment. To his dismay he noticed a mobile webcam was active in his bedroom, undoubtedly transmitting images to some guys who were after the same thing as that woman. No wonder she preferred not to be seen here. This had to be serious business indeed. He crushed the webcam under his heel, grabbed the pants he had worn yesterday and searched its pockets. His fingers touched a small object, which proved to be a sort of tiny phial. It clung to the fabric of his pants and was so minuscule and light that he hadn't even noticed its presence until now. He slid it into his pocket and threw the pants back on the bed. He figured unwanted visitors were on their way, and, if they didn't find the pants, they might decide to chase him down. If, however, they found the pants but without its treasure, they might assume it was lost, had fallen out, and as the owner had carelessly left the pants on the bed, it was clear he had no idea what he had been involved in and would be left alone. Or so at least he hoped.

He left his apartment in a hurry and rushed to the Pizza Palazzo. As the woman hadn't arrived yet, he took a seat, typed his order on a keypad and offered his eye to the payment scanner. As he waited for his pizza, he saw the woman appear across the street. As she headed for the pizzeria, a few men caught up with her and stopped her, and a discussion seemed to ensue. The heavy traffic on the street prevented him from seeing what exactly was happening, but it was clear things were not going according to plan. The woman did not show up at the pizzeria, and when he had an unobstructed view of the street for a moment, he saw no trace of her anymore. Had she been intercepted by her enemies? Had she preferred not to lead those people to the guy who had the prized treasure in his pocket? Would she get in touch with him later to arrange another appointment? Would he ever see the woman again? Would her pretty face keep haunting him forever?

A programmed Italian-accented voice said, "Thank you for choosing the Pizza Palazzo," and as he turned around, he saw Luigi, all smiles, with his

Mexican pizza. "Good to see you," he said. "Are you okay?"

"I'm fine, thanks. By the way, can I ask you something? Do you know what this is?" He produced the tiny phial and handed it to Luigi. He knew this guy and his reputation for all sorts of pills and stimulants. If Luigi didn't know what these were, nobody would. "There's a story behind it," he added. "I got these by accident and various people are after me to get them back."

"I'm not sure," Luigi said, studying the phial intensely without losing his smile. "I suppose the stuff in here is not quite legal, and consequently pretty expensive and well worth your time and interest."

"Any suggestions?"

"The best way out of your problem is to swallow what's in here. Then nobody can take it away from you anymore, you can't be arrested for having it, you're out of this game you were dragged into and you have a free ride of whatever new fancy stuff this is. Good luck, Roy. Let me know how the trip turned out."

"What if this stuff is dangerous, or lethal?"

"They don't exactly use these miniature containers for rat poison, if you catch my drift. I've seen them before, and if some guys are desperate to retrieve them, they just have to be some fancy new designer drug, just slightly illegal. I'd take my chance, if I were you. Get yourself a trip, man. Open the thing, press until it signals there's nothing left, and get rid of the phial. Good luck."

Luigi left to attend to some other customers, and Roy wolfed down his pizza. Then he went to the men's room and closed his eyes as he urinated. He just hated that holographic gnome that popped into existence at his feet, saying, "Stop feeling pissed off! Try our new line of MoodUpswings, and feel ecstatic every moment of your day!" The holo creature disappeared as soon as his urine stopped coming, and Roy felt relieved in more than one way. Much as he loathed this particular holo commercial, he felt tempted to give these new powerful emoboosters a try one of these days. But for now he had other plans.

It took him a while to open the phial. After a few frustrating attempts he finally managed to open it, shoved it into his mouth and pressed until he heard a beep. He hadn't felt anything go down his throat, but maybe this was miniaturized stuff. As long as the effects weren't minimal, he wouldn't mind. He flushed the phial down the toilet and headed for the exit, walking straight through a Fun Coke commercial spraying him with holographic foam.

He went back to his apartment, expecting to find traces of visitors. He was almost convinced they hadn't bothered to drop by after all, until he noticed the pants in his bedroom weren't exactly where he had left them. Now he could only hope these people would assume he didn't have what they wanted and forget about him.

Time went by. The woman didn't call him, and the stuff he had swallowed failed to produce any effects so far. Maybe a delayed effect had been built in? Or maybe Luigi had been wrong? But then again, there were no harmful side effects either. He would just have to wait and see.

When the time came to do his shift at the Lunch Mob, he took the CityNaut ride to the Airport and went to work. Would the woman perhaps drop by over there, preferring not to use her phone anymore? Or would the other guys wait for him there, hoping to catch both him and the woman? He walked in, ignored the WaterWhirl crocodile jumping at him, and greeted his boss.

"Hey, Roy," Kelvin said. "A few guys were here this morning. They wanted to talk to you. And I've had a few cops here too. Yesterday someone paid by having a cloned retina scanned. That's illegal. It also means we didn't get that payment. Remember that situation we had here yesterday? Don't tell me you're involved."

"I'm not, Kelvin," he lied. "If those guys come back, tell them I just work here. I won't have anything to do with this nonsense."

"I hope you're not involved; otherwise you won't be working here anymore."

"Believe me, Kelvin, I'm clean."

To his relief the rest of the day proved uneventful. There was one thing, though: for reasons that evaded him, he forgot to take any emoboosters or uppers, and didn't even feel the need for any. And towards the end of his shift, there was a text message on his phone. It invited him to drop by at eight PM at the Switchbleed, a bar on the top level of the Airport building. It added he should bring a suitcase, containing a certain item of clothing, look like a passenger having a drink before checking in, and swap suitcases with the person sending the message. The text was not signed with a name, but with a tattoo, one he had seen crawling around on that gorgeous woman's skin, which identified her unmistakably. He didn't relish the thought of getting ever more embroiled in this unwholesome business, but the idea of meeting that woman again was irresistible. Who knew what this might lead to? But would he ever find out what her name was, who she worked for, what all this frantic activity was all about? And, more importantly, would he get her where he really wanted her?

Roy had arrived a bit early at the Switchbleed, had ordered a drink and

155

now admired the view the bar offered of aircraft coming in and taking off as he waited for the woman to join him.

As a gigantic aircraft took to the air, he saw the woman enter the Switchbleed and head for his table. He shot her a smile, a natural one, not driven by emoboosters, and behind her he could see the aircraft take height. It had barely been airborne for a few seconds or something seemed to go wrong. Flames erupted from one of its engines, black smoke billowed up from the aft section of the fuselage, and the plane tilted at an impossible angle. A flash of blinding white light could be seen behind every window, and then flames sprang up all over the aircraft until it finally exploded into a dazzling orange fireball. Roy sipped from his drink and stared at the burning fragments plummeting down, converging toward the same point and eventually forming a string of fiery words advertising *Inferno in the Skies*, an upcoming disaster movie.

The woman put her suitcase down, took a seat opposite him, and said, "Hi. Nice view, right?"

"The day a plane really crashes here," he chuckled, "no one will pay attention and people will think it's advertising taken one step further."

"Well, it would fit the general atmosphere," she replied.

"Let me buy you a drink," he offered. She typed something on the keypad, and he turned his eye to the scanner. At least my retina is a real one, he added in thought. He also noted she still had the dazzling hairdo that was locked in cycles of color and style changes, as well as the artful tattoos. Sadly, the nipple ornaments were covered this time.

She cast a glance under the table and said: "You didn't bring a suitcase. I told you we were supposed to look like passengers, and swap cases as we leave. Will you make this simple transfer go wrong once more? Why are you making this so difficult? Why?"

"There's no need for all that," he said. "Can I ask you a few questions instead? What's your name? Who are you working for, what is all this about? And why was I drawn into this?"

"Believe me, the less you know about all this, the better. You don't want to be involved in this game."

"Now, what if I tell you I swallowed what was in that tiny phial someone slipped into my pants."

She shot him a piercing stare, was silent for a few moments. She barely noticed the waiter who brought her drink. Then she shook her head and said:

"You idiot. You have no idea what you've worked yourself into."

"Then tell me. Are we talking about some fancy new drug here? I must

156

say it has no effect on me. And what makes it so important some people are going to such lengths to get their hands on it? A few guys even broke into my apartment. By the way, why didn't you do that, instead of calling me? You could have simply picked up that stuff instead of arranging appointments that basically led nowhere."

"That was considered too dangerous. I might have been intercepted at your place, or arrested, or worse. You see, we're not talking about drugs here. What you swallowed were antidotes."

"Antidotes? Antidotes against what?"

"That's a long story, and we can't stay here too long. The moment they find out we're here, we'll be history."

"Who are 'they'? And who are you, for that matter?"

She chuckled, said he needn't know her name, took her glass and sipped from it. While there was a short silence, a wisp of smoke seemed to emanate from the middle of the table and unfolded quickly into a scantily clad woman with tantalizingly well-shaped curves, like a speeded-up video image of a seed blossoming into a flower.

"Would you be interested in our services?" the holo ad's audio system asked with its soft female voice.

"We're talking," he replied curtly, and the holographic hooker pouted at this rude refusal of the services of her flesh and blood counterparts and dissipated like a smoke-ring in a draft.

"You've just joined what seems to be a losing battle," the woman said. "And we're the ones that happen to be on the losing side. Follow me. We'll walk around the airport. Try to act natural. We shouldn't stand out, let's pretend we're passengers doing some shopping before we check in." She finished her drink, grabbed her suitcase and rose to her feet. He followed her, hoping he would finally find out who she was and what kind of game he had thrown in his lot with.

Soon they were part of the crowd milling through the shops and buying stuff compulsively. As they walked past a holographic vista of an exotic sun-splashed place, peopled with smiling men and women, and a voice said, "Happiness and unspoiled nature are awaiting you at our many destinations. Why don't you book your Time Warner Airlines flight now?", the woman turned around and asked:

"Why aren't you buying anything? Pills, emoboosters, all the other stuff you were buying all the time? Like everyone else here? Well?"

"I just don't seem to feel the need to buy that stuff now," he answered.

"And you know why? Perhaps because you've taken those antidotes?"

"All right. Tell me the complete story."

"Well, why not, as you're with us now, whether you want it or not. I'm sure you know most of what we eat and drink and the tons of pills we swallow so happily have stuff in it rendering it addictive and increasing our receptivity to advertising? You know most of the food and drinks these days are "sponsored" by big corporations that are controlling the market and intent on keeping consumers in an economic stranglehold?"

"Yes, but there's nothing illegal about that. They add the elements to our food and drinks that keep us going, that keep the economy and the world as we know it going. That's the way things evolved. We get quality stuff, and there's plenty of it, so why would we bother about those conspiracy theories?"

"It's not illegal because these big corporations are the ones wielding power. They're controlling the authorities as well. As a matter of fact, they're controlling everything, and they're still out to extend their control. We're fighting a holy war against this mad consumerism smothering our freedom."

"Oh, please, don't give me that kind of revolutionary crap. So you're fighting the establishment. And your so-called antidotes are illegal?"

"Of course they are. They're evil stuff cooked up by some rebel movement out to destabilize society and shake its consumerist foundations, according to the official view. And they're hot on or heels, both the authorities and the corporations' lobbyists, in a no-holds-barred kind of way. Especially because they're moving into the next big phase. They don't want us spoiling the fun."

"What's the next big phase?"

"Big religious organizations have understood the benefits of food and drink sponsorship, decided to buy their way into the system and added stuff that increases receptivity for religious messages too. They're definitely winning. We're clutching at straws, we may be fighting the last battle in a war we'll lose. Have you seen any empty churches recently? Mark my words, consumers are growing more devout with every mouthful of junk or swig of liquid shit."

"I think I'm getting the picture. Let me guess. You were at the Lunch Mob to meet someone who would hand you some of these antidotes, but your opponents got the air of the deal and intervened. Your contact only saw one option, slid the goodies into the pocket of an innocent bystander, hoping to retrieve them soon, and all the parties left empty-handed, wondering where the goodies were."

"Fair. And the goodies are now inside you, making you a formidable ally for Unholy Grail, and a hot target for the other side, as soon as they find out what's cooking in your bloodstream."

"Unholy Grail. The name has a nice ring to it."

"Never mention the name to anyone. The wrong ears might be listening."

"So what do we do now?"

"I'll have to talk about that with my friends. I'll get back in touch with you. In the meantime, don't give yourself away. Act naturally, buy some stuff even if you don't feel the need, tell your boss you're taking emoboosters even if you don't want to ever touch that stuff again. Make sure no one finds out about your altered condition. And enjoy it to the fullest."

"What exactly is this stuff doing inside me?"

"The antidotes are countering all effects caused by any active elements that enter your system and their programming identifies as intruders. No more impulsive buying. No frantic energy, artificial smiles and unnatural moods. No urgent need to go to church. You'll feel liberated. As everyone should be entitled to feel. The antidotes are nano-agents, self-repairing and reproducing in your bloodstream. You can't remove them, and they have no known side effects. You'll be fine, as long as you manage to stay alive. That's all you need to know."

"One more question," he said as they walked by a holo commercial of Nokia's new cell phone virus scanner. He looked all around him, but the woman was gone. She had disappeared into the throng of shoppers filling the place. He was alone. Well, not quite. He had joined Unholy Grail and had gained a number of merciless enemies out to get his blood. Quite literally.

"Don't let them get you," the holo ad's voice system said, accompanying a gigantic cell phone that was attacked by a monstrous creature, opening its mouth and sinking its teeth into the phone. "Protect your right to call and be called, get Gobble-X as quick as you can." While the voice spoke, the creature started gobbling up the phone, but at one point the holo image stopped, shimmered and flickered until it winked out. Was this holo ad malfunctioning? Had it been hacked, damaged by a virus? Now that would be a strange coincidence. Unless this was an intentional effect, a joke of the advertiser. But did it matter? Didn't he have more important problems on his mind than silly commercials? To hell with the damned nuisance!

Strange, he thought, that I'm starting to experience the countless commercials popping up around me as bothersome and irritating. The woman had been right. The antidotes in his blood were doing a fine job. But still he wondered what would happen now. How would he fit into Unholy Grail's plans? How would this Holy War end? And would he have any say in that?

He shook his head, turned around, walked straight through the

Gobble-X ad that popped up again, and headed for the exit. For now, he would go home. And all he could do was wait until that gorgeous woman got back in touch with him. If only he wouldn't have to wait too long. And if only he would be able to realize his own private ambition with her. The Holy War wasn't all that high on his list.

There was one effect the antidotes failed to cancel, as he discovered the next few days. He kept seeing that girl's pretty face before his mind's eye, any moment of the day, wherever he was. She haunted him, made him long to be reunited with her, made him daydream about the ambition he hoped to realize one day with her–basically positive, stimulating feelings he did not exactly regret.

What he did regret was that she failed to get in touch with him. The first day, he just thought she was discussing the problem with her revolutionary friends, but the days went by and there was no call from her, nor any other sign. Each time his cell phone rang he thought it was her; each time he was disappointed to discover it was another commercial for religious services or for nano-art body ornaments.

He kept a low profile, as she had suggested, acted as he always had, bought stuff he didn't really need so no one would harbor any suspicions about his unnatural thrift. The third day after their meeting, he could take it no more and decided to do some research. After his shift at the Lunch Mob, he went to an Internet café (preferring not to use his own computer, which might be monitored), and tried to find any information about rebel movements or underground resistance fighters. He even entered the word "Grail" into the search engine, but all he got was sites referring to history and movies. Hadn't the woman (would he ever find out her name?) said they were on the losing side? Maybe by now Unholy Grail was very much history indeed! Maybe the incident at the Lunch Mob, that had turned him into a player in the field, had been the final skirmish of the war.

The next day he dropped by at the Pizza Palazzo, and asked Luigi a few questions, carefully phrased so he wouldn't give away too much. All he learned was that a shady organization specializing in payment fraud using cloned retinas had been dismantled. Could there be a link with Unholy Grail? Or were the Grail activists merely using those cloned retinas so they couldn't be traced by their payment patterns? Maybe there was no direct connection between the two groups.

He hung around news booths as much as he could, hoping to pick up some news items that might offer clues, but there was nothing at all. The fact that the tidbits of information were embedded in thick layers of commercials was perhaps an indication that Unholy Grail had met with abject failure. And the fact that the commercials irritated him beyond reason reminded him that the antidotes were still inside his blood, and that Unholy Grail was still active, even if it might now be limited to a one man's army. For by now he felt privileged to be with them—he had grown to experience the antidotes as a cleaning, he felt liberated and relieved, as if a smothering embrace had been broken. But maybe the liberation had come too late.

As the days went by, he grew convinced he would never hear from the woman again, or from any other Unholy Grail representative for that matter. The guys from the "other side" hadn't tried to get in touch with him either, the ones who had broken into his apartment, had interfered with the woman's actions, had paid his boss a visit when he wasn't there. Perhaps they thought the enemy had been defeated, and were not aware of the full nature of his involvement. Did this mean he could consider his situation safe? He hadn't heard from the cops either. Was this another good sign? He decided it was, until proof to the contrary.

He didn't know whether the antidotes were a blessing or a curse— would he have to hide his "immunity" for the special substances in his food and drinks for the rest of his life? Would he have to be wary of the authorities for the rest of his days, would he be arrested and brought to trial if they discovered his secret one day? Would he end up a social outcast, a raving psychotic, a mental wreck?

On the sixth day, his weekly day off, several things happened that made it a special day in the full sense of the word. As he hung around news booths, he repeatedly caught images of a wrecked train, with a voice talking about this being the biggest catastrophe to hit the CityNaut network in many years, with a lot of victims and seriously injured people, huge material damage and an interruption of the regular CityNaut services in that area for at least a few days. Most people didn't seem impressed much. They probably thought this was another commercial on heavy rotation, but after a while it dawned on them this was a news item and a terrible accident had indeed happened.

Roy had been quicker to grasp the gravity of the situation, as he had been following newscasts with more interest than most people, and with a mind freed of the influence of uppers, emotional stimulants or other such products used to generate a revved-up, smile-driven mental stance. Lucidity, however, was not necessarily a typical effect of these products.

Later that day, as he was watching another holo newscast in a mall close to his apartment, his heart missed a few beats as he saw the woman that had been on his mind for days now. Was she looking for him? Had she been unable to get in touch with him by phone and was she on her way to visit him? He immediately went after her, and noticed a few things that didn't seem right.

She was different. For instance, she had a normal hairdo, one that wasn't in constant evolution. And she wore a cheap recyc T-shirt, sporting a garish Microsoft Moviedrome ad, a far cry from the fancy dress she had worn on previous occasions. Sadly, this cheap stuff covered the nipple ornaments, supposing those were still present at all.

He tried to call her name, and discovered how extremely frustrating it was that he still hadn't found out what her name was. So all he could do was run after her and try to catch her attention. When he was finally close to her, he grabbed her arm, forced her to stop and look at him, and said, "Hi, do you remember me?"

"Hi," she said. "Do I know you? Sorry, pal, but I'm in a hurry." She shot him a smile, the kind of empty smile only emoboosters could produce, and turned around, ready to continue on her way.

"Wait," he said, "please wait. We need to talk."

She shot him a blank stare, although the smile didn't disappear. "I don't think I know you. Maybe you mistake me for another person. But never mind all that, why don't you come along?"

"Where are you going to?"

"To church. Follow me."

That's it, he thought. She doesn't remember me, she no longer sports all her fancy stuff and she's going to church. Either she's desperately hiding the fact that she's an Unholy Grail activist, or the authorities saw through her disguise, caught her and "cured" her of all undesirable traits, setting her free again afterward in a world she was perfectly adapted to. But if her current appearance and attitude were only a cunning strategy to mislead the enemy, why did she pretend not to know him anymore? Was she implying it was too dangerous to re-establish contact? Had the war they fought against the consumerist utopia reached a decisive phase? And why was she going to church, when it was her goal to undermine the church's grand ambitions? Maybe she was simply luring him along, maybe all would become clear if he followed her and didn't ask any questions?

He decided to follow her, and no further word was exchanged as they wound their way to the church near the city's main CityNaut terminal. A service was apparently already underway, and the woman quietly took one of the few remaining empty seats. Roy followed her example after a moment's hesitation, choosing a seat from where he could observe the woman.

162

He had no idea religious services drew crowds this big. Was this due to the effect the woman had described to him, or were there other factors involved in this evolution? Frankly, he had never given the matter much thought, but the fact that this very same woman was sitting there, a few rows in front of him, seemed to indicate the true nature of things.

He barely paid attention to the ceremony that was presented to the crowd, although the tastefully choreographed holographic projections highlighting the sermon were very well done indeed. His thoughts kept going back to the woman, the role she was playing and the role he was supposed to play in the future. Would he ever find out, or was he on his own now? Had she invited him to follow her to church for no other reason than that was the normal thing to do, or was there a hidden agenda somewhere?

At one point the woman turned her head, vaguely looked in his direction, then shifted her attention back to the sermon. Was this a signal? Was this her way to tell him this was a crucial moment, was he supposed to catch a clue now? He looked around him, listened to what was being said: a plea for empathy, for compassion with those who were in need, for solidarity and sacrifice in favor of those stricken by fate. A reference was made to the CityNaut tragedy that had happened, a call was made to donate money for the victims, to give blood and convince others to go to blood drives. The sermon changed topics, and Roy got lost in his thoughts.

The CityNaut accident, money for charities, blood drives. Was there a clue here? Or had she simply looked around for no special reason? Maybe he was reading too much into all this, maybe she didn't even know where he had taken a seat, as he had entered the church after her, maybe he was looking for signals and clues where none were intended.

Wait a minute. Blood drives? Of course, big supplies of blood were required to help the huge number of victims. Let's just suppose, Roy thought, that this woman was indeed "cured" of her revolutionary ideas and the whole Unholy Grail movement had been wiped out, but that there was still a final vestige of those ideas smoldering within her mind, just enough to drag him along to a place where his attention would be drawn to the benefits of blood drives.

Especially if this was about his blood, possibly the only place left where some undetected antidotes were still alive and kicking. And by giving blood, these antidotes would be transferred to other people, maybe a fair number of people, who would become new supporters, even if unwittingly, of Unholy Grail's fight. If he went to enough blood drives, and the new recruits did likewise, his efforts might make a difference. The woman had told him

163

these nano-agents were self-regulating and self-replicating. They would do their job, in body after body that he "contaminated". Would the blood that was collected be checked? Probably it would be checked for the usual risks, but maybe not for the nano-agents that were maybe already considered history anyway. It was a chance he would have to take.

As he left the church after the service was over, he tried to find the woman, but she was nowhere to be seen. Had she wandered off, not even knowing he had been there, totally unaware of his presence or its meaning for Unholy Grail, or had she consciously severed the link he represented with what remained of Unholy Grail, if there were any members left at all, in an effort to increase the chances of his action plan?

Had this entire episode, from the incident in the Lunch Mob to the present moment, perhaps been a carefully planned set-up, too vast for him to grasp? Was he perhaps but a cog in a gigantic machine, a tiny pawn unable to fathom his place and role on the chessboard?

In any case, he understood the battlefield had now been reduced to his bloodstream, and he would act with that idea in mind. So he would give blood, whether this was the woman's intention or not, because that was the only option open to him now. I may be the only activist of Unholy Grail left, he thought, but I'll inject new blood into the movement, to use an extremely appropriate phrase. I'll give as much blood as I can the following days.

Unholy Grail isn't dead. As a matter of fact, it's about to be revived. And as this second attack comes from an unexpected front, a source mistakenly believed to be dried up already, it might well take the enemy by surprise.

Unholy Grail was back. After all, it was in his blood.

END

FRANK ROGER was born in 1957 in Ghent, Belgium. His first story appeared in 1975. Today he has a few hundred short stories to his credit, published in about 40 languages. A story collection in English, *The Burning Woman and Other Stories*, was published by Evertype in 2012.

Apart from fiction, he also produces collages and graphic work in a surrealist and satirical tradition.

Find out more about his work at www.frankroger.be.

EXTRA CREDIT

Paul Levinson

Originally published in *Buzzy Mag*, July 2012.

Jon 1

Jon slammed the piece of mail on the table, knocking off a buttered half of bagel in the process. It teetered on its edge on the floor for a moment, then fell down squarely on the buttered side.

"Another wrong credit card charge," he called up to Trudi between curses. "Seems we stayed at the Coach and Chariot Inn last month."

"With or without the kids?" Trudi walked in and sighed. She picked up the credit card statement and shook her head. "This is—what?—the third mistake like this since the new year?"

"Cancel the card." Jon scooped up the bagel, surveyed the sticky dust, and tossed it in the garbage. "If these people are too lame to get their charges straight, we'll go elsewhere."

"We need the credit line," Trudi said. "I just got a cash advance—"

"Do whatever you want, then." Jon waved his hand in disgust. "But let's at least call the company and explain that we were at your mother's house getting heartburn on her cooked-to-death chicken when they say we were in the whirlpool at the Chariot."

"Right," Trudi said, "as soon as I finish with the Motor Vehicles people about why my new registration isn't here yet. And my mother's chicken is manna from heaven compared to your mother's hydrochloric pot roast."

The woman on the speaker-phone was about what Jon and Trudi expected.

"Have you folks moved recently?" she asked.

"No, been here for four years," Trudi said.

"Has your mail been reported stolen recently?"

"Uh, no," Trudi said. There was that time several months ago when their mail had been mixed in with several of their neighbors' mail, but nothing

165

had wound up lost as far as she knew. It was pretty funny, though, seeing the kind of pornography that old Mr. Gleason up the street subscribed to.

"And you're certain you and your husband didn't sneak away for a quickie at the Chariot—"

"Believe me, we're certain," Jon replied.

"Well, I don't know what to tell you then," the woman said earnestly. "The hotel admits that they have no physical record of your being there—no signed receipts or that sort of thing. But their computer record is quite clear that you were there."

"Haven't you people ever heard of computer hackers?" Jon asked. Jeez.

"Well, of course we have, Mr. Goldman. But what would a hacker stand to gain by charging a room to your credit card, and not using the room?"

"I don't know," Jon said. "Look, I'm not Sherlock Holmes—I can't tell what makes a criminal tick. I just want this charge taken off my credit card."

"Well, of course. I already told you that the hotel has no physical evidence of your having been there, so of course we'll remove the charge. But we'd like to get to the bottom of this."

"So would we," Trudi said. "What do you propose?"

"Well, for a start, we're putting a special photo-hold on your card. Starting today, you and your husband won't be able to use your card without showing a photo-ID to the retailer. And of course no mail orders or phone or computer orders will be allowed."

"Fine," Trudi said, sarcastically. "We're the ones getting hacked, but we're the ones being treated now like criminals. Fine."

"We're doing this for your benefit, Mrs. Goldman."

"For your benefit, too—these credit thefts cost you time and money," Jon said.

"Which all comes back to you, Mr. Goldman, because these losses oblige us to raise the interest you and our other card holders pay us. Anything more I can help you with today?"

Jon rifled through the Saturday morning mail. "Card from Auntie Kira in Florida...bill from the plumber...something from Chandler at MIT, I don't know why he didn't send this to me at the lab—"

"Any mail for me, Dad?"

Jon smiled at his eight-year-old son. "Yep, here's a card from Ari. Looks like it has something scribbled on the back."

Noah laughed. "It's a code, Dad."

"Ah. And here's something for you, sweetheart." Jon handed a piece of colorful advertising over to Samantha, their two-year-old, who promptly put it in her mouth.

"No, no, that's not good for you honey." Trudi leaned over and pulled the advertisement away. "That's good to look at, not—"

"Goddamn charge again!" Jon exploded. He waved the statement in the air. "This one's nineteen dollars and twenty-eight cents—from the Parthenon diner three weeks ago. We didn't eat there then, did we?"

"No, and we wouldn't have gotten out of that goldmine for so little if we had." Trudi took the statement and stared. She pulled her phone out of her pocket and jabbed a number.

"Look, I know it's a Saturday," she said tersely into the phone after giving her credit card number, "but I want to speak to your supervisor. Right. It's about the fourth wrong charge to our credit card this year, this time from a diner that we last ate in maybe six months ago. That's right, we have a photo-hold on our card and everything. Thank you."

"We should sue them, Mom," Noah said. "I hate that place—"

"Shhh!" Jon held up a warning finger. Meanwhile, Samantha deftly pushed her father's plate so that it was just about half over the edge of the table, where it sat with the half-eaten scrambled eggs interrupted by the morning mail delivery.

"That's right," Trudi was talking again. "It's getting to the point where this card is more trouble than it's worth—my husband and I have to look at every statement like hawks to make sure we're not being charged for something that—Right. I know there's a lot of this kind of theft going on and you're doing your best to control it. But—"

Trudi took the phone away from her ear in exasperation and held it out at arm's length. The supervisor's voice was squeaking about people needing to be careful about crooks looking over their shoulders in department stores when charging merchandise. Then he said something about a new retinal scan that the credit card company was introducing—

"Cancel the card already," Jon said. "I've had it with this!" He jabbed in the air to make his point. His elbow brushed his plate—and pushed it over the edge. It landed face down on the floor with his eggs. There was something going on here that, given half a chance, was working against him.

Jon 2

A very slightly different universe, almost the same as ours in all respects...

Jon kissed Trudi full on the lips at the front door. "So we're finally making a little progress on the finances," he said.

"We're still in debt," Trudi said.

"I know, but at least we're starting to move now in the right direction." He blew Trudi another kiss and walked to his Prius in the driveway. The doors clicked open at his approach. This Prius was one of the reasons they were in debt so deeply. Jon knew this but also felt that the Prius was worth every penny.

The drive from home to Fordham University was precisely 18 minutes. This was one of the things Jon loved about his job. He parked his car, walked quickly to Everett Hall, and bounded up the three flights of stairs to the Theoretical Physics Digital Lab. He grabbed a cup of coffee from the shiny new machine and entered his little sanctum.

Eugene, the current grad assistant, was already hard at work, rendering some old analog video clips into digital. Jon clapped him on the back and proceeded to his own workstation. There was a piece of mail on the desk. Jon shook his head.

"Mail-room brought it up just a few minutes ago," Eugene offered. "Another missive from Scott Chandler—you going to just throw it out like the others?"

Jon played with the envelope and laughed. "You know, it's sad. He says he sends his really important messages through land mail because he's afraid his email doesn't always get read. And now I'm proving that the same can happen to paper mail." Jon tossed the envelope. It made a neat fluttering descent into the trash basket.

Eugene chuckled. "It's the price of your success. You attract crackpots."

Jon started up his desktop. No one other than Jon—not even Eugene—knew what Jon had here. Jon scarcely believed it himself. His Russian former graduate assistant, apparently a budding computer genius, had left it in this machine. "My gift to you," she had told him, "to thank you for being such an inspiring teacher."

Jon called up the program, started work on a transaction—

"Jon." Jill Barnes, a colleague, was in the doorway. "We're due at that faculty meeting in 15 minutes."

"Right." Jon cursed to himself and logged off the machine. He'd forgotten about the stupid meeting, which he was obliged to attend. He shut off his computer and smiled at Jill. "Let's go then."

He took his coffee and waved goodbye to Eugene as he left the office.

Eugene thought about it for a few minutes after Jon was gone, then quickly fished Chandler's letter out of Jon's trash.

Jon 1

Our universe...

Jon entered the digital lab, sipping a cup of perfectly brewed coffee. He wrestled his suddenly ringing cellphone out of his pocket, flipped it open, narrowly missing the coffee as he put the phone to his ear and mouth. "Yah, good, honey," he said to Trudi. "We'll do fine with just the bank card. We did the right thing canceling the Ameri—" He realized he was talking loudly, and Eugene could hear. "Okay, good," he said quietly to Trudi. He snapped the phone shut, nodded to Eugene and sat at his temporary computer station.

It had been temporary for almost two months now, and he felt bad about that, not only because he had been deprived of his own workplace, but because his old desk had had Sasha's present upon it. She had given it to him as parting gift before she'd decamped for her doctorate at Cal Tech. "Something very special for your computer," she had told him. "My gift to you, to thank you for all the extra credit and belief you have had in me."

Not a hundred percent comprehensible, but that was Sasha, better at code than words. He looked at the computer now on his temporary desk, his current computer, and sighed. Some student had spilled soda on his computer with Sasha's present the day after Sasha had left. Hey, if faculty didn't follow the no food and drink in the lab rules, why should the students? And he had never had a chance to even touch his original computer since then. It had been out for repair, the techies still not clear exactly what was not quite right about it—

"Jon." That would be Jill Barnes, here to walk with him to a faculty meeting as per their appointment. "We're due at the meeting in 15 minutes." He'd have rather walked himself, but what could he do, he couldn't be rude to a colleague.

"Right." He stood and knocked over his coffee. He'd barely had a sip. He cursed to himself but smiled at Jill.

"I'll clean it up, you'll be late," Eugene said.

"Oh, thanks!" Jon said. He turned to Jill. "Let's go then."

"Some mail came in for you," Eugene called out as Jon joined Jill at the doorway.

"I'll get it when I come back," Jon said.

Jon 2

The slightly different universe...

"What do you think they'll tell us about the salary freeze?" Jill asked Jon, as they walked across the campus.

Jon winced slightly in the sharp February breeze. "Won't make much difference to me, one way or the other, given my mortgage." And also the fact that he'd tapped into the new source of income.

"Yeah, tell me about it," Jill said, referring to the high cost of living.

Jon nodded. He didn't like talking about this.

"I just think it's wrong that they increase the number of students in our classes, but keep our salaries on hold," Jill continued. "I mean, I know the economy's still bad, but enrollment has been up and—"

Jon's ringing phone interrupted Jill's critique. Jon was grateful. He smiled apologetically at Jill, threw his nearly empty coffee cup into a nearby receptacle and took the call. "Hey, on my way to a meeting," he said to Trudi.

"Oh, right, sorry," Trudi said. "The meeting about the salary freeze?"

"Yeah," Jon replied.

"Well, don't let them intimidate you. You're entitled—"

"I know."

"Okay. I just had a quick question—about a new after-school possibility for Noah. Can you talk?"

"Sure. More or less," Jon replied.

"Well, the school has some wild bird expert who'll be running a special program in ID'ing birds in the New York area. You know how much Noah loves that."

Jon nodded. "Absolutely."

"But it'll cost us $200," Trudi said. "I know we've been doing better with that long-range installment plan you worked out for us online, but—"

"Let's do it." They'd been doing a lot better with that "installment" plan, which required no payment at all, not even for the purchases themselves.

"Okay," Trudy said, mostly happily, but with a tinge of unassuaged concern.

"We're here," Jon told Trudi, as he and Jill reached their destination. Jill scowled, in continuing anger at the university administration.

Jon 1

Our universe...

The walk across campus was uneventful. Jill was droning about the outrage of the salary freeze, but Jon had more pressing financial problems to think about. What the hell was going on with his credit card? Okay, he'd canceled the one with the phantom charges, but why couldn't the credit card company get to the bottom of it? And if he was being targeted by some super hacker who had acquired his credit card, what was to stop him or her from moving to another one of Jon's cards?

His cellphone rang. It was likely Trudi. Jon didn't answer. He needed to think about this more. But he didn't blame his wife in the slightest for being so worried. He supposed the next step would be to go to the police, but Jon didn't relish being an official victim of anything, and the time that would take out of life.

He and Jill reached the meeting hall. Her talk subsided into a scowl about the university administration.

Faculty were milling around the hall, breath visible and frosty this early February afternoon. Jon looked them over. He was not particularly close to any of them—he often said he preferred his students to his colleagues—and—

Wait a minute! Jeez! Was that Chandler? Yes, it was him, and he was walking right towards Jon, and it was too late for Jon to pretend he didn't see him.

"Jonathan!" Chandler extended a big, beefy hand.

"Scott—good to see you—what brings you to the Bronx?"

"I was visiting Liu in the Math Department—we're doing a conference together next year—and I called your office, and your grad assistant told me you were on your way here. I've been trying to talk to you about something for a few weeks now. I'm not completely sure what it means, but—"

"Why didn't you call or send an email?" Jon knew the answer but saw no advantage in making this easier for Chandler.

"I don't like talking about these things on the phone," Chandler said in a conspiratorial tone. "Same thing with email. I was only calling your office to see if you were in, so I could drop by. I have sent you a few letters, by the way—in fact, I sent one just last week, letting you know I'd be on campus today."

Jon shook his head derisively. "Mail's getting less and less reliable."

Jill, who had been talking to a gaggle of faculty nearby, waved at Jon. "I'm going in," she mouthed at Jon in exaggerated motions and walked to the entrance way.

171

Jon was glad for the excuse to get to the point with Chandler, who had seen Jill's departure. "Okay, so what did you want to talk to me about?" he asked Chandler. "I'm sure it will be more stimulating than what I'll hear in there." He gestured to the building. He realized that that was likely sadly true.

"I ran into a student of yours in California last month," Chandler's tone was lower and more conspiratorial, "Sasha Humek?"

Jon nodded.

"And, well, I guess she had too much vodka," Chandler continued. "She's brilliant, you know. Her paper on inter-alter-matrices was really something—raised a lot of eyebrows. All hypothetical, of course."

"Yes," Jon replied.

"But she had had a lot to drink, as I told you," Chandler said, "and I couldn't completely understand her—you know, between the accent and the drink—"

Jon nodded again.

"But I think she said something about actually developing a program that could do that," Chandler said, "and I've been thinking about that ever since, and it's been bothering me—"

"Do what?" Jon asked.

Jon 2

The slightly different universe...

Jon looked around at the faculty walking and talking around the front of the building, like geese honking on a lawn. Jeez—there was that noodge Chandler! What the hell was he doing here, stalking Jon? Jon spun around quickly, neatly, and walked away, to the other side of the building. He thought he heard Jill telling him she was going in. He waved over his shoulder without turning around. He didn't want to risk Chandler spotting him, if he hadn't already.

Jon thought he knew what Chandler wanted to talk to him about—he had read Chandler's first letter. Jon had thought then that it would be best to avoid this conversation for as long as he possibly could. He had the same opinion now.

Jon ducked into a side door, then into a men's room, and hoped this would be the last he would see of Scott Chandler. He'd hang out in the bathroom until the meeting got underway, walk carefully to the rear entrance, and look around. He doubted Chandler would wait around if he didn't see Jon

172

either entering the meeting or in the meeting once it had started. Then Jon realized that the safest course of action, if he wanted to avoid Chandler, was to leave this hall altogether, and just go home without attending the meeting at all. Jon knew he could count on Jill to attest that he had indeed been here, even if she didn't see him leave after the meeting. What kind of psycho, after all, would walk all the way across campus to a meeting, only to walk out before it started?

As for Chandler, he'd survive. True, Chandler had sent Trudi and him congratulations cards when Noah and Samantha were born, but that wasn't the important thing now. Jon had to protect his kids and from the financial vicissitudes that sooner or later struck everyone, especially in the current world.

Jon 1

Our universe...

Four faculty walked by Jon and Chandler—Chandler pulled back from Jon and held a finger to his lips. "We shouldn't just be standing here, talking in the open like this," he said, in a volume so low now that Jon could barely hear.

Jon looked at the hall in which the meeting was about to commence, and thought quickly: No one will miss me at this point if I don't attend this. Jill would say to anyone who asked that she had walked with me to the meeting, and who would be so crazy as to walk all the way to a faculty meeting, only to walk away before the meeting started? Well, maybe not so crazy, for anyone who knew how boring faculty meetings could be, but—

Jon realized that Chandler was waiting for a response, and beginning to edge even further away. "Of course," Jon answered. "You're right, of course. Let's just take a nice little stroll around the campus—we'll be able to see anyone we're approaching, or approaching us, and we can stop talking if need be." Jon took Chandler's arm and began escorting him away from the building.

Chandler nodded slowly, reluctantly. "But your meeting?"

"It's okay," Jon replied. "My colleagues will fill me in.... So, you were about to tell me what Sasha told you, in her Russian accent, when she was a little drunk."

"A lot drunk," Chandler said.

Jon nodded.

"And she—" Chandler started and stopped talking in deference to two students who were walking by.

"Hi, Professor!" one of them said brightly to Jon.

"Hey, Angela, how are you doing?" Jon replied. Then, to Chandler, "And?"

"And your student Sasha told me she had written a program that permitted inter-alternate-universal transactions."

"Come again?"

"Don't play dumb with me," Chandler replied, suddenly losing all of his trepidation. "You know exactly what I mean—she was your student, if she really wrote such a program she must have learned it from you."

Jon considered. "She was one of those students who already knew a lot more than I did the first day she stepped into my class, that's why she was my grad assistant," he said, truthfully. "Did she tell you what she intended to do with such a program?"

"She said she was leaving it and the decision about whether and how to use it in your hands."

Jon said nothing. He knew where the program likely was, now.

"You going to pretend you know nothing of this?" Chandler pushed.

"Some student spilled sticky soda on my computer before I even had a chance to load Sasha's program."

"So you've never used Sasha's program?" Chandler asked, not completely believing what Jon had just told him.

"No," Jon replied, and his eyes flared with the beginning of understanding. "But that does not mean it has not been used."

Jon 2

The slightly different universe...

Jon was in his Prius, ignition on, when he realized he had left the transaction he had started in his office incomplete—interrupted by Jill and their apparent need to go to that stupid meeting. But the meeting was no longer an issue. So what was keeping him from his desk and that transaction?

Chandler could come looking for him in the office, after not being able to locate Jon in the meeting, but Jon had no intention living the rest of his life in fear of a conversation with Chandler. And completing the transaction in the office shouldn't take more than a minute.

Jon grinned as he turned the car off, stepped out, locked it, left it, and made his way back to his office. The nice thing about being so way beyond the cutting edge was no one could see what you were doing, even if you were doing it right before their very eyes.

Well, he supposed one person could. Not a person in this universe, this reality, though. But the Jon in that other universe, the Jon whose card was being charged for his, this Jon's, purchases: He would certainly see the results, he of course would see the charges and would feel their impact.

But a few charges certainly couldn't bankrupt anybody. They might cause a little discomfort, a little concern, but, hey, for all Jon knew, his alternate self was a rich man, a millionaire, who wouldn't feel or mind the little debits at all. Hey, Jon had come close to making it big in this world himself—a better book deal, more high-paying jobs as a consultant to complement his teaching career, any one of a dozen slightly different breaks could have put him in the upper strata right now. For all Jon knew, his alternate self had done all of this and more, and wouldn't notice or care at all about a charge from a hotel he had never slept in.

Jon bounded up the three flights of stairs to his office.

Jon 1

Our universe...

Jon was determined to get a look at Sasha's program and get to the bottom of this insanity. Could the inexplicable charges on his credit card really be the result of his alter-self, in an alternate, parallel universe, having made the charges, but via Sasha's program somehow gotten those charges to show up on Jon's credit card right here in Jon's universe? Jon fingered the card in his wallet inside his jacket pocket, then clenched and unclenched his fist in anger. "I think I know where my computer with the program is right now," he said. "You want to come with me to our tech repair center?"

It couldn't hurt to have Chandler standing by, in case Jon had trouble using the program—assuming his beleaguered computer was in some sort of working condition now. Jon was good with computers, but Chandler was better, a classic nerd case of clumsy with people smooth with equipment. Conceivably he could get Jon's computer to work, when Jon and the techies could not.

"Sure," Chandler replied. "Locate the program and destroy it—leaving it out there in the world, especially with techies around, is not a good idea."

"Exactly," Jon lied as the two approached the gleaming new tech center. He had no intention of destroying Sasha's little present to him—at least, not before he'd had a chance to use it, and set the universes straight. And maybe make a little profit for himself. He thought for a second about dis-

175

inviting Chandler—no, unless Jon was able to resurrect his computer, he would not be able to even get a look at Sasha's program.

Jon 2

The slightly different universe...

Jon sat at his workstation. Eugene was nowhere to be seen—he was probably out to lunch. Good. Although Jon didn't worry much about doing his special transactions with Eugene around—who would not have known what he was looking at, if he'd happened to have glanced at Jon's screen—Jon still preferred doing this with no possibly prying eyes around.

Jon booted up his computer. He went directly into that miraculous little program Sasha had provided. He clicked the icon that would make it work now in the background, as Jon went to the Fieldstone school web site— Fieldstone was Noah's school—and made the $200 payment for Noah's after school bird identification course. And the sweet, incredible thing was that this charge would never show up on his credit card. Sasha's program would shunt it to the parallel universe, where it would be charged to Jon's alternate self's card.

He finished the transaction and leaned back in his chair, with his hands clasped around the back of his neck. Ethical issues aside, this was indeed one fine piece of business. It thrilled him as much as it had the first time he had attempted it. Trans-universe transactions were positively addicting.

Jon 1

Our universe...

Jon walked into the head-tech's office, with Chandler a little behind him. "Professor Jon Goldman," Jon announced to the head-tech, and pulled out his faculty ID.

"I know who you are," the head-tech said, without a trace of a smile.

"Good. Well, I'd—"

"You'd like your computer back and working. I know. Your office has called here, what, a dozen times?"

"The computer's been out of commission for nearly two months—all because a little soda was spilled on it?" Jon had long ago realized there was no point matching attitudes with these tech people. They held his equipment in their hands—they held all the cards. Still, it was hard to resist the bait.

"As I know I already told you, it's something more than the ginger ale," the techie explained, his patience already strained. "We replaced the damaged parts, but we can't get it to keep working for more than a few minutes once we turn it on. We think it's some kind of virus that got in there before the soda, and it's incompatible with the upgrade hardware we put in. We're still trying to identify it. We have an obligation to make sure it doesn't spread to other computers on the campus."

Chandler spoke up. "Can we—Professor Goldman—see the machine? If that's possible."

The head-tech shrugged. "Won't do you much good."

"I know," Chandler said, soothingly, "but—"

The techie pointed to the other room. "It's against the far wall in there."

Jon and Chandler proceeded to the room. "Glad I brought you along," Jon told Chandler. "You have a good way with these people."

Chandler just nodded. Jon looked at the far wall. "Ah! There it is."

He and Chandler proceeded to the computer. Jon sat right down and turned it on, Chandler looking over his shoulder. "He said it only works for a few minutes at a time, so you have to do this quickly," Chandler advised, quietly, urgently.

"Right." But Jon really had no idea what that "this" was—Sasha had left no instructions in her little note. He supposed he could call or email her— he had her contact info in his online address book. Jon looked at the screen. No, that probably wouldn't be necessary. As the icons popped into place, Jon noticed a shimmering new gift-wrapped box on the screen, named "Sasha's present."

Jon hesitated for a moment. He wasn't thrilled about doing this in front of Chandler. But he had no choice at this point, and Chandler could still be of help if the program proved balky.

Chandler saw the icon on the screen and pointed to it.

Jon nodded, and clicked.

The screen that came up said: "Pay for anything you like online with any of your credit cards, and let my present do its work for you. You won't notice anything different immediately, but watch for what is on your bill—or not on your bill." And the words were followed by an animated little smiley icon.

"Good, that seems to be it," Chandler said nervously but happily. "Now just drag it to trash—"

But Jon went instead to his favorite online wine store. He had a strong feeling he and Trudi would soon have something to celebrate.

Jon 2

The slightly different universe...

Jon moved to shut off his computer, but got a chime from his email that he had a new message. It was a receipt for purchase of a bottle of Black Dirt Red Wine from Warwick. He and Trudi loved it—a great $12 wine they'd discovered at a farmer's market in the Fall—but why would Trudi buy a bottle now? They still had two bottles in their little rack the last time he'd looked—which had been maybe two days ago.

He called Trudi. "Nope, I didn't buy it," she told him. "I don't mind another bottle, though—maybe some grateful student bought it for you as a present. You really shouldn't accept it, I know. Or maybe some Dean wanted to thank you—"

"I doubt if it's either," Jon said. "I don't see how either could have gotten my credit card."

"Yeah, that's right," Trudi said. "But then—"

"No big deal," Jon lied. "All right, I'm on my way home—anything I should pick up? We okay with orange juice and milk?"

Jon got off the phone with a grocery order and a thought that rang as painfully clear as day in his brain: This was a very big deal. He got up, paced around, and tried to find some balance on this. A credit card in his name for a bottle of wine he hadn't bought. The price was indeed no problem, but the process surely was. Maybe this was just some sort of credit card error? Jon smiled, ruefully. No, he knew that it wasn't. This was likely just what his alter-self had been going through. And now Jon in that parallel universe, the Jon who had been receiving this Jon's charges, had turned the tables.

Jon hoped his counterpart would continue to be this sparing with the charges. Jon certainly had not been with his. Was there a way this program could be disabled?

Jon 1

Our universe...

"No!" Chandler cried out, and lunged at Jon's computer. But Jon had already clicked on the wine. He had set this online store for express, one-click purchase, so he could get in a last-minute order when he was late for class.

Jon stood and restrained Chandler.

The techie stuck his head in the door. "It's okay," Jon said. "We're just rehearsing for a departmental play."

The techie looked at Jon and Chandler as if they were both crazy, but didn't see enough of a problem to warrant his continued intrusion. He walked back into his room.

Jon's computer promptly went off.

"You used that program to charge something to your alter-self," Chandler said, still somewhat furious. "That's not right."

"No, it is," Jon said. "Here, have a seat. Let me explain what I think is going on."

Chandler looked at the computer as if to confirm it was off, and could do no further harm, then sat.

"I think I've been a victim of my alter-self's charges for several months now," Jon explained. "I don't know if there's any way I can undo them, now. But I can rectify this by charging my counterpart back."

Jon 2

The slightly different universe...

Jon shut his computer off, patted it, almost affectionately, regretfully, and headed for the door.

So this would be it. His computer, Sasha's extraordinary little program, had done well for him. But now that his counterpart in the parallel universe had finally gotten a clue about this, there was really no point in continuing. If each charge that this Jon shunted to the parallel Jon was matched by a charge from the parallel Jon to this Jon, there would be no net gain for either Jon. One Jon of course could make bigger charges, and charge more frequently, than the other Jon. But the other Jon would know this as soon as the trans-universe charges arrived, and could easily retaliate. So the net gain, sooner or later, would be zero. All that escalating charges in both universes could eventually engender would be mutually assured bankruptcy.

Jon got into his Prius and drove out of the university parking lot. This had been one wild ride, no doubt. Financial transactions across alternate universes. Had other pairs of parallel people being doing this? Had they started like Jon, with one doing it to the other, and then the other catching on? He still wondered why it had taken his parallel Jon so long to get going on this. He

179

wondered if there was any way he could yet turn this back around to his own advantage, or at least prevent his alternate from transferring any more charges.

Where did the the program, the technology, come from? Jon had heard rumors, conspiracy theories, about parallel universes, for years. Pathways to alternate realities brought into being by fast-moving quantum particles. Hypothetical informational super-luminary highways...

Sasha was the key to this. Her program made this real. He owed her a call. No point doing this in the car, though. He wanted to concentrate, take notes, if needed. There could be a career-making paper in this, for him as well as Sasha.

Jon 1

Our universe...

Jon turned the computer back on, on impulse. It made some strange noises, but stayed dark. He banged the table hard. "I wanted to see if I could get it to do it again," he said to Chandler.

The bang brought the dour techie back in. He shook his head. "I told you, it only stays up a few minutes. Banging the table won't change that."

"I know," Jon said. "Sorry. Could you see if you could get it working again now, even if for just a few minutes?"

Chandler, who obviously had been struggling with how to react to this, finally spoke. "Yes," he said to the techie, "if you could do that, it would be very helpful. He has notes for a new paper on that computer, which he doesn't have anyplace else, and lots of people are eager to see it."

Jon nodded and smiled at Chandler, grateful for the support.

"I'd like to see those notes myself," Chandler added.

The techie grunted, motioned Jon out of his seat, and got to work on the computer. He put in four different diagnostic and boot disks. None had any effect. The techie frowned. "It may be permanently brain dead," he said. "I can have someone else look at it, but usually when these things are gone they're gone."

"But—" Jon started, but realized there was not much more it was safe to tell this techie. Letting him know that this half or completely dead computer contained some extraordinary program was a sure ticket to the techie saying any repair was futile, and keeping the computer for himself. "Okay, thanks for trying," Jon said. "No need to do anything more about this now. Could you pack it up for me so I can take back to—"

The techie shook his head no. "Lots of reasons I can't do that. You need a form signed by the Chair of your Department. I'm about to pack up and leave—closing the shop early today, I have an appointment—"

"Okay," Jon knew all about the forms, and how intractable the techies were about requiring them. The money would be deducted from their salaries, maybe worse, if any computer went missing. "Thanks," Jon said. "I'll see if I can come back with the signed form tomorrow—that okay?" Best Jon could do—his Chair was in Manhattan today.

The techie shrugged.

"Thanks," Jon said, again.

He and Chandler left the building. Ordinarily, Jon would have complained about the repair facility closing early, it would have driven him a little crazy, but not today. Let the techie shut down the room and go to his appointment. With a new set of broken computers to deal with tomorrow, the techie would likely not give Jon's computer another thought. And then Jon could get his computer, and try to find someone who could get it to work.

Meanwhile, the best thing to do now, Jon considered, was call Sasha. Maybe it was the best thing in any case. If she could send him another copy of her program that Jon could install on a fresh computer, that would take care of everything. He didn't see why she wouldn't send it to him.

But he didn't want to call Sasha right in front of Chandler. He started to thank Chandler, and say he had to be getting home.

"But there's a lot more I'd like to know about this," Chandler objected, "a lot more we need to discuss."

"I know," Jon said. "But I can't do it now." Not before he spoke to Sasha. With no evidence in hand, Chandler couldn't do much, not anything really, with what he had just seen. Anyone other than Jon and Sasha would dismiss Chandler as a nutcase if he'd try to inform them about what he thought had just happened.

They approached the garage. "Can I give you a lift to the train?" Jon asked Chandler, in a bid to get him off campus and as far away from the computer as possible.

Chandler was clearly still not happy about the way this day was concluding, but he accepted the offer. "Sure, thanks."

Jon dropped him off at the Metro-North, and swung over to the parkway. He'd call Sasha as soon as he got home and gave Trudi a long hug.

Eugene 2

The slightly different universe...

Eugene had been keeping an eye on the lab from a safe distance down the corridor . As soon as Jon left, Eugene went right over to Jon's computer. He turned it on, called up the program Sasha had left Jon, and then the program Sasha had left on Jon's computer for Eugene. He smiled broadly.

He Skyped Sasha. "I think we can move on to our next couplet now," Eugene told her. "The Jons seem to have reached their equilibrium."

"Good," Sasha said. "Took the Jon in the other universe long enough."

"Yeah, we need to look into that, could be an important data point," Eugene said. "The soda on the keyboard was of course my doing—part of our protocol for seeing what happens when real life throws in a monkey wrench. But I can't figure why the computer techie was taking so long."

"Could be another monkey wrench—unexpected—could be he ran some diagnostic and found something unusual about our program," Sasha said,

"It's supposed to be self-disguising to the usual scans."

"I know. You should get the computer out his hands in any case," Sasha said.

"Yeah, the tech center should be closing in under an hour. That'll be my next stop today."

"Good."

"Meanwhile, you proceeding well with Professor Ramapuram out there?" Eugene asked.

"Yah," Sasha nodded.

"Excellent. I've been accepted as his grad assistant in the Fall. You leave him the code at the end of this term, and move on to another school. I'll come out there to keep watch and we'll be in business, just as with Jon and the others."

"Jon will likely be calling me, to get a little more clarity on what's been happening to him."

Eugene laughed. "Tell him the usual. You stumbled on to this program with the quantum mechanical app, wasn't really sure what it could do, so you left it in his wiser hands. Give him your heartfelt apology for not telling him more up-front... He'd need a nova of light to understand what's really happening—hey, we're not much better, are we?"

"But I'll shut him down, tell him the program is unstable, that I need to do much more work on it before I set it loose again—give to anyone as a present," Sasha said.

"Right," Eugene said, and his eyes were thoughtful. "You think our alternates, Eugene and Sasha in the parallel universe, are having something like this same conversation right now?"

Now Sasha smiled. "I'll do you one better: You think there may be another group of happy researchers, much like us, in yet another parallel universe, and they're running us, testing our responses, just as we've been doing with the Jons?"

END

PAUL LEVINSON is an American author and professor of communications and media studies at Fordham University in New York City. Levinson's science fiction, sf/mystery, and popular and scholarly non-fiction works have been translated into twelve languages. As a commentator on media, popular culture, and science fiction Levinson has been interviewed more than 500 times on local, national, and international television and radio.

His most recent novel is *Unburning Alexandria* (2013) and his newest non-fiction book is *New New Media* (2009). *The Silk Code* won the Locus Award for Best First Novel of 1999. His novel *The Consciousness Plague* won the 2003 Mary Shelley Award for outstanding Fictional Work. His novella "Loose Ends" was a 1998 Hugo Award finalist, a finalist for the 1998 Sturgeon Award, and a finalist for the 1997 Nebula Award. The radio play of his novelette "The Chronology Protection Case" was nominated for an Edgar Award for Best Mystery Play of 2002. His Amazon Author page is www.amazon.com/Paul-Levinson/e/B000APZZZK.

AFTERWORD

We would like to personally thank you for buying and reading this book. Producing this anthology has been, and continues to be, quite fulfilling for us and we hope that it is enjoyable for you as well.

Please consider taking a little extra time to help others find this book by leaving feedback where you purchased it. Your opinion about this book truly matters, both to our authors who have contributed to the anthology and to other readers.

If you have any questions, comments, suggestions, or just want to say hello, please visit our publisher's webpage on Indie Authors Press (www.salgado-reyes.com) and follow our publisher's Twitter: @Indie__Authors

~Indie Authors Press~